Vietnam,
The Making of a Sniper

Jerry Melvin Mitchem

authorHOUSE®

AuthorHouse™
1663 Liberty Drive
Bloomington, IN 47403
www.authorhouse.com
Phone: 1-800-839-8640

© 2010 Jerry Melvin Mitchem. All rights reserved.

Cover photo of author by Sheena Ratliff

No part of this book may be reproduced, stored in a retrieval system, or transmitted by any means without the written permission of the author.

First published by AuthorHouse   7/30/2010

ISBN: 978-1-4520-6189-4 (e)
ISBN: 978-1-4520-6187-0 (sc)
ISBN: 978-1-4520-6188-7 (hc)

Library of Congress Control Number: 2010911048

Printed in the United States of America
Bloomington, Indiana

This book is printed on acid-free paper.

Dedication

This book is dedicated to the thousands of Army Special Forces and Marines who served America bravely in South Vietnam as military advisors and in intelligence from 1962 to early 1965.

I wish to thank the following people who played a role in my writing this novel.

Without their support and hard work, this book would not have been possible:

My pastor and friend, the Reverend Ron Williamson for encouraging me to write this book.

My wife Virginia, for her dedication and support through the long months I labored with this book.

I wish to give thanks to my Lord Jesus Christ for giving me the desire to write a novel without the filthy language that so many novels have today.

Many thanks to my cousin, Donna Daniel, for her time and professional help in getting this novel edited.

I wish to acknowledge my dear departed mother-in-law, Ruby Roberts, who believed in my abilities to write this novel and encouraged me to continue.

Also, thanks to Uncle L. Brown for being a fatherly figure when I needed it the most and for having the patience to teach a young boy how to shoot, hunt, track game, and live off the land.

Many instances in this book are true. Some of the characters names have been changed and scenes were added or omitted to make the book come alive. Therefore, this book must be called a fiction.

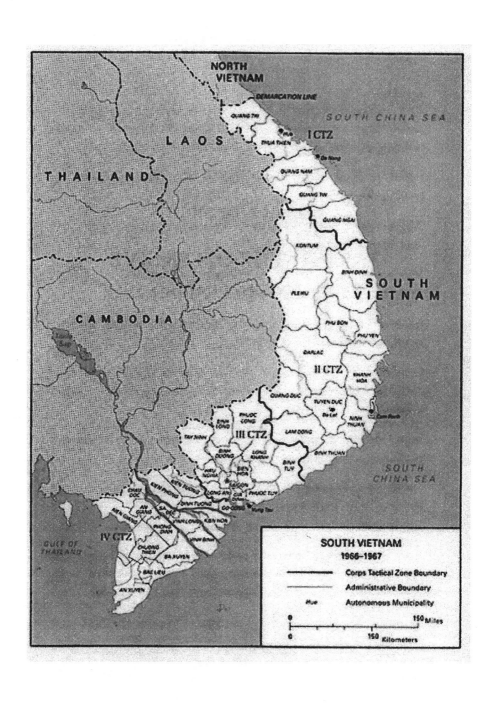

Foreword

Upon arriving in Vietnam, I was assigned to Southeast Asia Marine Corps Headquarters, Intelligence Battalion, Company 'M', Saigon, South Vietnam. I was an advisor, training the South Vietnamese in the proper use of American supplied weapons. I was part of a 4,000-man build-up of U.S. Military Advisors to the government of South Vietnam by order of the President, Lyndon B. Johnson. The United States sent thousands of Army Special Forces and Marines as combat advisors to instruct and train the armies of South Vietnam.

The U.S. Army 'Green Berets' accounted for nearly 80% of our advisors, while the Marine Corps accounted for 20%. Some Marine units and Green Berets were *assigned covert operation orders, to search out and observe the Viet Cong guerrillas, and discourage or stop their efforts to wage and escalate the war against the South Vietnamese government.*

No American ground combat forces had arrived in Vietnam as of 1964. However, the war began to escalate in August 1964 when North Vietnamese torpedo boats attacked two U.S. destroyers in the Gulf of Tonkin. President Lyndon B. Johnson had ordered two Navy aircraft carriers and task forces to the region to increase U.S. air power in the region; and, along with the Air Force, the Navy began retaliatory bombing of select military targets in North Vietnam.

It is mandatory that annually all U.S. Marines qualify with their rifles. Three weeks after arriving, I was assigned to the rifle range for qualification with the M-14 rifle. I shot in the high expert range and was four points from having a perfect shoot.

I was asked to attend a five-week sniper school, which was conducted at our base. Major (Maj.) H. A. Sims was the commanding officer (CO) and Gunnery Sergeant (Gunnery Sgt.) Richard P. Davis was the senior noncommissioned officer (NCO) instructor.

Classes included physical conditioning; intense field training; proper use and care of a sniper's rifle and scope; camouflage and concealment; stalking; survival classes; escape and evasion; and last, but not least, the many, many hours of shooting at human silhouette targets on the rifle range.

In early 1964, the Marines did not have a true sniper rifle. We used sporting rifles, and most shot the 30/06, 308 or 300 caliber. When asked *what was my favorite hunting rifle and caliber,* I answered, "300 Weatherby Magnum bolt-action, firing 180-grain .300 caliber soft nose bullets."

About 45 days later, two specially designed Weatherby Magnum's, with flash suppressors and a Redfield 4X9X variable match scope mounted on each, were delivered from a Marine armory stateside for my use. I was issued 173-grain ammo in .300 caliber that provided muzzle velocity of 3,230 feet per second (fps), sporting the knockdown force of 2,037 foot pounds of energy (fpe) at 500 yards. It could literally put an exit hole the size of a golf ball in a boar hog or a man.

In the first half of 1964, we tried many different variables on the range and in the field. The Marine Corps in 1965 adopted the Winchester model 70 in 30.06 caliber with the 9X Redfield scope and firing 173 grain soft nose bullet as standard sniper issue. This became the Corps standard sniper rifle, scope, and ammunition issued to Marine snipers in the Vietnam Theater in late 1965.

CHAPTER 1

This is about a time in my life when I should have walked away from trouble, but being a young gung ho Marine with no fear of death, I ran toward it.

As a 22-year old Marine, I found myself sitting nestled down in 3-foot tall grass, on a ridge in South Vietnam, overlooking a prime Viet Cong village that we had code named Cong3. It was October 21, 1964, and I waited, watching for my target to appear. He was a lieutenant colonel (Lt. Col.) who had been trained by the Russians in Hanoi. Our intelligence had information that he was an expert at breaking code. Intelligence was determined to end his services to the North Vietnamese and the Viet Cong.

Lt. Col. Huc Po Pauhu was a communication expert who could speak five languages — Vietnamese, Russian, Chinese, English, and French. We were afraid he would intercept our messages from intelligence and combat units in the field. My orders were to take him out before he could break our code and train others.

For three days, I had waited, from dawn to sunset, and he had not arrived at this village as scheduled. It was so hot that the blowflies were fanning each other. For about the fifth time I checked the windage on my special designed sniper rifle, a 300 Weatherby Magnum in .300 caliber, bolt action, with a 4X9X variable Redfield scope and flash suppressor. I was using a 173-grain soft point bullet that would be lethal on most all North America game animals and three-fourths of the big game in Africa. I had to have the windage precise to insure the 540-yard shot to the mayor's house in the village was dead-on target. I needed to hit a target the size of my fist at this distance. This Weatherby Magnum delivered about 2,037 foot pounds of energy upon impact at 500 yards with a bullet drop of 26.04 inches.

I was growing tired and only catnapped for a few hours each night after the Viet Cong (VC) patrols called it a night. The grassy spot I selected was 30 yards below the crest of the ridge at the eastern end overlooking the village, and it was as close as I dared get. Their patrols were searching up to 300 yards out from the village. I had an excellent view of the village plus a quick and silent escape route back through the high grass, over the ridge and down to a large marsh 100 yards from the hill, where I could silently continue my diversion tactics and, hopefully, reach my pickup point.

I had 48 hours left to complete my mission. A helicopter would fly over the primary pickup points, only once, every other morning for six days. There were three designated pickup locations. If I didn't reach one of these three locations by the morning of the sixth day, I would be left, which required walking back to the base camp through 16 miles of VC held territory — something I was trying hard to avoid.

The sharp sound of a vehicle horn brought me back to reality, fast! A rusty colored old car was trying to avoid pigs and chickens as it headed toward the west end of the village, where the mayor lived. I looked at my watch, 0856 hours.

I quickly laid flat on the ground in a prone firing position. Making sure I still had a good view through the grass, I eased the rifle to my shoulder, pulled the stock in real tight, and just melted around the weapon, trying to become one unit, while peeping into the 9X variable special Redfield scope. I checked the windage again. It had dropped to near 3 knots, so I readjusted the windage on my rifle and quickly picked my spot — the porch steps. This should not be too difficult a shot.

Everything was ready, and my target was now fast approaching. I had about 20 seconds before the old car reached the house; and in less than two minutes, I would be leaving. The driver of the old rusty sedan jumped from behind the wheel and hurriedly opened the rear door for Lt. Col. Huc Po Pauhu, who was all of five feet five inches tall at best, thin as a toothpick, and wore the traditional Viet Cong dirty brown uniform of a senior officer.

My scope centered on his left shoulder as he quickly climbed the steps. As he neared the top step, I had already found his shoulder blade and centered the cross hairs near his heart. His lifeless body fell face first onto the old wooden porch. I knew the 173-grain soft point sniper bullet had found its mark, creating an exit hole the size of a golf ball. Recoil on the 300 Weatherby Magnum is something that takes a while to get use to — *'It's a Bad Mama.'*

Only after firing did I hear the shot as it echoed across the small valley. Looking around very quickly, I saw that the patrols had not pinpointed the shot origin, and there was a lot of confusion in the village.

I had the morning sun at my back. No one looking up in my direction from the village or from the slope down below my position could see me, for the rising sun would blind them.

Quickly, I slipped on my gear and cautiously moved up toward the crest, going back over the hill and down toward the marsh and the river.

Thirty minutes later, I reached the edge of the marsh. I quietly eased into the slimly water, crouching low to keep most of my body underwater with only my head and my weapon above the surface. I quickly moved further out into the slimy green marsh. I had 200 yards of swampy marsh to cross before I could reach the river and the thick jungle just beyond.

Instinctively, I suddenly decided to turn north, going deeper up into the marsh, instead of crossing it. The VC trackers could be arriving anytime now. I wanted them to assume I had gone on east toward the river. I had only moved about 50 yards away from the crossing when nine VC entered the marsh at a run. I eased behind an old rotten tree stump that was next to me and slowly lowered myself even deeper into the water, trying to avoid detection. They were moving fast, splashing water with every step; the slime was near their waists, but they kept moving, without saying a word, toward the river. I froze until they passed, keeping my weapon and only part of my face above the surface.

I knew I might have to deal with them later, but right now, I just wanted distance between them and me. After they passed out of sight, I slowly moved northward up the marsh, crouching all the while to keep my body under, and only my head and the Weatherby above the slime. My knees and legs hurt like crazy from crouching so low.

Four hours later, I emerged from the marsh on the river's side, about two miles north of where I entered. I was totally exhausted, having moved so slowly in the marsh with just my head and weapon above the slime. I had stopped for 10 minutes every hour to catch my breath and relieve the cramps in my legs. I suspected some of the trackers would possibly double back when they did not find any sign of me crossing the river and could be close because the natural sounds of frogs and birds had stopped, and there was now a deathly silence in the marsh. I still had about three hours until sunset.

Time to move again — moving so slow that I appeared to be a part of the terrain. This was a real key to staying alive out here.

I changed directions again, this time I headed straight for the river where I would cross and head southeast.

I chose to stay in the thick undergrowth and slip ever so slowly that it would be difficult for anyone to see my movement or me. I knew that 'getting in a hurry' would get me caught or killed. That was not what I wanted.

When being hunted by other humans, it does cause one to used extra precaution. By knowing that the hunters are as intelligent as the hunted, it becomes a mind game.

With me now being the hunted, I remembered Uncle Leroy Brown teaching me to track wounded wild hogs and deer and how the animals used their sense of survival to try to get away. Staying off trails, they would move along the thick swamp undergrowth. Even one big old hog had hid himself from me by finding a narrow ditch full of leaves and limbs and crawled under all that with just his big old black snout barely sticking out so he could breathe. It took me almost a week to find him. Then, and only with the aid of nearly a dozen buzzards, I saw how he had evaded me and died right there in that ditch.

Back to the present — suddenly, through the undergrowth, I saw a movement about 30 yards to my left; it was the barrel of a rifle moving back and forth. A lone tracker was moving along a path that would bring him within a few yards of me. He was moving slowly, bent over at the waist, searching the ground for my tracks in front of him. Occasionally he looked up. He was slipping along a narrow trail that connected the upper area of the slimy marsh and the river. This VC tracker was hunting me — I began to sweat.

I strained my eyes looking for others, but saw no other movement. I had two choices, let him go, or kill him! I knew what I had to do, so I began to position myself for the task. Very gently, I placed the Weatherby on the ground. Then, I eased the K-bar from its scabbard just below my right knee. I knew I was taking a big chance trying this. I could not use my rifle; and I could not let him fire his weapon, alerting the other trackers of my location. He slowly closed the distance between us.

I was standing in thick undergrowth, which gave me excellent concealment. My tiger stripe clothing blended well in here. I had painted my face black and green earlier this morning, and I just hoped my face paint had not completely come off after my morning episode in the marsh.

As long as I made no sudden movement, he wouldn't see me. He was getting very close. He smelled like raw fish! With the big knife securely in my right hand, I waited.

With almost no movement other than my right elbow very slowly bending backwards, I eased the big knife up to thigh level. I could almost reach out and touch him now.

He was searching for me. He was so intent on looking at the ground, trying to pick up my trail, that he was totally unaware I was less than eight feet from him. I just knew he could hear my breathing or my heart beating like a drum. My knees began shaking uncontrollably. Large beads of sweat were running down my face.

I waited for the right moment. I saw his nostrils flare, as he slowly lifted his head and smelled the air. Suddenly! He stopped, he didn't move. Did he smell me? He turned his head around very slowly and looked over his left shoulder back toward the river. I made my move. In one quick stride, I was within killing range and the big eight-inch razor sharp blade rapidly plunged upwards, under his ribcage, toward his heart. His eyes and facial expression showed disbelief. Our eyes met and I saw his fear, his mouth opened and his own bloody bile oozed out and ran down his chin before depositing itself onto his shirt. He clutched at my hand that held the knife and tried to push it from his body, but I held it steady and then gave it a violent twist, letting the big blade cut his insides even more. His eyes rolled upwards as he took his last breath.

His weapon fell from his hand to the ground. His finger never made it to his trigger.

He was actually dead before I let his young muscular body slide down to the jungle floor.

Hurriedly, I searched him and found nothing useful. Grabbing his arm I quickly dragged him into the thicket where I had been hiding. I picked up his weapon and threw it in there on top of him. I noticed my knees were not shaking anymore. I located my Weatherby and slowly made my way to the river, still some 60 yards away. I still had a long rough road ahead of me.

When I reached the river, I replenished my water supply and then began searching upstream for a sharp bend that would allow me to cross while limiting my exposure to others. In less than an hour, I found where the river made a sharp bend. There, just above the bend, I crossed the river and knew it was only a matter of time before the trackers would find the VC's body and my trail. They were like bloodhounds.

The Viet Cong really were excellent trackers, so good they could follow a trail that was two days old. I walked backwards from the edge of the jungle out into the river; then as I emerged from the river, I made sure I walked backwards into the jungle again, hoping to fool them for a little while and, just maybe, adding a few more minutes of distance between them and me.

I decided to go to my primary pickup point first. If things got rough, I would still have 24 hours to make it to the final pickup point. The pickup locations were set in a large triangle, with each point of the triangle designated as a chopper rescue point — these three locations were five miles apart. The chopper would be over the first point at a certain date and time. If I had not arrived, the chopper would be at the second point exactly 10 hours later and follow the same scenario for the third and final pickup point. Therefore, I conceived a plan to go to my first pickup point; if for whatever reason I missed the chopper, I would make my way to the third pickup point. This pattern gave me a better chance for survival and the best chance for pickup by the chopper.

There were now eight trackers somewhere out there still searching for me. By doing what they didn't expect would help me make it back alive. I did not want to end up missing or having my body never found. The Viet Cong were very ruthless fighters. They would chop me up like liver in a heartbeat. So to have the best chance to stay alive, I had to think positive and keep them guessing and leave as few tracks as possible. Far into the night, I continued moving southeast. I only stopped when I thought it was necessary to check my position, using the compass and map. I didn't know how close the other trackers were. I just knew they were relentless in pursuit by nature.

Suddenly, it began to rain very hard. This was very common here in Vietnam. I could move a little faster in this downpour. I still had another two miles before I reached pickup point Alpha — that should take maybe two hours at most in this weather. The chopper was due at dawn — 0538 hours. It was now 0210 hours. The signal for my pickup was to set off a green smoke flare when I saw the chopper approaching.

The rain was so hard that vision was limited to 20 yards. But the rain was also a blessing, as it would wash out my tracks, making it impossible for the Viet Cong to follow my trail.

The ear shattering sound of many semi-automatic rifles firing suddenly shattered the night's stillness. Many weapons were firing at once. Instinctively I found myself hitting the ground trying to get under the first layer of mud, wanting the earth to swallow me up — but all I managed to do was pee all over myself.

I thought, '*They've found me!*" I didn't feel any pain from being shot, so after discovering I was not hit, I began to concentrate on my situation again.

It's raining like cat and dogs, so they couldn't have gotten a good target of me." I didn't know how many VC there were, or where they were. Soon, I discovered they were not shooting at me after all. The firefight sounded like it was somewhere off to my right, maybe 150 yards away. In this weather, it was hard to pinpoint exactly the direction or distance. I knew one thing for sure, now was the time to ease out of this area.

When the rain stopped just before dawn, I was waiting at pickup point Alpha. I had not heard or seen anyone else since the firefight during the night. I just hoped the chopper would be on time. Knowing how my luck worked, it would be late or something would happen when they tried to pick me up. I had made a sweep around the entire landing zone (LZ) prior to daybreak to insure the VC had not set an ambush. I heard the familiar sound of the chopper rotors; and as it approached at about 300 feet above the clearing, I set off the green flare. Once airborne, the pilot radioed that he had picked up the hitchhiker.

A military policeman (MP) driving a jeep met us at the airfield. The MP said, "I am to take you directly to Headquarters Intelligence." Minutes later, I gave a full briefing upon arrival to the duty officer. By 0900 hours, I had taken a shower and begun the task of cleaning my weapons.

One hour later, as I crawled into my cot, Gunnery Sgt. Davis came by to talk about the mission. He told me that last night a squad of South Vietnamese Marines and a few of our Marines had gotten in a firefight with a group of VC up near pickup point Alpha. I didn't mention to him just how close we were to each other. I just grunted, told him I had heard it, and then I turned over and passed out.

In the afternoon, Private First Class (Pfc.) Daniel Gibson, my spotter and partner on most missions, came by and offered me a beer; and, we shot the bull about the mission. After several beers, I crashed and was thankful my buddy had put me in my bunk.

Dan woke me at 0700 hours saying I needed to report to Headquarters Intelligence (HQI). Gunny also dropped by a few minutes later to make sure I had gotten the word. Gunny and I walked over together and reported to Maj. Henley. Soon Colonel (Col.) Bowers, our CO, and the intelligence officer Captain (Capt.) Swanson, joined us. Each had heard about my briefing and wanted to question me personally. Swanson wanted detailed information about the Viet Cong village that we called Cong3 so he could update his intelligence maps immediately.

Henley wanted details on how I avoided the trackers. Gunny's interest was in the operation of my weapons and any related problems. Col. Bowers wanted to know if everything went as planned. Each man was very thorough, and so was I. This was the time and place to correct anything that may have gone wrong, so the next mission would have a chance to be successful. We discussed my mission for two solid hours.

At the end of the meeting, Capt. Swanson mentioned a new target near the Cambodian border. Pfc. Gibson would accompany me on this trip, which would last about 10 to 12 days. Our target was a political figure planted by the Russians who had the backing of Hanoi. We had nine days before debarkation. Details would be provided in five days at our next scheduled meeting with Capt. Swanson.

Dan and I spent the next four days as a team on the firing range, continually striving to improve our accuracy, timing, and running, or trying to sleep. We cleaned our weapons after each day on the range. Our rifles were as accurate as we could get them. I consistently grouped five shots within a four-inch diameter at 600 yards with the help of Dan and his spotting scope. We saved the equipment checks until we knew exactly what we would be taking with us. At that point, our responsibility was to ensure everything was operational and ready for the upcoming mission.

****

Pfc. Gibson and I had finished breakfast by 0530 hours. After reporting to HQI at 0600 hours for the upcoming mission's briefing, we spent the next three hours with Swanson, Henley, and the Gunny going over maps, communications, and the assignment. This mission's target — a political commissioner and advisor attached to the VC 514th Battalion, which was fighting in the Delta and in the Cambodian triangle. He was from Hanoi, and he had a lot of authority. Hoa Lu Thayn often decided when, where, and who these battle-hardened Viet Cong regulars attacked.

The next four days we spent readying our equipment and studying personnel profiles of the target and the 514th Battalion Commander. We just might be going into the triangle!

We would be carrying a PRC-77 radio with us. Capt. Swanson shared information that suggested there could be a big VC gathering close to the border with Cambodia during our mission. Headquarters badly needed this information. Since the beginning of the war, the Viet Cong used Cambodia as a safe haven from which they regrouped or re-supplied by the North Vietnamese Army (NVA). Our pilots could not bomb either the NVA or VC in Cambodia or Laos.

We legally could not cross into Cambodia or Laos to fight the VC. If we were in Cambodia, *by accident*, we also had to be on the lookout for the Khmer Rouge guerrillas, who were allies with the VC. They had been bought off by the NVA. Khmer Rouge guerrillas were almost as bad as the VC, having killed thousands of their own people in a Communist-attempted political takeover of the Cambodian government. They now had control of the entire countryside in Cambodia.

Our mission was southwest of Saigon, near where the Mekong River flows out of Cambodia and enters South Vietnam on its journey down to the sea. It's one miserable place where temperatures reach 105 degrees in the shade. Humidity is near 100% almost every day, making normal breathing difficult. It rains there nearly every day, and the blood-sucking leeches are up to five inches long in those flat marshes along the river. Spiders, half the size of crabs, deliver bites that can kill or make you wish you were dead. Mosquitoes were as big as houseflies. Ticks the size of your thumbnail could quickly suck a pint of your blood.

November 8th, the afternoon before departure, Dan and I inventoried the equipment. Besides our ponchos, extra shoes, socks, and skivvies, we each would carry two canteens, a 782-pack full of C-rations (C-rats) of our choice, five M-26 grenades, three claymore mine bandoleers, and an M-57 electrical firing device. In addition, I packed 10 half-pound bars of C-4 explosives, and Dan packed the timers. Besides carrying a mission's normal weapons and ammo, Dan would also be lugging the radio, an M-49 spotting scope, and a waterproof canvas bag with our flares and flare launcher.

After making sure my scope lens was dry and cleaned, I put the protective caps over the scopes' lens. I taped the barrel on my Weatherby real tight and packed an extra 10 rounds for it. Finally, everything was packed — the maps with case, 1/2 gallon of extra drinking water, even a special net shirt to test for some manufacturer stateside. If it would help keep the big mosquitoes off us, we would gladly give it a try. I decided to take an old stand-by that belonged to Gunny. He offered to lend me his Thompson .45 caliber semi-automatic weapon, and I packed extra ammo and magazines for it.

We each took time to write letters home, assuring our families we were OK and would be writing again soon. This was procedure before departing for any mission.

Little did we know this mission would demand so much from each of us.

But, this is getting ahead of my beginnings that led to my service as a Marine.

CHAPTER 2

I was born in a little country hospital in Crestview, Florida, on January 14, 1942. My mother was a young 18-year-old-girl named Luevenia (Lou) Mitchem. She was filled with love, patience, and understanding. She was beautiful, vigorous, and hard working. But, she named me 'Melvin' — life has been an uphill fight every since.

I can't remember very many things in life that came easy, unless it was getting into trouble, and boy was I constantly good at that. I was not a troublemaker, but trouble usually found me.

I grew up in Niceville, Florida, just 18 miles south of where I was born, without my father. I was an unwedded child, raised by my mother, her four sisters, and my maternal grandmother. I learned early in life no one was giving me anything, except a hard time. If I wanted something, I had to scratch and fight for it.

My greatest joy as a young boy was deer hunting with Uncle Leroy Brown. He was everything I wanted to be — a great hunter, tracker, and one of the best riflemen in six counties in northwest Florida. He had this keen ability to live off the woods and swamps, which was abundant in our area of northwest Florida. Seemed we had to keep an eye out for water moccasins even walking the streets downtown. They would slither in from a nearby swamp or small creeks, which we called branches, and crawl up beside some stores or under your house — and even slip inside sometimes. A bite from a big snake could be deadly.

Once while hunting squirrels with Uncle Leroy in Alaqua Swamp when I was a young boy of 12, I had a bad experience with a water moccasin, which is also known as a "Cottonmouth" due to the inside of its mouth being white as cotton. I was sitting on a pile of fresh fallen leaves with my back up against a big white oak acorn tree. I spotted several gray squirrels playing in the tops of tall trees nearby.

I shot a squirrel out of a large sweet gum tree and watched it fall to the ground. Soon, I had killed three more squirrels, and I knew where each had fallen. I got up to begin retrieving the squirrels. When I reached the tree where the first had fallen near the big sweet gum's base, there was no squirrel to be seen. I eased around the side of that big sweet gum tree and saw a good-sized opening that was almost a triangular shape. I just knew that old squirrel had crawled into that opening. Using the barrel of my .22 rifle as a stick, I poked it into the hole and moved the barrel around in there as much as I could to flush the squirrel out. Nothing came out. But, I could hear it moving in there on the dry leaves. I pulled my .22 out from the opening, propped my rifle against the tree, and got down on my hands and knees so I could reach in and drag him out.

I knew Uncle Leroy had counted my shots and would expect me to show him a squirrel for every shot fired. That's just how he was. So, I wasn't about to let a squirrel get away if I could help it — looking inside hollow trees or into a sweet gum's hole was my normal way of sometimes retrieving squirrels.

As I tried looking into the opening, I was struck just above my left eye by a four-foot water moccasin, which was bigger around than my upper arm. Talk about messing in your drawers! I immediately fell backwards and saw the big cottonmouth slithering away. I panicked big time! I began screaming at the top of my lungs and running. I remembered screaming, *"I'm snake bit!" "I'm snake bit!"* I was crying, screaming, and scared to death of that big old moccasin. I just knew that I was going to die and had only maybe a few hours to live.

I don't know how Uncle Leroy caught me, but he did. I didn't run towards where he was hunting, but he heard me screaming and took off to intercept me. I just remember he grabbed me, picked me up in his big arms, and flat-out run to his old pickup parked a quarter mile away. He was telling me as he ran that I would be all right.

In less than 40 minutes, he and I were in front of Dr. Williams, who was inspecting my snakebite. Dr. Williams worked around my eye for a long time.

Finally, he said, "Young fellow, you sure are lucky. Both of that snake's fangs struck you in your eyebrow, and its fangs went clean through the eyebrow and exited out in your upper eyelid. His fangs went through this soft tissue so quickly that his venom hardly had any chance of getting into your system. Most of it ejected out onto your cheek. You will be sick for a few days, and I'm giving you a shot to help you to rest."

Once, a few years later, Uncle Leroy was teaching me to shoot a .243 caliber rifle at a sandpit, when a crow landed in a tall pine on the other side of the pit.

Pointing, he asked, "Do you see that crow across the sandpit in that tall pine tree?" I began to look very hard and finally saw the crow sitting in a tree at 70-plus yards from us.

"Yes sir, I see him," I said.

Uncle Leroy then said, "I'll show you how to shoot that old crow's head off with one shot."

After about 10 seconds of looking through his scope, he fired, and that dumb crow fell out of that tall pine. I was shocked!

Uncle Leroy said, "Melvin, go get him and check his head, because that was what I was aiming at."

That crow had almost all of his head missing. I absorbed anything and everything he was willing to share about tracking, hunting, and shooting from that moment on.

I spent a lot of time at his house. Aunt Evelyn and my cousins Sharyn, Donna, and Buddy got used to me poking my head in after I had run home from the bus stop and helped Grandma Williams with chores. For the next four years, Uncle Leroy took me under his wing and taught me what he knew. Buddy was just six — not old enough to go with us everyplace we went.

At every opportunity, my uncle taught me how to identify different birds and animal tracks. He showed me how to tell the sex of a deer by looking at its tracks. I learned to track game, the characteristic of game animals, and what these animals did when wounded, hunted, or frighten.

Then we ventured into the swamps where I learned how to track animals in this habitat and how to tell north from south in a swamp without the aid of the sun.

One basic point *I've always remembered was that man's instincts are like animals when they're wounded or hunted.*

* * * * * * *

September 2, 1961 after graduation from high school earlier in June, I ended up going into the Marine Corps. I voluntarily signed up. Well —

that's almost the truth! My closest friend was Billy Wayne, a big "bad" dude who was six feet one inches tall and 192 pounds. I was only five feet nine inches tall and weighed all of 165 pounds.

We considered ourselves very lucky to have grown up within three miles of Eglin Air Force Base (AFB). Eglin is located in the panhandle of northwest Florida. The small city of Niceville, located on Boggy Bayou, was one of the small towns close to the base; and it happens to be where Billy was born, and I was raised. It was our home.

When we were high school seniors, we became famous for starting fights with the base airmen for dating the local girls. Anytime we caught airmen with Niceville or Valparaiso girls, we usually beat the living crap out of them. We generally did our fighting from Friday evening through Sunday night at the skating rink, drive-in-theater, or one of the local burger hang outs. We didn't care if airmen dated girls from Fort Walton Beach or Crestview. We just hated them encroaching on our turf and dating "our" girls.

The base commander finally went to the community leaders to let them know the Air Force intended to put Niceville and sister city Valparaiso OFF LIMITS if these attacks did not stop immediately. We earned the distinction as the culprits. The cops took us out of school and drove us to Niceville city hall in a police cruiser. My mother, Billy's parents, and the mayors of both Niceville and Valparaiso, along with their police chiefs and two Air Force officers, were waiting for us.

After the two police chiefs finished reading the riot act to Billy and me, the two officers began telling us how we had been hurting not only airmen, but these two cities as well. The officers said that we could be responsible for the emergency room bills for three airmen, on top of the fines or jail time if we were found guilty of assault with bodily harm on any one of three dozen airmen.

When our parents had a chance to speak, it more accurately resembled "Yelling." Anyway, both of our parents promised everyone strict measures of punishment would be handed out, and they would make sure that these two boneheads would not be involved in anymore fighting . . . period, if the Air Force and the Twin Cities would choose not to prosecute us.

The two mayors asked that the police chiefs and Air Force officers meet with them privately in an adjoining room. Neither Billy nor I would say anything to our parents unless asked a question. I sat very still and with my head in my hands, looking at the floor.

Shortly, they all came back into the room. Both mayors told us how much money each of the cities could lose if they were put 'off-limits'. The amounts were staggering!

The two Air Force officers asked our parents if they would agree to let us go into the military service after school was out for the summer, in exchange for not pressing charges against either one of us. If either one of us did not enter the military service, we would be taken before a judge on the charges previously mentioned.

The choice given was to spend 6-12 months in jail for assault or join the armed forces soon after we graduated. We both chose the latter. Our parents also agreed to this. After graduation, we tried to go in the Navy on the buddy system. At the recruiting office, Billy failed the entrance exam. We then tried the Air Force in July — they certainly didn't want us!

Near the end of August and with time running out, we decided to try the Marine Corps. Bingo! Two hours later, we both were laughing and joking about the ordeal of going off to be "Jarheads."

Five days later, I was at the Trailways bus depot in Fort Walton Beach waiting for the bus that would take us to Montgomery, Alabama, for our physicals and swearing in. Billy was late as usual. Less than 10 minutes before the bus arrived, Billy called the old stand-up glass phone booth that was located outside the bus station.

A woman who was standing close to the phone answered it and yelled out, "Anybody named Melvin here?"

I went over to the phone booth and said, "That's me!" The woman handed me the phone.

Billy said, "I'm not going in the Marine Corps with you; I'm leaving for the Army in two days. My parents got things changed for me."

I began to curse him for everything I could think of, telling him how yellow and chicken he was. I promised to put a beating on him he wouldn't soon forget when I saw him again.

He just laughed and said, "You better pack a big lunch buddy boy; whipping my butt won't be easy."

* * * * * * *

Sixteen weeks later, I graduated from boot camp at Paris Island, South Carolina, and went up to Camp Geiger, North Carolina, for six additional weeks of weapons and combat infantry training. I was now Pfc. Melvin Mitchem, United States Marine Corps (USMC).

Upon completion at Geiger, I took 10 days' leave and came home on a train. I had never rode a train until then and that train had a club car. I was drunk as a skunk when my Mom and my Grandmother met the train at the nearest train depot over in Flomaton, Alabama.

After being home a few days, I tried looking up my old pal Billy. His brother, Randall, said he was stationed at Fort Gordon and only got to come home about every three or four months on a three-day weekend pass.

I had grown quite a bit and put on some weight while away at boot camp. I now was six feet tall and weighed 186 pounds. It would have been one heck of a fight! I could pump out 50 pushups, turn around, and do 100 sit ups without stopping.

Visiting Aunt Evelyn and Uncle Leroy again was great. He and I went off mullet fishing and had a ball talking about old times when I was younger. She fried up the fresh mullet and made hush puppies, pork-n-beans, and cole slaw. Mom, my sister Vivian, and Grandma came, and I got to see my cousins Sharyn, Donna, and Buddy again. We had one of the best times of family fellowship and eating that I can remember.

I knew that I must also visit Aunt Lorene and her family while I was home. This included my cousins Larry and Wayne and my Uncle Cole.

I had to stop by and see my Aunt Viola, Uncle Bob, as well as my cousins Darlene and Linton. Linton was also one to stay in trouble all the time. He and I were really close — guess one could say we had a lot in common. He really was a great baseball pitcher; two years later, he would receive a big bonus from the San Francisco Giants to pitch for their organization. Later in his career, he also pitched for Pittsburg, Atlanta, and the Dodgers' organizations.

One other thing I wanted to do while home was pay a visit to Eglin AFB. Since I was now in the armed forces, I could visit the enlisted men's club and enjoy its benefits. Dressed in my Marine Corps winter green uniform, I thought I was something with that single stripe on my sleeves.

I intentionally tried to bump into airmen as I entered the club. The few that I bumped into moved out of my way, apologized, and stepped back. Later, I decided to get a serving of cake and ice cream, but I was not going to wait in line. I walked up close to the front of the line and asked two airmen, "Do you mind if a Marine cuts in front of you guys?"

Those two and others nearby said, "It's OK for you to jump line, but airmen can't."

I stayed to play pool for a few hours and realized that strangely, I had mellowed out and actually enjoyed playing pool with these fellow servicemen.

CHAPTER 3

My next duty station was Sea School at Norfolk, Virginia. I was selected as one of the 10 outstanding Marines in our platoon at Parris Island. These either were assigned to serve two years' sea duty in a Marine Detachment aboard a Navy ship or selected to serve two years on Embassy Duty overseas. Traveling the world and taking in the sights would be a real adventure, considering my entire lifetime prior to entering the Marines had been spent in two states, Florida and Alabama. And, the largest boat I had ever been on was a 52-foot shrimp boat owned by Mr. Walter Owens of Niceville, Florida.

It seemed an old nemesis of mine followed me up to Norfolk. I had spent part of my paycheck on something that I could use to share my adventures with my family and friends. I bought a real nice color camera with two lenses, and one of those was a real nice seven-inch zoom lens for taking close up pictures.

The first Saturday that I had off, I walked around the base taking photos of me and my friends. Everything went so smoothly that day, so on Sunday I eased off down to the other side of the base where the large navy warships were tied up in port. Armed with two new rolls of 35mm color film, I set out exploring.

Finding several large ships, I took photos of an aircraft carrier, a battle ship, and a tanker.

I walked further down the pier; and through an opening between two smaller ships, I looked across the way and saw a couple of submarines tied up on another pier. Being full of energy and wanting to show my family back home all these big ships, I ventured on over to where the subs were tethered to also get some nice photos of them.

I was busy clicking pictures of the subs and didn't realize that I had caused sort of a stir among the Navy guys. There were maybe five sailors that walked up, curiously watching me taking pictures.

I turned and asked, "Do you guys wanted me to take a few pictures of y'all also?"

Most of them shied away, excitedly expressing, "No!"

But two sailors stepped forward with some sort of arm bands on and both wore a .45 caliber pistol side arm. These two sailors wanted my camera paraphernalia.

One of them asked, "Can we have your camera, bag, and film?"

I quickly answered, "Not on your life!" That sure got them all fired up in a hurry.

The next thing I saw was a .45 caliber pistol pointing at me and both of them yelling, "Get down and spread eagle, now!"

I soon found out that <u>no one</u> was supposed to be taking pictures of the Navy's ships.

I believe those Navy boys thought I was a spy. They kept asking me my name and who were my contacts. Over and over I told them my name and said that I was in Sea School here on base and had bought the camera to shoot some photos to send home to my family. I was taken in a jeep to a building where others, including several Navy officers, now questioned me for almost an hour.

Finally, they called the Marine Sea School and my superiors confirmed that a Pfc. Melvin Mitchem was currently going through Sea School training, but that he had signed out to go on base that morning at 0958 hours.

The Navy kept my film of all the ships and subs. I was taken back to Sea School in a jeep. One of the Navy officers who questioned me went along. He kept my camera bag in his possession until he had given the Sea School's Officer of the Day a full briefing, along with the instructions that Pfc. Mitchem was not to take photos of Navy installations or ships on this or any base in the future. He then gave my camera to the Officer of the Day.

I lost my camera and any free time that I might have gotten until I graduated from Sea School. After eight weeks of inspections, spit and polish, drills, and more spit and polish, I had orders for the USS Constellation CVA-64 — the largest conventional powered aircraft carrier in the U.S. Navy fleet. Its current homeport was New York City, New York.

Wow! And to think, until I joined the Marines, the largest city I'd ever been in was Montgomery, Alabama. Now, I'm going to New York City.

I thought about Billy, who I wouldn't see again until after finishing my two-year tour of sea duty — how he might be stuck on some desolate Army base, while I would get a world tour. Talk about justice! This was it! A world tour and they pay me to take it. Wow!

The USS Constellation was big like a city. There was everything on board ship that a city had, except traffic lights and women. I met some really good Marines and sailors; some of them became close or good friends. We shared quarters, duty together, liberty, playing fast pitch softball, sightseeing in foreign lands, the loneliness of being away from home, and the spirit of the Corps. We became a band of brothers! We were U.S. Marines and sailors.

This was a peaceful time in my life. I had met this girl in New York City named Peggy, and we began to see each other for the next four months when the ship was in port. We went to the many parks, either sightseeing or on a picnic when the opportunity would allow. Every other date, we would take a sightseeing trip around the city. We even managed to take in a few Yankee's baseball games. The ship, *Connie* — short for her name, "Constellation" spent the next four months in the South Atlantic Ocean and the Caribbean Sea. We operated out of the U.S. naval base at Guantanamo Bay, Cuba.

The Constellation went back to New York and departed New York City one month later for San Diego, California. San Diego was going to become our new home port.

Before our arrival in San Diego, the ship made port calls in Saint Thomas, Virgin Islands - Trinidad - Rio De Janeiro, Brazil - Valparaiso, Chile - Panama City, Panama - and Acapulco, Mexico.

Peggy traveled across country and met me in San Diego upon our arrival. For the next five months, we dated almost every other weekend. She lived with her relatives in Burbank, a suburb of Los Angeles, California.

In February 1963, the Constellation left San Diego for a Pacific Far East (Westpac) cruise.

Our first port of call was Hawaii. There, my cousin Eva Thompson met the *Connie* when we docked in Pearl Harbor. Being a Marine Orderly meant you were the personal bodyguard of the ship's Captain or Executive Officer (XO), and there were times when special favors could be arranged. When Eva met the ship, I was allowed to bring her aboard and give her a grand tour. Eva was married to a sergeant in the Air Force stationed at Hickman Field in Hawaii, and they had a baby girl.

After leaving Hawaii, while cruising in the Philippine Sea, our long range radar planes picked up two unidentified aircraft that turned out to be two huge Russian Bear long-range bombers approaching the ship. Six of our fighter jets raced toward the bombers and intercepted them about 300 miles out from the ship.

The *Connie's* Captain was *'COOL'* — he asked a Senior Chief Petty Officer *(senior NCO)* to hurry and signal a proper greeting to our Russian friends. Three of our jet fighters flew right alongside each giant Russian bomber when they flew by the ship.

This Senior Chief ordered all flight crews to line up on the flight deck in a formation which provided a curious jester of a wrist with fist attached and a *'finger'* giving a salute to the Russians. Our fighter pilots that were escorting those bombers could also see the *'BIRD'* and all of them thought it was great.

Shortly afterwards, we visited Subic Bay, Philippines. The *Connie* then headed for Hong Cong, China, and finally Yokosuka, Japan — our home away from home.

In July 1963 while steaming close to the island of Formosa, China, we encountered the leader of the Nationalist Chinese people, President Chiang Kai-Shek, his wife, and his high-ranking officers who led the revolt against the Red Army of Communist China. He and a few million Chinese made their way by boats to the island of Formosa lying off the Chinese mainland.

The U.S. Navy acted as host and provided the President an 'Air Show' demonstrating the capabilities of the aircraft on board the *Connie*. I must say it was impressive!

We also visited the Japanese ports of Kobe – Iwakuni – Sasebo - and Beppu before heading toward Buckner Bay, Okinawa. Then it was back to Hawaii where I spent more time with my cousin Eva Thompson and her family. This time, Eva, her little daughter Sondra Kay, and I took a grand tour of the area. *What beautiful islands!*

This Westpac cruise lasted until we returned to San Diego in early September 1963.

After exclusively dating Peggy again for every weekend I had off since returning to San Diego, we decided to get married. My best man at my wedding was my best friend, Lance Cpl. Harry Boling of Bristol, TN.

Harry and I 'sort of' watched each others' backs during our port calls around South America and the Far East.

I was part of a large group of Marines on the *Connie* transferred to either Camp Pendleton or Camp Lejeune.

* * * * * * *

I was stationed at Camp Lejeune, North Carolina, in K Co., 3rd Battalion, 6th Marines. I was selected for special assignment in the Panama Canal Zone in early February 1964. I was part of a special Marine training team that instructed certain Army, Navy, and Air Force personnel in escape, evasion, and jungle survival.

The trainees included Army helicopter pilots, truck drivers, supply personnel, and cooks and Navy and Air Force pilots and aircrews. Our country was close to war in Vietnam, and these guys needed to know how to survive if shot down or captured. One hundred fifty Panamanian soldiers played the part of the Viet Cong. They were instructed to speak only Spanish and wore black pajamas and straw hats. When, or if captured, the trainees were treated like prisoners of war (POWs). Each school session ran for two weeks, and then a new group was assigned for training.

The last day of February, I had orders to return to 3rd Battalion, 6th Marines. The Battalion flew out by helicopter to the waiting helicopter battle group carrier USS Coral Sea, which was cruising off the Carolina coast. This ship was taking the 3rd Battalion down to the Dominican Republic, near Cuba. Communist radicals had overthrown their own government and threatened to invade the U.S. Embassy. Our mission was to secure the Embassy, to ensure its personnel were safe, and, finally, to eliminate the communist trained force that threatened to overrun our Embassy. These guys were shooting at anyone who stepped outside any of the buildings inside the Embassy compound.

The Coral Sea arrived on the scene our fifth day after boarding. It stayed miles off shore, cruising back and forth near the Dominican Republic. Marines were airlifted off the Coral Sea by helicopter and landed on a golf course on the outskirts of San Domingo, the capital city. As our group of helicopters approached the golf course, it was easy to see the tracers that the insurgents were firing at us as we flew in to land. The choppers were armed with rocket pods, so when they got a fix on where the insurgents where…it was "Rockets away!" Actually, only two were fired.

We landed without any further incidents.

As soon as all companies and equipment were on the ground, the 3rd Battalion quickly assembled into its four rifle companies and one weapons company. 'K' Company and the Weapons Company were assigned to enter the city via the main four lane highway that ran alongside the golf course. It was only two miles to San Domingo and another mile after reaching the city to the U.S. Embassy.

The other rifle companies were given different assignments and routes to take.

One company traveled up the four lane highway going in the opposite direction from the city. They were to establish road blocks at a large four-way intersection a half-mile from the golf course and act as a rear guard and secure the area around the golf course LZ. Two other rifle companies took different routes to the Embassy.

'K' Company and Weapons Company left the golf course and kept 40 yards distance between companies. 'K' Company put 1st Platoon up front as point to make sure the way was clear for both companies to move ahead. Once we actually entered San Domingo, our Platoon Leader Staff Sgt. Corbin split the platoon into four squads. There were two squads on each side of the four-lane highway; both squads moved forward two men at a time from tree-to-tree or building-to-building. Moving slowly due to the potential of possible sniper attacks and always alert, we all finally reached the Embassy safely.

The Embassy had two other buildings on the grounds with a five-foot high wall around the four-acre compound. The wall was one and one-half feet thick and consisted of reinforced concrete and solid rock.

After ensuring that U.S. Embassy personnel were safe, Marine fire-teams were assigned to areas along the walls to watch and defend. Snipers were taking pot shots at anything moving. That night we sent out patrols to locate the many sniper bases of operations. I was assigned to a recon patrol. Our mission was to determine the number and location of enemy snipers taking pot shots at us and embassy personnel within the compound.

Our squad leader, Sgt. LeBlanc, was a nine-year veteran of the Corps. Smart and level-headed, LeBlanc was also as tough as they come, never taking crap from anyone. After receiving orders to grease-up, we checked each other to make sure the camouflage (camo) paint was properly applied. Each of us was issued 100 rounds for our M-14s.

The Embassy was surrounded on three sides by much taller buildings that were about five to nine stories high. We were to search each of the three buildings on the east side for snipers. Sgt. LeBlanc decided he would keep the squad together at each building and assign a fire-team to each floor. None of the three buildings we were to search had electrical power.

I was a fire-team leader and had five men. Assigned the first floor and basement, our job was to make sure the enemy was not in our area of responsibility and that no one entered or left the building. Once all levels were searched, Sgt. LeBlanc marked that building inspected. My fire-team was the first to enter the darkened building. In my mind, I thought there might be a sniper or two waiting for us. Butterflies were as big as dragons in my stomach.

Everyone had taped a flashlight to the side of his weapon. I first sent a rifleman inside the front door to set up and provide cover fire for the others as we went in one at a time, until everyone was inside. I had already assigned two men, one with an automatic weapon and the other a rifle, to watch the stairs going up, as well as those going down to the basement, and to guard the elevator. The rest of us moved one door at a time down darkened hallways until we had searched the first floor. At that point, the fire-team moved down the steps into the pitch-black basement one at a time, until everyone was down there, except the two Marines guarding the stairwells and elevator.

We searched every room and closet in the basement and discovered this area was where the building supplies were stored. The basement had an exit door in the back, which opened into an alleyway. I suppose this was where delivery trucks dropped off or picked up supplies.

Sgt. LeBlanc was calling for me to come up to the main lobby. I detailed two men to secure the back exit door, and then meet the rest of us in the main lobby.

LeBlanc asked, "What has your team found?"

Quickly, I informed Sgt. LeBlanc that there were mainly just small office rooms on the first floor and our fire-team had thoroughly inspected each room. I also told him about the basement situation with the back supply entrance door. There were no booby traps in our search area. Most of the rooms appeared to be offices of some company.

LeBlanc said he could use my help on the third floor. So I assigned three guys to watch and secure the first floor; my rifleman and I then went up to the third floor to assist. One third floor window was knocked out in a room facing the Embassy, and a lot of sand bags had been set up about five feet back from the window so someone could shoot at the Embassy without getting hit by return rifle fire. Sgt. LeBlanc noted the exact location of that window on paper. At least one sniper position was discovered in each building.

These snipers were not in the same league with Marine sharpshooters, but still good enough to cause concern. With any kind of luck, they might just hit one of us if they were allowed to continue shooting. We were not worried so much about the bullet with our name on it, just the one that had *'to whom it may concern'* on it.

Soon after daylight, the shooters returned and began taking pot shots at anyone who moved from either of the housing buildings or presented themselves as a target.

During our second day at the Embassy, the Captain held a meeting with squad leaders. In about 10 minutes, Sgt. LeBlanc emerged and summoned the fire-team leaders to join him. What we heard was unbelievable! It didn't make sense. There had to be a mistake.

"Washington has said you cannot shoot at the enemy until he first fires at you, and then, we cannot use excessive firepower."

I was hoping LeBlanc would say, "Just kidding guys." But, I could tell he was as mad as we were about these new orders.

He said, "Maj. General Greene, 6th Marines Commanding Officer, tried talking with the Pentagon, but they told him, this order came down from the White House."

During our fifth day, while eating lunch, we came under fire from two of the three buildings in our area of responsibility. The snipers had changed their schedule, trying their luck during the middle of the day. Normally, they would fire a few rounds in the morning, then again in the late afternoon. They had never taken pot shots during midday — until today. The snipers used a flash suppresser that made it real hard to see a muzzle flash during daylight. We believed it was possibly Russian made.

"Corporal Mitchem, get that sniper off of our back." LeBlanc ordered.

"He's history Sarge!" I replied.

After getting the signal that the sniper was still firing from the third floor of the first building, my team moved out. He was using the second window from our left to take his pot shots. The third floor of this building was the only logical place to fire at the embassy compound. It provided the best view of the compound. The large old oak trees hindered the view from the second floor level, and from the fourth and fifth. The sniper had switched rooms since yesterday.

The team was now in a good observation position. I waited until he fired again, then I had Pfc. Okie Hammond, the best M-79 man in our company, place one round of white phosphorus (WP) in the sniper's lap. As the room exploded with a white flash and fireball, we knew we would not receive another attack from that same location. The second sniper, obviously deciding he was not ready to die after seeing his buddy blown to pieces, hightailed it out of the area.

That night, I asked Sgt. LeBlanc about taking my fire-team to set a few surprise booby traps for the snipers to contend with when they arrived before daylight. Sgt. LeBlanc explained my idea to the Captain and received his OK. At about 2300 hours, my fire-team exited the compound rear gate. With stealth swiftness, we crossed the street and entered the buildings the snipers had been using. A few M-26 grenades were set with trip wires so that anyone using the stairwell leading to the third floor would detonate the grenades. Inside the second building, the grenades were set just inside the doorways on the third floor with a trip wire installed six inches above the floor.

At the third building, we planted small amounts of C-4 explosives with detonators secured to trip wires on the stairwells. This method would surely give a big lift to whoever was trying to reach that third floor.

At 0415 hours that morning, a loud explosion in one of the buildings awakened everyone in the Embassy. Along with the explosion came screams of pain and cries for help in Spanish — all coming from the first building where we had set the grenades.

Three days later, I took a five-man team on a recon patrol at 2200 hours. Our objective was to locate the enemy's staging area for their sniper attacks. We knew it was outside our perimeter, which was now a 300-yard radius around the Embassy. Although we had expanded our security perimeter, the snipers continued taking pot shots from just beyond that point.

The recon team, moving slowly under the cover of darkness after leaving our perimeter, kept our backs against the wall of every building, thus eliminating a rooftop sniper getting a shot at us. Each building could potentially harbor a sniper or a rebel force waiting for a chance to waste a Marine. Building by building we moved; several times movement in a doorway turned out to be a friendly, which would hurry back inside and close the door.

We had been gone for a little less than an hour, having moved just nine blocks, when suddenly a voice from inside a dark tobacco store doorway uttered in broken English, "I can show you where rebels are."

I turned suddenly, looking at this man, standing four feet away, and asked him his name.

Nervous and scared, he gave me his name and then said, "They come here and steal my tobacco every day. I cannot have business if they continue stealing from me. You kill those rebels who murder and steal from me?"

He pointed toward the back door and said, "We go now, this way."

Telling him to "wait a minute," I radioed the Captain to pass this informant's name and address onto headquarters, asking for a security check on a Roberto Silva Garcia, the shop owner. Within minutes, I got the okay regarding Mr. Garcia. So I asked him to show us where the rebels were. With the team at ready, we followed him down back alleys for 30 minutes, when finally he stopped and pointed.

"There," he said, pointing to a gray two-story house on the other side of the street from us. I thanked him, and then assigned Private (Pvt.) Lewis to stay with him and keep him at that present position until we returned.

After surveying the layout, I determined the best way to observe the house was from the roof of a four-story building, on our side of the street. It was within 80 yards of the gray house. I had sent two of my men to watch the rear of the gray house, and Lance Cpl. Jennings and I went to the roof of the four-story to observe the target. I had instructed everyone to regroup at 0315 hours where Pvt. Lewis was guarding the informant, Mr. Garcia. With any luck, this would allow ample time to reach our lines before daybreak.

Jennings and I had been on the roof for 20 minutes when we observed two men entering the target house. They soon came out, and each was carrying a rifle. Time went by fast because there were lots of people going in and out of the house. Most exited with a weapon. At 0315 hours, Jennings and I were the last to reach Pvt. Lewis' position. The other two team members reported that there were six men who exited the back door with weapons. The location and address of the house was noted so the information could be relayed to the Captain.

Before leaving Mr. Garcia at his shop, I assured him the U.S. Embassy would replace the items that had been stolen, after we removed the rebel force. The Captain made this assurance when I called for the security check on Mr. Garcia. I reported the exact location and activity we observed in the gray house to Headquarters, and I thanked Mr. Garcia for his assistance.

"The Ambassador personally thanks you for your help," I stated to Mr. Garcia.

We then headed toward the U.S. Embassy. As we approached an alleyway, a man fired at us and ran down the darkened alley. Upon reaching that alley, Jennings saw the man run into a small white house located at the back end of that alley. Suddenly, the sound of a heavy machine gun was almost deafening. The machine gun was a heavy .50 caliber set up inside the white house, firing out one of the windows — we were the target! The large bullets were tearing out massive chunks of concrete whenever they hit a building. From where we were on the street, I worried about other rebels joining in the fight or possibly already being in position to attack us. I grabbed the radio, but a lucky shot from the sniper who had run down the alley wiped out any hope of reaching the Captain.

Along part of the alleyway at the street was a low stone wall about two feet high, affording a way to cross the alley. But to reach the small stone wall required crossing nearly 10 feet of open alleyway. Small arms fire also started coming at us from the direction we had come, indicating two or three people were shooting at us from our rear position. The way to the Embassy would have us crossing the alleyway which the .50 caliber guarded.

Lewis and Jennings kept the rebels heads down that were shooting at us at from our rear, spitting out steady streams of M-14 rounds. With Lewis and Jennings covering our rear, I decided we would have to cross that 10-foot open alley, one at a time.

The first person to cross would lay down cover fire when he reached the next building. Pvt. Taylor went first, and as soon as he entered the open alley space, the .50 caliber opened up again.

Pvt. Taylor dove head first behind the small wall and began crawling to the next building on our street, where he set up cover fire for the rest of us by firing at the machine gun. Pvt. Ates followed him, and then I went next. Ates and I set up a cover fire to assist Pvt. Lewis and Lance Cpl. Jennings in getting safely across the alley. The .50 caliber was consistently tearing up the top part of the small wall, knocking out small chunks of stone. Jennings made it, but it was close. There wasn't much wall left in certain places. Lewis, being a little overweight and slower than the rest of us, thought he would have difficulty crossing the alleyway and so began by trying a different approach — crawling across on his stomach.

Just before Pvt. Lewis reached the small wall, the enemy spotted him as he rolled onto his back. He was trying to unhook his ammo belt, which had snagged on a short piece of old rusty pipe protruding a few inches above the sidewalk, while he was on his stomach. When the .50 caliber opened up, Lewis was caught cold turkey out in the open.

"I'm hit! I'm hit!" he screamed.

There was panic for a second; Jennings then crawled to the end of the low wall and held out his rifle barrel, screaming for Lewis to grab it and hold on. Jennings then pulled him behind the little wall as the rest of us provided cover fire. I was able to carefully examine Lewis' wound, as it was now getting daylight. A single .50 caliber bullet had just creased his lower stomach, cutting it open like a scalpel for nearly seven inches just below his navel. None of his organs were damaged, but his intestines kept trying to fall out. He was bloody and wet from his own stomach fluids oozing out.

We feared his intestines would dry out since we did not have water canteens on this mission; so, we urinated on his intestines to insure they stayed moist. If Lewis' intestines dried out, he could have very serious complications or die. This was a technique that was taught to all of us back at Lejeune in Emergency Field First Aid class.

We worked together to make a stretcher, using his poncho and two M-14s; and, we fashioned a make-shift bandage for his wound from torn pieces of one of our T-shirts.

A half-hour later, we were still receiving hostile fire from our rear. Pvt. Taylor laid down cover fire that kept the rebels at bay, as we slowly made our way toward the Embassy.

"Marines coming in," Pvt. Ates called out from up front.

Sgt. LeBlanc led a dozen men to aid in our rescue. His men quickly took the stretcher carrying Lewis and quickly passed out additional ammo. Within 10 minutes, we were out of that area and near a park that was open enough for chopper egress; so, we took Pvt. Lewis there to be airlifted back to the Coral Sea for surgery. The last week in March, with the fighting over and our Embassy again safe, we received orders to board ship and return to Camp Lejeune, North Carolina. We arrived back at base on the 3rd of April.

I took two weeks of leave time after signing up for "Special Assignment-Vietnam."

CHAPTER 4

After returning to Camp Lejeune, I immediately signed up for "Special Assignment" in South Vietnam. On April 27, 1964, I flew into South Vietnam on a big military jet.

The United States military was already involved in Vietnam as military advisors and U.S. weapons trainers and functioned as an intelligence-gathering source for the South Vietnamese and our government. This was President Kennedy's 4,000-man task force that was approved by Congress a few years earlier to assist the South Vietnamese people seeking Democracy. President Johnson gave the order to continue personnel rotations in this theater.

I saw this as a chance for me to help stop the spread of Communism in the world.

I was gung-ho, and I wanted to get back into some kind of action where I could use some of my skills. After all, I assured my wife Peggy and my mother, it wasn't like I would be in combat. I was just going over to instruct the South Vietnamese on the proper way to use American weapons and equipment in whatever situation arose.

Approaching Bien Hoa airfield near Saigon, I looked at the landscape from my window of the large jet and thought, *"How could fighting even exist in this peaceful and beautiful green countryside?"* Talk about first impressions being wrong!

I had heard all the wild stories — where a little Vietnamese girl would sell you cokes during the day, then provide information to the enemy for artillery fire on your position during the night or little boys selling you their mother or sister one night, then the next night they would plant a grenade in your area, trying to kill you and other Americans. There was also a story about cute young girls in Saigon that were suicide bombers who had the tires on their bicycles filled with nails and explosives. They would sit on their bike's seat wearing a split skirt that showed they were not wearing panties trying to draw a crowd of U.S. Army, Marines, or South Vietnamese soldiers, and then blow everyone to hell and back that gathered around her.

* * * * * * *

Our call letters were "Delta–Two-Foxtrot" on the PRC-77 radio. HQI still used "Hotel-Nine-Alpha." They would be operating on frequency 88.63; and, if the communications band became overloaded or the weather turned bad, they would switch to 79.29 as a backup. Both of these frequencies are monitored by HQI at all times.

My sniper assault team was being airlifted by chopper to within six miles of our Delta destination. We would have to walk in, through elephant grass, rice patties, and low flatlands, until we reached the marsh. Upon reaching the Hoy River, we were to turn south and travel about three miles. Sounded easy, the way Gunny Davis described it! This all had to be done without the VC knowing a Marine sniper team was in their backyard.

The helicopter set us down at 1030 hours; then it was quickly airborne again. After leaving the helicopter, I shot a compass reading to take us to our next grid square. I then had Dan radio *'Hotel-Nine-Alpha'* telling them, *"The pigeons are on the roost."* We then slowly eased into the high elephant grass and disappeared from human sight in a few seconds. We are now just two crazy Jarheads looking for trouble in Charlie's backyard.

Our only chance to see this mission through was to move very slowly. I don't want to risk the mission by being careless or cause us to get shot by not being cautious. We have 10 days to complete our mission. It started raining, slowly at first, then harder with every minute. We slipped our ponchos on and continued our journey.

This whole area was a worm-bed for VC. As I said — this is their backyard! They would like nothing better than to be able to hang our hair on their belts. The feat of killing a Marine sniper team would really elevate any VC's status. If I screwed up, they just might do that, too. 'HQI' holds me responsible for the mission, along with the safe return of an essential and experienced sniper team — Dan and me.

Dan was not only my friend, but on missions he was my spotter, my flank security, my radioman, my flare man during night shooting — a very vital part of this team. Me, I only kill, bark orders, make decisions, and hope the decisions are the right ones.

We reached the end of the high grass. I waited five minutes after looking around before we emerged from the grass, crawling low down an embankment. It had taken us 90 minutes to move through the grass.

"Smoking lamp is lit," I said while thinking this may be our last smoke for a while. We enjoyed the smoke, then put the butts out, and put the butt in our pockets. I was not leaving a trail of American cigarette butts that would lead VC trackers to us.

I surveyed the patties while I smoked and saw the maze of dikes through the rain. The dikes appeared to be real muddy, and that would make our footing very bad. I decided we would move slowly as we walked in the patties — staying low, sidling up next to the dikes for added security. I estimated it would take about an hour to travel 300 yards across the rice patties, moving ever so slowly; but, this maneuvering would give us a better chance of staying alive.

To provide extremely fast reloading when necessary, Dan taped his magazines together in an inverted position before we departed base. He also painted the tape on the magazines with green dye.

The mud on the bottom of the rice patty was clinging to our shoes, making them feel like 10-pound weights that were sucking our shoes off our feet. I wear sneakers and require my spotter to do the same, which allows slipping through woods or jungle much quieter, running a lot faster, and traversing distances more easily than with heavy boots on our feet.

When I was first selected for sniper missions, I explained to Gunny Davis that I would have a much better chance of survival if I wore my Corps-issued sneakers. Gunny just wanted results. He didn't care what I wore — just get him positive results. I also scarfed up an extra pair from a short-timer, and I borrowed a can of green dye from an army jeep parked outside a supply shed. Presto! — two pairs of green high-top sneakers.

We were halfway across the rice field, and I suddenly signaled for Dan to drop. Four Vietnamese men were walking on an adjoining dike in our direction.

"Where did they come from?" "Did they have weapons?" "Could they be VC or sympathizers?" "Had they spotted us?" These questions raced through my mind as I peeked over the dike at them.

They were indeed farmers, for they carried the tools of their trade across their shoulders on their way to do some afternoon work. As suddenly as they appeared, they exited onto an adjoining dike and were busily discussing what farmers discuss. They had appeared from the opposite side of the dike that we were walking next to — the slow movement, the low profile, and the earthen dike kept us from being spotted.

Even though they had come no closer than 100 hundred yards to us, I surmised they had not seen us because they were walking along with their heads down, watching their footing.

After leaving the rice fields, we entered a large flatland full of small trees and large insects, which apparently had not eaten in a year. They feasted on our body sweat, biting and sucking on any exposed human flesh. Three hours later, we dragged our tired, worn out, insect-riddled bodies up under a small grove of banana trees, ate a few bananas, and rested. I suggested that we swap out getting a few hours shut-eye. Dan agreed! He was instructed to awaken me at 2130 hours. My body screamed for rest. Moving for hours in a squat position is very painful to one's back and legs. Soon, I went into a dead sleep.

Dan knew to keep a sharp eye back toward the rice fields, just in case those farmers by day turned into Viet Cong by night.

Dan remained alert and watchful, but allowed his thoughts to wander to his girl friend Kathy and his family. He was from Baltimore, Maryland. His father was a sergeant in Baltimore's police department, where he had walked a beat since Dan was a small boy. His mother was working at Sears, where she had been supervising store clerks for years. His dad also was a deacon at the Harvest Life Baptist Church, a few blocks down the street from his house. His mom could make the best apple pie in all of Maryland.

Kathy was eighteen, with short dark brown hair and the world's cutest smile. Kathy wrote him a letter every day. Dan had wanted them to get married before he left for Vietnam, but Kathy said, "No, we'll wait until after you return from Vietnam."

Dan was an offensive tackle on his high school football team. His coaches kept him lifting weights, and when he played his senior year, he was six feet three inches tall and weighed in at 259 pounds. His team went undefeated during the regular season, but lost in the state playoffs. He had high hopes for a football scholarship from the University of Maryland. During Dan's junior and senior years of high school, most all the guys followed the news concerning Vietnam. Each knew they could be drafted to answer their country's call to arms if a war broke out. Dan and a few of his friends decided to go ahead and join the Marines. The day he got orders for Vietnam, he remembered Kathy's exact words to him.

"Please come back to me, and promise me you won't do anything foolish to get yourself hurt," she had said.

* * * * * * *

A smile crossed Dan's face as he thought of the number of missions he and Sgt. Mitchem had been on — each one seeming more dangerous than the previous. Sometimes, they had a slim chance of making it back alive, or so it seemed — like this one now. But Sgt. Mitchem was one sharp Marine. His instincts were like those of an Apache Indian, even though he wasn't Indian. Those keen instincts had saved both of their lives more than once.

Dan remembered one mission in particular. The target was a real spark plug, a smart senior officer in the regular Viet Cong Army — Colonel Loa Hu Minh. Col Minh was an expert at guerrilla warfare fighting. Minh was very hard to locate. He moved constantly and kept select bodyguards with him at all times. Mitch trailed him like a wolf, after we spotted him in a village. For two days and nights, we stayed on his trail. Mitch wouldn't let us sleep. We were constantly moving and eating on the go just like these VC were doing.

"We are getting real close to them," Mitch stated as he stopped to observe the sign left by the three-man security team surrounding Col Minh.

"I hope they are no better at protecting Minh than they are at concealing their trail," Mitch whispered.

We moved silently through the dense undergrowth, so slowly that it took us 10 minutes to move 20 yards.

Mitch found half of the group asleep along the side of a small brook in the jungle. It appeared that Minh and one guard slept while the other two guards were lookouts, somewhere near camp. Mitch left me and began to crawl slowly, trying to spot the lookouts. After 40 minutes, Mitch returned and signaled for me to follow him. Again, very slowly we began crawling toward the two sleeping men some distance away.

I was crawling very cautiously just 10 yards to the left of Mitch when suddenly, one of the sleeping VC jumped up and charged right at me, screaming at the top of his lungs. He was about 30 yards out in front of me, firing his AK-47 from the hip as he ran at full speed in my direction.

Surely, he couldn't see me lying in the undergrowth in the dark. He must have smelled me or sensed my presence, because bullets were clipping vegetation off all above and around me.

I was stunned and couldn't move or think clearly for an instant. My M-14 was still across my arms, under my chest. I had not tried to raise it to fire. I did not have time! I would surely die right here. He was so close now, I was afraid he would run over me.

Before I could move my weapon, he tripped over me and fell onto the undergrowth. I rolled over on my side to shoot him, but I was shaking too badly. He remained motionless, his body twisted in an awkward position; he was piled up lifeless, four feet from me.

Someone grabbed my arm. It was Mitch, wanting me to follow him. I got to my feet and moved with numbness. My aching body couldn't believe I was alive. My heart was pounding so hard that my chest hurt. My stomach lurched, and I almost threw up.

We stopped and Mitch whispered that he'd disabled one posted guard, but another VC had taken off when the shooting started. Mitch thought the one that ran away was Minh.

We had traveled about 50 yards beyond their campsite when Mitch grabbed my arm and jerked it, wanting me to get down. We had just hit the ground, when the night lit up with AK-47 automatic rifle fire. The Viet Cong were 60 yards away, above us, on a hillside; and, even though they had our position, they were firing too low. Mitch and I both returned their fire. We were aiming at their fire bursts. Screams of pain let us know that we had hit them good because the screaming stopped in a few minutes.

After dragging all four bodies into the campsite, we were able to identify Col Minh. He was the one who ran firing at me. I noticed a single large hole in his chest and asked Mitch if he had shot Minh.

"Gosh, I was beginning to think you were fond of him and didn't want to shoot him. But, really I just didn't want to go through training another spotter," Mitch stated.

Heck, I had been so scared of dying that I didn't even hear Mitch shoot. Col Minh's personal identification and a few papers that were in his pockets were taken for HQI. We then headed toward our pickup point, hopefully without running into any more of Minh's friends.

Hours later, well after daylight, we luckily found a small cave about a mile from our first pickup point. It was about 30 yards off the trail and fairly well concealed by vegetation. The cave opening was eight feet above the jungle floor on the side of a small cliff. After examining the cave, Sgt.

Mitchem gave the all-clear signal, and we moved in for the day to sleep in shifts for the next eight hours until the helicopter arrived.

In the afternoon, thick overcast skies and light rain persisted. I went outside, so I could transmit and receive on the radio. I tried raising HQI.

"'Delta-Two-Foxtrot' calling 'Hotel-Nine-Alpha',...nothing!

"'Delta-Two-Foxtrot' calling 'Hotel-Nine-Alpha', come in. . .come in," I tried again.

"'Delta-Two-Foxtrot' this is 'Hotel- Nine- Alpha', over...," came the reply.

Mitch wanted to let them know the mission was a success and to ask when we could expect the chopper.

"'Hotel-Nine-Alpha', three rude guests evicted along with boss. Over...," I said.

"'Delta-Two-Foxtrot', thanks for escorting guest out. Any trouble with our staff? Over...,"

"'Hotel-Nine-Alpha', staff is fine. When can we expect airmail? Over...," the radio barked.

"'Delta-Two-Foxtrot', weather should clear later this P.M., will deliver at 2010 hours at designated mailbox. Over."

"Hotel-Nine-Alpha', Roger on airmail at 2010. 'Delta-Two-Foxtrot' out!" Silence.

The VC was probably out looking for us already. I hurriedly climbed back inside the cave as soon as the transmission finished.

An hour and a half passed when I spotted a group of VC at a distance coming our way. There were 10 of them dressed in the traditional black pajamas. These boys also wore the long black bandannas tied around their foreheads, and most of them carried the AK-47. Even though there was some vegetation concealing the opening, these guys probably knew the cave's location — probably played in it as kids. They could really put a hurting on us by tossing grenades into the cave. They came closer! We knew that they had us already pinpointed when they began to suddenly spread out and slip toward the cave.

Mitch picked up his sniper rifle and grabbed a handful of his 173-grain cartridges from his sack. I could keep their heads down, plus do some serious damage with my M-14. It was too late for us to try and slip out. They had us cornered like pigeons in a cage.

I had to keep them from getting close enough to use grenades, thus giving Mitch a chance to do some good with his rifle. Mitch fired first, his sniper rifle sounded so loud in the cave that my ears were ringing. Outside, the lead VC went down as the large round tore through his chest. I began firing, and Mitch fired again and again. Each time he fired, one died. We were lucky that the cave was a little above the jungle floor. The receiving rifle fire was hitting the walls and ceiling and ricocheting away from us.

The remaining VC were getting closer. I laid down firepower in five to seven round bursts, trying to stop their advance.

One suddenly stood and tried to lob a grenade into the cave's opening. Before his hand could start forward with the grenade, I put two holes in him. He fell backwards, the grenade falling to the ground, exploding, and sending vegetation and pieces of shrapnel flying everywhere. The other VC were still trying to get closer. It became almost impossible to locate them, unless they fired.

Darkness began creeping into this remote valley, and it was still raining — just continuously light, not hard like it normally rains.

"We'll have to make a move to get out of this cave if we want to catch our ride home," Mitch said.

Knowing the VC would be watching and waiting to pick us off, one at a time, as we tried to escape, Mitch devised a little surprise that just might be our ticket out of here. He gently laid a grenade with the pin pulled almost all the way out inside our flare bag, letting just the tip of the pin remain in the grenade — enough to keep the spoon in place.

His idea was to toss the flare bag toward the VC and hopefully at impact with the ground, the pin would release the spoon and the grenade would set off the bag of flares. Mitch counted on the fireworks blinding the VC and diverting their attention just long enough for us to slip out undetected. Mitch said I was not to look at the flash or fireworks, for it would cause me to lose my night vision, and I wouldn't be able to shoot effectively.

We discussed the plan, and I knew what I had to do. Now, we were just waiting on complete darkness in the rain. Darkness came early, due to the weather.

When Mitch gave the signal, I opened up with a 20-round burst and received fire from a VC in front of the cave. Mitch located him and heaved the sack full of flares toward his position. Suddenly, the night sky became a brilliant light as the grenade exploded, setting off the flares in the bag. When the flash of bright light exploded upon the darkness of the jungle, we immediately exited the cave, each going a different direction and taking cover.

Once outside and safely concealed, I tried to pick out the location of any VC on my side of the cave opening. I saw one easing toward where the explosion and flares went off, about 30 clicks to my left. I dropped him with a well-placed shot with my M-14. In a few minutes, Mitch gave our familiar bird whistle; and, when I repeated it, he moved to my position.

"That last guy must not have been as committed to Buddha as his other nine buddies. He hightailed it out of here when his friend got blown up," Mitch said wryly.

"We better leave, too! It's time to meet the chopper," he added.

CHAPTER 5

Someone was tapping my arm! Sgt. Mitchem was kneeling next to Dan asking him if he'd seen or heard anything.

This brought Dan's thoughts back to the present; they were down in the Delta.

"Nothing, Sarge! Everything is quite," Dan said.

After eating some C-rats and chatting for a while, Dan snuggled up to his M-14, put his head on the flare pack, and once again thought of Kathy.

I woke Dan at 0400 hours to resume the trip to meet up with one Hoa Lu Thayn, the civilian commissioner who was active in selecting which U.S. military targets to hit. Thayn received his training in Moscow; and now, he was selecting and hitting targets that Russia felt would be the most damaging to the American advisors. In a way, he was part of Russia's extension into the war. The U.S. had long suspected the Soviets were advising the North. Now through Thayn, they were assisting the Viet Cong Communists in their attempt to overthrow South Vietnam.

Thayn gave suggestions to other Battalion Commanders, currently commanding the VC at this time. Once he decided on a certain target, the commanders were compelled to carry out the attack — if they wanted to stay in command. This made Thayn a very dangerous man, even among his own fighters. He was both loved and hated by the officers and men under him. He demanded and received respect from them.

Two hours later, Dan and I were entering the marshes. It wasn't long until I felt the hairs on my lower right leg stand up. I stopped and slowly eased my pants leg up to my knees. There were three black leaches almost three inches in length doing their best to suck the life giving blood out of my leg. I took out my lighter and burned each of them off with it. I checked my other leg and found it was leach free, for now. I didn't have to tell Dan to check himself, he had both pants legs up over his knees looking and feeling for leaches on his legs. Other than the episode with the leaches, we navigated the marshes safely.

One and half hours later, we reached the eastern bank of the Hoy River. We could not cross the Hoy, a small river about 40 yards wide that flowed into the huge Mekong River further south. We turned south, slipping quietly toward where the Mekong River flowed out of Cambodia into South Vietnam.

Our designation was about three and one-half miles to the south of our present position. Our area of operation would cover a five-mile square and be as busy as a beehive with VC guerrillas moving back and forth. I believed Commissioner Thayn would stay close to the border, or even stay in Cambodia and use it as a base of operations. Wherever he was, I now had nine days left to locate and snuff him.

I asked Dan to quietly call HQI to report our location. He got on the horn; and after several attempts, his voice quietly stated:

"'Hotel-nine-Alpha', this is 'Delta-Two-Foxtrot'. Over...,"

"Go ahead 'Delta-Two-Foxtrot'," said the radio operator of *'Hotel-Nine-Alpha'*.

"We've met Hoy, proceeding to his big brother. Over...," said Dan.

"Roger, 'Delta-Two-Foxtrot', and good hunting," came back the reply.

We reached our target zone around mid-afternoon without seeing or bumping into any Cong moving south along the Hoy. I looked at Dan and said, "You and I now need to find a good safe base camp for us to operate from for the next eight days."

"Move extra slow; we don't want to give ourselves away by running up on any VC. Also, we've got to remain silent and invisible until target time," I reiterated.

"Lead the way Sarge. I'll be close behind you," Dan whispered.

I then began the search for a good base camp, from which we would do our scouting to locate the 514th Viet Cong Battalion that was re-grouping in this area.

Every blood-sucking insect in this part of Vietnam had bitten both of us within the past two hours, or so it seemed. But, I kept searching. I was looking for a place the VC wouldn't routinely just enter. Soon I located the ideal hiding place — a very small, isolated island in the vast swamp where the Hoy joined the Mekong. The island was about 40 yards wide and maybe 50 yards long. There were sinkholes everywhere! Part of the island was five inches underwater. A small 20-foot section was three feet above the water where we made camp. The insects were already unbearable there.

Just the place any other sensible human being would avoid. We broke out our one-piece mosquito net shirts that completely covered our upper body, including the entire head, face, neck, chest area, arms, and hands. It was specifically designed for jungle conditions where insects were a major problem. The net was an ultra thin, see-through type camo green and black; it was a pullover, which had straps to tie around the wrist and waist. It had an elastic band under the neck that kept it snug. We kept the camo net shirts on day and night, while staying on *"Bug Island,"* as we had dubbed our base camp.

We made a cold camp *(no fires-no smoking)* and placed stacks of large broad leaves on the ground for bedding. We used one exit only, being very careful of the sinkholes. A misplaced step could mean trouble.

At 1500 hours, we were ready to begin our hunt in the selected area I had chosen to search for the Battalion. Dan and I had green and black paint on our face, neck, and hands. Our bodies were camouflaged with mud and vegetation from Bug Island. The sniper rifle and Dan's M-14 were camouflaged with green and black mossy tape.

When either of us was lying still, standing beside trees, or crouched near any vegetation, it was almost impossible to distinguish us from the landscape — even from very close range. We were ready to hunt! We moved so slowly that it was almost impossible to detect us.

At base camp, Dan and I had blue-marked the map's trails the Battalion would possibly use to assemble. Now, we only needed to check those trails for signs and wait.

There wasn't any way a force as large as a Battalion could move and not leave some sign, but we were not expecting the Battalion to move just yet. The fighters who were coming to join the Battalion would leave signs. We hoped to capitalize on their carelessness in thinking that no one but themselves was in this area.

By nightfall, we observed maybe two dozen fighters heading into Cambodia. We watched them cross the Mekong River on small rafts that were hidden from sight. By 2200 hours, another four dozen went across. They were being shuttled to the Cambodian side; then, someone would bring the rafts back. We returned to Bug

Island where we ate, rested, and planned for tomorrow's hunt. We both went to sleep at the same time, without worrying about any VC patrols finding us.

I tapped Dan's foot to wake him from his sleep. We would be leaving shortly. He got his canteen and splashed a little water on his eyes, trying to get the sleep out of them.

We ate cold C-rats of ham and eggs for breakfast; we stuffed our pockets with candy, then took care of business, and were soon applying new paint where it was needed.

I went over today's plans a final time, making sure we were both on the same page and that nothing we discussed last night was forgotten. Today, we would watch a trail just a mile away, checking the traffic on it, and hoped to find the place where Charlie crossed the river. I wanted to know where every crossing was located and where they kept their rafts hidden. This could become 'life saving information' later on. We set up today so that Dan was near the trail, and I was closer to the river. I selected a spot next to a large burned out tree trunk that was nearly 10 feet tall. It had good vegetation around it, so I blended in well. Still, I used the black ash on the tree to blacken my face even more.

Shortly, men talking broke the silence. A large group of fighters approached and a sergeant barked out orders. The column stopped 20 yards from my position and began looking for a place to sit. Two came over and sat down at my feet, not two steps from me. One guy broke out a pack of smokes, and they all lit up and talked about who knows what.

The sergeant yelled again as a VC approached from the river, and everyone scrambled to their feet. The men followed their sergeant, soon disappearing downriver.

I had to know where that crossing was! I waited 10 minutes, and then eased off in the same direction. One hundred clicks later, I came upon a wide beaten down area where the rafts had been hidden.

The rafts were halfway across the river — six of them, loaded with the VC fighters. I had noticed earlier that not all of the fighters carried an AK-47. Those that had weapons were the veteran fighters; the others would be issued new weapons soon.

I was lying on my stomach, five feet from the place where the rafts had been kept, when a young VC fighter approached, said something to someone close by, unbuttoned his trousers, and took a leak — not 10 feet from me. Upon finishing, he walked back toward the other person and began talking. Just the two of them were here; the other raft tenders, who were escorting the rafts across the river, would return soon.

I eased backward, turned, and started back to my original hiding place by the burned out tree trunk. I had crawled 20 yards when I heard more VC approaching. Lying completely still, I let this group of six VC pass within a few yards of where I lay. I soon reached the old tree and spent the next seven hours taking mental notes. There sure was something big coming down. Today, I had counted more than a 180 Viet Cong going into Cambodia. That would be where Thayn was.

Counting just part of yesterday and with today's count, I saw 213 VC fighters cross the river into Cambodia from Vietnam. HQI needed to get this information tonight. Maybe with something this big, they would send up a forward air spotter. They fly in a small twin-engine aircraft that is equipped with a camera, radio, and four air-to-ground rockets on the wings. I sure was going to ask for one. It had a way of quietly easing over an area and taking aerial photos. Maybe it could locate the Battalion, if the weather allowed.

After dark, I left the old burned tree and headed off toward Dan's direction. After sitting by the trail for 20 minutes without any sign of VCs on the trail, I decided to use our birdcall signal. Shortly after I made the call, Dan's answering call provided his location. Soon we were on our way to our little Bug Island camp in the swamp.

After reaching the island and knowing for sure we had no visitors, I asked Dan, "How many VC have you seen?"

Upon getting his count of 63, I told him what I had observed down near the river. I decided to use my count because I had seen the VC fighters approach the crossing from two different directions, whereas Dan had only seen VC on the one trail he had watched.

I wrote down the information I wanted Dan to pass on to Capt. Swanson. I wanted Capt. Swanson to get personally involved tonight. I did not want to take a chance the HQI radio operator would wait until tomorrow morning to give Swanson this message. I was hoping he was on base and had not gone into town tonight.

I needed Swanson, Maj. Henley, and Col. Bowers to be in the HQI radio shack tonight. Col. Bowers or Capt. Swanson would probably also get Regiment involved.

Dan set up the radio, and in a few minutes began calling in a low voice.

"'Delta-Two-Foxtrot' calling 'Hotel-Nine-Alpha', over...," He paused for one minute, and then begins again.

"'Delta-Two-Foxtrot' calling 'Hotel-Nine-Alpha', over...,"

Dan paused for nearly one minute.

"They've got to answer," I mumbled.

"They might be able to hear us on the other frequency — I'll try it," Dan said.

Dan turned the frequency knob from 88.63 to 79.29 and began again,

"'Delta-Two-Foxtrot' calling 'Hotel-Nine-Alpha'. Over...,"

In just a few seconds, we heard —

"'Delta-Two-Foxtrot,' this is 'Hotel-Nine-Alpha'. Over...,"

"'Hotel-Nine-Alpha', request following gents: Swanson-Henley-Bowers be present for vital information in 20 minutes. Over...,"

"'Delta-Two-Foxtrot,' Roger on gentlemen, will notify. Over...,"

I eased out into the swamp, listening for silence, and was thankful to hear only the normal insect sounds, which meant we were still alone here in the swamp. Shortly, I eased back into camp and saw that Dan was wolfing down his C-rations, so I took out my favorite meal package, and we both ate a meal while waiting on HQI to respond.

"'Hotel-Nine-Alpha', calling 'Delta-Two-Foxtrot'. Over...,"

"'Hotel-Nine-Alpha', this is 'Delta-Two-Foxtrot'. Over...,"

"'Delta-Two-Foxtrot', requested gents are present. Over...,"

"Roger, 'Hotel-Nine-Alpha'. *Have been very busy, have verification from one and a half days of 213 people gathering for a large party across river. Request that you have FAO* (Forward Air Observer) *take some photos tomorrow, weather permitting, of other side located in grid section 3. We'll be crossing over at 0330 hours. Over...,*"

"Roger, 'Delta-Two-Foxtrot', *gentlemen in process of making decision. Over...,*"

"Roger, 'Hotel-Nine-Alpha', we'll wait for their decision. 'Delta-Two-Foxtrot' Out."

Four minutes later:

"'Delta-Two-Foxtrot', *Roger on all requests. Be careful crossing over, that's a bad place. The gentlemen said thanks for telling them about party. Over...,*"

"'Hotel-Nine-Alpha', we thank them for granting request. 'Delta-Two-Foxtrot' Out!"

I discussed with Dan the equipment we would be taking across the river into Cambodia.

"We will only eat twice a day, so take six days' supply of food. Take water, ammo, weapons, and demolitions. I can't risk carrying the PRC-77 with us, so turn it off and leave it concealed here, and we'll pick it up on our way home. Anything not taken has to be hidden under palmetto limbs, here on Bug Island. Any questions Dan?" I asked.

At 0230 hours, I awoke to a hard rain, reached over and shook Dan's shoulder, and roused him from his sleep. We quickly ate our normal breakfast of ham and eggs, again stuffing our pockets with gum and candy, and making sure our canteens were full. We checked to ensure our weapons were ready, and then painted our face and hands. We concealed our equipment left at camp and moved slowly in the heavy rain toward the old burned tree. I knew that if this downpour did not lift, no FAO aircraft would be flying.

With any luck, we should locate the Battalion within the next day or two and, hopefully, return in six days or less.

We approached the area of the burned tree without sighting or hearing any VC fighters. I eased on to the location where the VC had been watching the hidden rafts, about 150 clicks farther along this path. Yesterday, seven or eight VC soldiers were working raft duty. This morning before daybreak, I wanted to take a raft and cross the river into Cambodia. It would take a great deal of skill, plus some downright luck to get the raft; but, we had to cross. It was either secure a raft or swim the quarter mile in swift currents.

We crawled the last 50 meters on our bellies and now were within 10 clicks of the rafts that were staked to the ground and tied together. A single guard lay asleep on cut bamboo close to the rafts, a rifle lying beside him. I motioned for Dan to take him and I would provide cover fire; he acknowledge by nodding his head. Leaving his M-14 with me, Dan slowly crawled toward the sentry with his K-Bar in his hand.

He inched his way one foot at a time toward the sleeping sentry. He had to cross 15 yards of open area without making any noise that might alert him or his friends, who were sleeping some 40 yards farther up the path from the rafts.

The sleeping VC sentry guard reacted instantly when the knife went deep into his chest, and Dan's hand went over his mouth about the same moment; very little sound escaped his lips. His body arched as the knife found its mark, and then he slumped back onto the bamboo. Quietly,

Dan pulled him off into the jungle and covered his body and weapon with leaves. Hopefully, it would be hours before his buddies found the body.

I saw Dan was now crawling toward the rafts. I joined him as he cut the raft free and we eased it down the bank into the river. After we stored our explosives and weapons on the raft, we each grabbed hold of a side of the raft. Dan pushed the raft away from the shoreline, and we began to kick our feet as the current began to take us away from the shoreline of Vietnam. Soon, we were kicking like crazy, trying to get the raft to move closer to the Cambodian shore.

Twenty minutes later, the raft was still moving downstream and had gone around a big bend in the river. Each of my legs felt like 50-pound weights, and my lungs were on fire. My left arm was almost numb, and I questioned how much longer I could hang onto the raft. I looked across the raft at Dan. He appeared to be in much better shape than I was.

"We're only about 50 clicks from the Cambodian shore," he said kicking almost effortlessly.

I raised myself up and surveyed the shoreline.

"Let's ease the raft toward the overhanging vegetation and conceal it," I managed to whisper.

Together, we managed to get the raft up underneath a group of wide, long-leafed plants and secured it with one of the ropes we had included in our equipment must-haves. Anyone on a boat passing by would be unable to detect the hidden raft.

As the heavy rain continued, we slowly eased off into the Cambodian jungle. The VC fighters had crossed yesterday by raft a mile upriver from us.

Somewhere near there, we would locate their trail and somehow find the Battalion. However, we could not stay on the trail because at daybreak, the raft tenders would miss the guard who had been asleep on duty. Soon thereafter, they would discover his body, and then all hell would break loose. It wouldn't take them long to put things together — a missing raft and a dead guard equaled intruders.

They would start a hunt for us soon. I had to get the Commissioner before they found us.

Daybreak came, revealing a low cloud ceiling and more rain. I was cold and wet, and wishing I could be any place besides this hellhole. I found the main trail by accident, suddenly and unexpectedly stepping from dense jungle onto a narrow road.

This was the trail used by the fighters crossing the river on the rafts yesterday. It would lead us westward and to the 514th VC Battalion and our target — Commissioner Thayn.

As quickly as I had stepped onto the trail, I stepped back into the dense jungle for concealment and protection. Luckily, no one saw my blunder. We were about 300 clicks from the river, and I needed to move inland, staying off the main trail until I spotted the Battalion's camp. We began moving parallel to and about 40 yards off the trail in the dense jungle.

In a short time, many voices came from the trail as more fighters were coming to join the Battalion. We walked parallel with them, quickening our pace to stay abreast with the column of fighters.

Within a half-hour, they became quiet; so, I signaled for Dan to stop. The column was probably getting close to the Battalion's base camp.

"Move very slowly, make no noise to alert any VC security that might be nearby," I whispered to Dan. He nodded! I knew he understood.

In another 15 minutes, we were within sight of a large encampment situated under a huge canopy of trees in a large valley — a location that would hamper any aerial surveillance.

Dan joined me as I peeked out from just inside the jungle upon this large camp that was about 350 yards from our position. I located their headquarters tent easily — as a Viet Cong flag was flying over it. Using the M-59 spotting scope, Dan did not see our man any place; it was possible he had not yet arrived.

Dan pointed out two large ammo and weapons tents to me. There were only a dozen large tents in the compound. Dan pinpointed the communications tent, several large supply tents, and the cook's kitchen tent.

The other tents were for senior officer quarters. We watched the camp for another two hours, until I knew their layout. During the second hour, Dan and I gave our attention to the officers to get their routine down.

I was trying to locate the Battalion CO, because he could lead me to Commissioner Thayn. The CO must be out of camp because we did not locate him. It was time to find another spot from which to view the camp. If only this rain would stop — but it didn't and wouldn't.

Slipping through the dense jungle was difficult — there were so many vines and other objects to trip us up. As we neared another location from which to watch the camp, I suddenly dropped to the ground, signaling for Dan to get down. Dan fell flat on the ground only moments before the battalion's five-man security patrol came into view, some 25 yards away.

They appeared suddenly, out of nowhere. We watched them stop as the squad leader assigned a guard post to one of his men.

He was assigning them positions along the outer flank for security. One guard was now less than 20 yards from our position as we both lay on the jungle floor watching the sentry standing in the rain. The rest of the security detail disappeared from view almost as quickly as they had appeared, moving in the same general direction we had just come from. There had to be other sentries nearby. Maybe word had reached the camp about the dead guard and missing raft, or maybe this was normal routine for camp security.

Whatever the reason, Dan and I were caught in a bad situation. I blamed myself for letting this happen because I knew there might be flank security. But now, I had let us get caught inside their security lines, like a green amateur.

"How can I get us out of this fix?" I mused.

These darn vines were everywhere, and we would surly give ourselves away trying to do much moving now. We could not move toward the sentry without alerting him.

I could see Dan looking at me. He also understood our situation. I eased ever so slowly toward Dan, watching every stick, twig, or vine that could give me away. Here I was crawling right in front of a Viet Cong sentry who would love to blow this dumb Marine away. I could see him, but he was unaware we were in his world. I had to wait for a chance to take the sentry out quietly, if we wanted to complete this mission and get back alive.

We stayed right where we were, watching and waiting for more than an hour. Killing him was no problem, but shooting him would be suicide — as a shot would draw everyone to us. Finding a way to get close enough to the sentry to kill him without shooting him was the problem we faced. Neither of us was any good at throwing a knife at this distance, so we waited.

For an hour and a half, we laid on our bellies waiting. There came a faint voice to our left, another sentry was calling to the one in front of us — probably wanting to smoke some pot with him. When the sentry in front of us moved off toward his buddy, we moved further into the jungle to avoid any other sentries that might be posted. In our situation, the heavy downpour had helped us. It was hard to hear anything but the solid beat of raindrops falling on the jungle vegetation.

I managed to get us to our destination without further incident. We were able to watch the camp for another two hours before dark and observed fighters that were coming into it in large groups. Soon the Battalion would be at full strength. When these guys were trained and turned loose, they could cause a big shift in the balance of power.

Some of the South Vietnamese soldiers would leave and fight for the VC, if they thought the VC had the best chance of winning the war. One more major victory by this 514th VC Battalion and the Viet Cong could have a lot of influence on the decisions of some South Vietnamese soldiers. A big victory for them could bring a quick end to the war, and thus defeat the South Vietnamese Army and their American advisors.

If a fight were to develop between just the South Vietnamese army and trained Viet Cong fighters, the VC would win hands down. A good VC battalion could whip two battalions of South Vietnamese regular army on any given day. Without the assistance from the U.S. Advisors, the South would fall in a matter of months.

Dan and I needed a place to hold up and to operate from each day; we found just the place before 2000 hours. It was 300 clicks south of the perimeter security lines. Dan and I broke out our C-rats and wolfed down a cold meal. My meal was beans and franks, with all the extras.

"I need my butt kicked for allowing us to get caught in that situation with the sentry up on the ridge today," I said after finishing my meal.

"Don't let it bother you Mitch," Dan stated. "But tell me, how did you know they were there? I just know if you hadn't signaled for me to get my butt down when you did, we would've been spotted."

"I saw the squad leader turn around suddenly to look at his men," I answered. "If he hadn't done that, it might have been over for us. The patrol didn't make any noise; they moved like cats — it was the sudden movement that I saw. I guess it was just plain luck that saved us Dan!"

I went over the plans for tomorrow and included our emergency plan, making sure I covered everything. The near miss today really got my attention. We had to complete this mission and get back home safely. This was my responsibility.

Seventy percent of the success of this mission depended largely on us not being discovered. The other 30 percent depended on how well Dan and I carried out the plan. I decided we would take turns getting some shut-eye. I took the first watch, which also gave me another chance to go over tomorrow's plan again. We had gathered enough information today to know the camp's daily routine. If I got the opportunity to waste Thayn tomorrow, I would do it. Dan knew his responsibilities, and I knew he would perform them like the pro he is.

I got Dan up for his watch at 2345 hours; and before I sacked out, I let him know I wanted to get up at 0330 hours. At 0330 hours, Dan woke me. We ate, went over our plan one last time, and then set out for the chance of taking care of Commissioner Thayn today.

I had chosen to position Dan and myself on the east side where we had watched from late yesterday. It was an excellent position from which we could observe and shoot from, and we would be close — just 150 clicks from the kitchen. We would be able to look inside the tents of the CO and officers from there. Their patrols were scouting a perimeter about 350-400 yards out from the main camp, and here we would set up less than 200 yards from the kitchen. This would also put us on the side closest to the river.

There was no way Dan and I could make our kill from even 300 yards away in this situation. The only way to get everyone together was when they went to the eating table. At any given range over 250 yards, the canopy of large trees blotted out the targets. Dan and I would have no chance of setting our explosives inside the camp if we had to slip in and out on our bellies from any great distance, as it would require quite a few more hours that we didn't have.

We painted our faces and hands and set out for our position in the morning darkness.

At 0530 hours, we arrived at my selected location. In the faint light that was beginning to break the eastern skyline, I found the large dead tree and snuggled up against it. I set the .300 caliber sniper rifle beside me against the tree, pulled my binoculars out so I could get a good look, and waited on the first rays of daylight.

Upon reaching his position right next to me, Dan settled in waiting for light to break the eastern sky. He planned to set out two claymore mines, just in case. He was now set to earnestly begin looking for Thayn. He could also take out quite a few VC, if needed. Charlie would have to step on us to know we were there; that's how good the natural camouflage and paint was. Dan also knew that Mitch looked much more like a tree with moss on it than a man. Each would be difficult to spot.

To the naked eye, the large tree trunk appeared to have grown moss along part of its trunk. This really wasn't moss, just Mitchem. He was looking at the officers' tents. The mess cooks served breakfast at 0530 hours and the VC fighters ate sitting on the ground. Only the highest ranking officers ate at 0605 at a makeshift table with a tarp over it to keep these officers dry. The Commanding Officer was not at breakfast this morning, nor was he in his tent. Now, I knew for sure neither he nor Thayn was in the camp. I knew Dan and I would have to make sure both of them were in camp before we set the explosives — the last thing we did before the shooting started, thus insuring the VC had the least amount of time to discover them.

Around 0930 hours, some of the VC troops were practicing hand-to-hand combat, while others were sitting in a rudimentary class with the instructor demonstrating the use of booby traps. Each group practiced for two hours, then stopped and traded activities. There was no lunch break.

These little guys were fed two meals a day, each consisting of rice, fish, and a hoecake, which is a small piece of bread; and, they drank water from their canteens. I made mental notes of what time the sentries were posted outside of camp, and when they were relieved. Sentries pulled a six-hour watch and then were relieved. The fighters in training were fed again around 1900 hours. Everyone followed the same routine as they did during breakfast. About 30 sentries were posted for each watch. Those not on watch were lying on straw mats sleeping or just relaxing in a shade.

Before daybreak the next morning, we were back by the large fallen tree, waiting again for our chance. Maybe, just maybe, the CO and Commissioner Thayn had returned to camp during the night!

Breakfast time would let us know. The cooks were busy, and soon the troops were fed. The officers, the same ones as yesterday, came to breakfast at 0605 hours.

The sun rose today without a trace of rain. It was a beautiful sight as its rays peeked through the jungle and finally flooded the valley. As the sun climbed higher into the sky, the temperatures soared close to 110 degrees. I laid my entire body on top of the large fallen tree. Even though the VC couldn't spot me, the fire ants were the first insects to be attracted to my body sweat. As they marched slowly in single file up the tree trunk to my position, I declared war on them. This I did without making any sudden movement that would give my position away. In 20 minutes, I slowly mashed all that I could. I caught them between my thumb and forefinger and executed them swiftly.

Some that escaped made me pay by crawling into my shirt from the back of my neck and biting me a half-dozen times. These would surely cause sore puss festers on my neck and shoulder areas. It seemed like the fire ants and the mosquitoes could communicate fairly well, because soon swarms of big mosquitoes were buzzing my head and biting and eating my sweaty flesh. They would land upon my face and ears, gently sucking my blood, and then fly away bloated.

Before the sun had reached midway in the sky, even the spiders and ticks had gotten in on the feast. My body ached as any other man's would from the constant biting from these insects. But, I had to shut off the pain from my brain. I had to get my brain somehow to disconnect the flesh feelings from registering in my brain. This is the only way a man can remain horizontal, not moving his body, for hours and hours waiting for his target to appear, without continually swatting these insects and being spotted by the enemy.

The Viet Cong fighters again went through their training cycle, the same as yesterday. The posted sentries kept the same schedule we had observed yesterday. The cooks also served breakfast and supper at the same times. Slowly, this day ended; and, after dark fell upon the valley, I slipped off the tree, and we eased back through the jungle to where Dan and I had made our little campsite, all the while avoiding the posted sentries around the encampment.

On day four before daybreak, we were again back at the same observation point. It had started to rain around 0400 hours. A smile came to my lips. The rain kept the insects at bay. Today, I wanted an all day rain. The harder the rain fell, the better — my aching body deserved a rest.

About an hour before nightfall, a small five-vehicle convoy rolled into camp. Two men exited from a jeep in the convoy. They had my full attention as they walked toward a small group of officers. The CO stopped and spoke with these men, but Hoa Lu Thayn walked past them and went into his tent. The Commanding Officer and the Commissioner had finally arrived. Orders were barked out, and men began unloading the supplies from the vehicles and storing them inside tents.

I watched and waited, hoping finally to get the chance to look at Commissioner Thayn up close, through my scope. I wanted the opportunity to detail the man, but he stayed in his tent. The CO was now also hurrying toward his tent to get out of the rain.

Over and over in my mind, I went through each step in my plan to make this mission successful. Again prone upon the large fallen tree, I rehearsed every detail in my mind. Rain beat down hard upon my head, but I hardly noticed as I was so involved repeating our plan in my mind.

After dark came to this valley, we slipped away and made our way to our small campsite. Dan and I ate a hardy cold meal of rations, and then

I reminded Dan of our mission. Taking out Commissioner Thayn was our number one priority. Then, killing as many senior officers as possible was next. Eliminating their radio communications and ammo storage was next. Getting back to base safely after completing the mission was paramount.

That night we talked about what we needed to do tomorrow. I told Dan to bring along the C-4 timers and I'd take the explosives. We discussed the targets designated as C-4 marks, where to reset the claymore mines, and the route we would take back to the river and the raft. We could only hope no one had discovered the raft. Tomorrow would be Dan's and my last day with the insects at the big fallen tree.

Dan would be a big help when the shooting began. I had plotted a route on our map from the large fallen tree to the raft's location at the river and on to Bug Island. Then I selected an exit route to our pickup point.

We would have to move fast to evade the wrath of this Battalion. But after Thayn's demise and before we headed for the raft, I also wanted to snuff the CO and as many of his senior officers as possible — if I got that opportunity. In addition, I wanted to take out their communications and destroy the ammo and weapons tents. All this destruction would surely put a big damper on Hanoi's plans of using this Battalion anytime soon.

Time was what the U.S. needed — time to get U.S. combat troops to Vietnam.

If I failed, the North Vietnam Communists could launch a major offense with the support of the 514th VC Battalion in the Delta. They could overrun the important cities of Chalon and then Saigon. After a few weeks, they could advance north toward Da Nang.

At 0345 hours, Dan and I were prone on our stomachs, crawling in the rain toward the ammo and communication tents located approximately 190 yards from the fallen tree. Five half-pound C-4 explosives were in my pouch; Dan had the timers and detonators. We had an hour and 35 minutes to plant the C-4 and return to the tree by 0520 hours. This should give us plenty of time.

Only the cooks were active this early in the morning. Security guard details would eat at 0500 hours and would leave camp as relief details at 0545 hours. I wanted us to be back at the tree long before the security details left and the officers arrived to eat.

I crawled slowly. The rain had eased off a bit — not coming down as hard now. It was just a steady, cold rain. I glanced back toward Dan, who was about 10 yards behind me, then moved on slowly toward the two ammo tents.

I was close enough to hear the cooks talking and laughing with each other as they prepared the morning meal. We had to crawl within 25 yards of them in order to reach the ammo tents, located 40 yards farther away. The communication tent was fairly close to the group of officers' tents, but deeper inside the camp, and another 40 yards farther away.

As I approached the cooks' kitchen area, I kept to the shadows. The dim lights they were using would blind them from seeing anything outside their lighted area. Soon, we reached the first ammo tent. I gave Dan a half-pound of C-4 to place on the boxes containing grenades and told him to set the timer for 0610 hours. At the second tent, I placed C-4 on boxes of mortar shells and set the timer for 0613 hours. I noticed about 30 new Soviet built rocket propelled grenade (RPG) launchers and cases of rockets were stacked in the corner.

We both crawled off in the direction of the communication tent. An operator would be on duty there. Forty yards more! The time was 0425 hours.

Upon reaching the back of the Communication tent, you could hear the low constant whine from the radio; so, I cut a small slit in the tent and peeked inside. The operator was slumped over with his head on the table. He appeared to be dozing, but I wasn't sure because his back was toward me. Slowly, I allowed the K-Bar to cut a longer slit in the canvas. I paused; still he had not moved. I cut the slit even larger so I could slip inside. Once inside, I crawled slowly toward his chair. I was only five feet from him, when loud talking from outside woke him. He got up from his chair, walked to the tent entrance, and looked out into the night. A dim light was on a pole near the radio table; I crawled behind the radio table and waited for him to return to his seat.

He mumbled something in Vietnamese, probably cursing the weather, and started back to his chair. I had to act quickly before he had a chance to react. I grabbed him as he came around the radio table, using one hand to pull him down on me, my other to ram the K-Bar deep into his chest. I pulled the dead body to the rear of the tent, and Dan dragged it outside and dumped it into the officers latrine ditch a short ways behind the tent.

I put a half-pound of C-4 on the back of the radio and set the timer Dan provided for 0615 hours. Outside, I placed one C-4 on the antenna and set the timer to detonate at 0615 hours. All explosives were now in place, with timers set in sequence.

Soon, all hell would break loose. Men would die! I hoped the number would not include Dan and me.

I pulled a stool and a chest with spare radio parts on it over to where I made the slit, placed them in front of the slit canvas, and backed out. Dan soon returned and instantly we headed back toward the tree at a crawl.

I glanced at my watch — it was 0450 hours. We now had 30 minutes to reach the old fallen tree. Security guard details were lining up at the kitchen for breakfast. They would begin eating in a few minutes. Their talking and laughter were kept low.

The sergeant of the guard did not want his men waking up the officers. His butt would be in hot water for that. So, he allowed them to smoke pot, if they kept the noise down. This had saved his rear end all week long.

I stayed in the shadows all the way to the camp's perimeter — only then did I stop crawling. On our feet and crouched over low, we eased the final 30 yards toward the large fallen tree.

Checking my watch after reaching the tree, I saw it was 0517 hours. Good! We had made it with three minutes to spare. Now I had to get busy; I had more work to do.

I took out a cloth sack containing my 30 extra .300 caliber rounds for the sniper rifle. I was hoping to get the opportunity to use them in a few minutes. I also checked the Redfield 9X scope. No moisture was inside, which meant I would have a clear sight picture. I knew the precise yardage to the officers table was 153 yards. My .300 caliber Weatherby Magnum has a flat trajectory out to 250 yards. This meant I could clean their plow without having to readjust the yardage, unless I was shooting at distances greater than 250 yards. Here, today, I would be close enough to smell their stinking body odor.

I eased the clip out of the Weatherby and put the maximum of four shells in the clip. I also loaded the extra two clips I had included in our supplies.

I tied the camo cloth sack containing extra clips and ammo to my belt, making it easier to get shells when I needed them. I then slowly opened the bolt, eased a round into the chamber, and reinserted the clip into the rifle — I could fire five rounds before reloading.

Easing the rifle to my shoulder and letting it snuggle in real tight, I looked at the officers' table through the 9X power scope. At this range, I could see the splinters in the chairs and each raindrop as it rolled off the tarp. It was good to be able to get this close.

Dan looked through the M-59 toward the communication tent. Everything looked normal. Apparently, the radioman's body was still concealed in the latrine. Slowly Dan moved the M-59 to view the ammo tents; everything looked normal. The explosives were set to detonate after the officers sat down and began to eat breakfast.

I had asked Dan to set out a 'welcome committee' for the VC, so he used two claymore mines and the M-57 electrical firing devices to slow down a frontal assault on our position. In addition, Dan rigged two of the C-4 plastic explosives — with both trip wires and electrical detonators — behind us, just in case they tried to come in our back door. A claymore mine slung out more than 100 No. 1 buckshot pellets, at two to five feet above the ground, killing or crippling anyone in its path. Awesome!

When Dan came back, he placed four grenades out where he could reach them and then made sure his M-14 was ready for action. Looking at my watch, I saw it was 0555 hours. Almost time to start! I looked through the scope again and concentrated on the officers' tents and latrine area. Hoa Lu Thayn was still in his tent. I wanted him out before all hell broke loose, so he would be an easier target. I needed to take him down first. He was the reason we had come to this insect-infested part of the war.

The CO came out of his tent and stopped briefly at Thayn's tent before proceeding on to the breakfast table. Senior officers were served meals; they didn't have to wait in line. So as soon as the CO sat down, a cook had a plate of hot food in front of him. I looked at the CO through the scope. He had one gold star on each collar, the insignia of a Brigadier General.

He was an averaged-size man who carried himself well. He had a weathered face, with a touch of gray in his dark hair, and wore tiny spectacles. This man had served his superiors well — a brave solider — and a man I hoped to kill today.

A chair was vacant next to the CO and the other seated officers were talking and already eating. One place remained and was soon to be occupied, for Thayn was walking toward the mess table to join the others. As he approached, I saw that he was a tall stocky man, who was dressed in casual attire. Everyone but the CO acknowledged his presence at the table, which was a sign that they either respected or feared him. He greeted the CO with a nod of his head, and then the cook served him a hot plate of food. Hoa Lu Thayn had a thick head of black hair, a small scar on his left cheek, and the big wide shoulders of an athlete. Little did this man know that his life clock was about to stop forever!

Slowly, I ensured my rifle was tightly tucked into the fold of my right arm and shoulder; my sling was tight around my left forearm, and my elbow was tucked nicely into my shooting position for the upcoming shots. Everything was ready. Dan had his spotting scope on the CO, my next target. I glanced at Dan, and then centered the cross hairs upon the commissioner's forehead as he ate.

Dan and I had practiced many long, hot hours to become a precision shooting team; it had paid great dividends in the past, and I knew it would again today.

I whispered, "It's time to shoot turkey's old buddy."

"Let's do it," Dan softly murmured.

I took a small breath of air into my lungs, exhaled half of it, and methodically squeezed the trigger. As the rifle cracked, Thayn's head just exploded like a melon.

The powerful impact of the 173-grain soft nose bullet sent his lifeless body sprawling 10 feet from the table. As the echo of the shot still ricocheted across the valley, I worked the bolt smoothly and moved the rifle an inch, centered my scope on the CO's chest, and fired. Both shots were just three seconds apart. With a gaping hole in his chest, the general joined Thayn's lifeless body on the ground behind the table.

Hurriedly, I sought the Executive Officer (XO). Dan had him in his spotting scope and directed me to him as the XO was trying to get away from the table, but he was a tad too slow. As he turned to run, my bullet caught him in the middle of his back. Down he went, falling forward into another senior officer.

As fast and as accurate as I could, I shot one officer after another, as Dan found them in his spotting scope, until my rifle was empty. Quickly, I put another round in the chamber, then extracted the spent clip and inserted a fresh one. Again, I had five killing shots.

By now, some of the VC fighters, having reached their weapons, began wildly firing in all directions. An officer or sergeant was selecting areas at which they should fire.

Dan again directed me on specific targets.

I began to take out any officer or sergeant we could locate, shooting until the clip was empty. They could not detect my muzzle flash and did not know where I was located.

But once Dan began firing his M-14, the muzzle flash would give away our position; so, he would fire only after our position was discovered. This maneuver also gave us another advantage — if they were thinking there was only one sniper, they just might get careless.

Suddenly, a bright flash and a loud explosion split the air. The first ammo tent blew to 'kingdom come'. Men were dying everywhere — from a sniper who never missed and from the exploding ammo.

A sudden burst of enemy rifle fire cut into the fallen tree trunk. A grenade was tossed toward us. The dirt from the explosion pelted our position. Lucky for us, it landed a little short.

The second ammo tent went up in a big fireball, killing or wounding a large number of troops near it. People were scrambling around, trying to find a place to hide; somewhere they would be safe from the sniper and the explosions.

Dan's M-14 rattled off a short burst. He had spotted some of the VC soldiers who had located us. Dan slipped away from me even further, trying to draw their fire away from my position. He continued firing, hitting one of them in the chest. The others directed their fire toward him, thinking he was the sniper.

The communication tent and tower went up in a ball of flames. The last of our planted camp explosions took the base radio and tower out of operation — no more messages from that big radio. A lot of smaller size radios were also stored in that tent; hopefully, they were all destroyed. Maybe there would be few, if any, radios left that they could use for communication. This would be to our advantage; having difficulty communicating with each other would make it much harder for them to catch these two jarheads before reaching our pickup point.

A sizeable force of fighters nearing the camp's outer perimeter was coming our way at a run — only 30 yards from our position.

Dan scampered back in behind our tree trunk, picking up the M-57 electrical firing device. When the fighters' were 15 yards from where he had set a claymore mine, Dan detonated it. Screams filled the morning air as men were dying right in our laps. Wounded fighters lay out in front of us screaming in pain.

Another group of fighters to the right of Dan was trying to overrun our position. When they were 10 yards in front of the other claymore, Dan flipped the switch on that M-57 firing device. Claymores can be nasty, and these were living up to that billing. Fighters were dying all around us from the mines. Those not lucky enough to have died were crippled for life and lay there on the ground just crying or screaming.

I told Dan, "Get your two bars of C-4 and detonators. We're leaving as soon as you return." In less than four minutes he had the C-4 and was back. "It's time to leave," I said, as I pushed the map case at Dan. "You lead the way to the raft, old pal."

Staying low, we eased back into the jungle and headed toward the river, a mile away. We had some rough terrain to cross before getting to the river. Hopefully, the VC fighters from the 514th Battalion would be too busy licking their wounds to worry about us. Our main objective now — *get home safely*.

I noticed that it had stopped raining, and the sun was trying to peek through the trees. Maybe this was a good omen. We continued moving toward the river at a slow pace.

"Want me to pick up the pace some?" Dan asked as he stopped.

I was about to say "no" when Dan suddenly put his finger to his lips and pointed to our rear! Holding up five fingers, he mouthed, 'Khmer Rouge'. I turned slowly on the ridge and saw them on our back trail, tracking us. They were maybe 100 yards away.

"Time to move fast," I whispered. I took the point, and Dan followed. I eased us out of sight from the Khmer Rouge; and, once we had good cover between us, I struck a fast trot, keeping that pace up for a couple hundred yards. Stopping only long enough to get a bearing on the compass, I returned to the same trot — a pace that would allow a lot of distance to be put between them and us, fast.

The one thing I didn't want was to get into a firefight with the Khmer Rouge or any more Viet Cong fighters. There is a time and place for fighting. Now, was not the time! Now was the time to skedaddle.

I hoped our raft was still where we had hidden it. We would need to stay well ahead of the trackers in order to escape with the slow moving raft. Our luck would have to change in order to get that far ahead of the trackers.

As we neared the river, I knew we needed a plan quickly. What could we do? How do we slow them down without getting into a firefight?

When I thought we were about 150 yards from the river, I asked Dan, "Do you still have C-4 detonators?"

Dan said, "Sure," and I nodded and smiled.

"This looks like a good location to set a trip wire rigged to C-4," I suggested.

Dan agreed with me and selected a large tree to put the C-4 on — insuring the blast was directed outward toward the trackers. A trip wire was placed at a six-inch height across the narrow path in a sharp curve.

Using a trick from an old honored VC enemy, I inserted some .45 caliber shells into the soft C-4 explosive. This trick was guaranteed to make them very unhappy.

Upon finishing, I said, "We'll move real slow the rest of the way to the river." Dan nodded in agreement.

The sniper rifle was still in my hands; and as we neared the river, you could hear the rippling of water as it passed by. Everything appeared peaceful. But still, I wanted to stop here, not rush down to the raft. This would be a good place for an ambush — just when we thought we were home free, the VC could surprise us. I had this gut feeling! I wanted to get us both back to base safely, and the only way I knew to do this was to be extra careful. I had to find out if we had a surprise party waiting for us?

I whispered, "Watch our back trail and provide cover fire if I need it."

Dan nodded, and I crawled toward the river. About 35 yards from the river, I stopped abruptly, as I smelled a familiar old smell — 'Pot'! Yes, we had company waiting, and I'd bet money it wasn't the U.S. Marine Corps.

A loud explosion reverberated from back in the jungle, and then screams. The Khmer Rouge had stumbled across our welcome mat. Whoever was here waiting for us was keeping out of sight. But, thank God, someone in the group liked to smoke pot.

I turned around and slowly crawled back to where Dan was waiting. "They're there; I don't know who or how many, but they're waiting for us," I said.

"What do you want to do?" Dan asked. "You heard the boys on our back door screaming when they got caught by the C-4 just a few minutes ago," I said.

"Yeah," Dan replied.

"What do you think these guys at the river would do if you screamed and hollered for help in English?" I quipped. "They would think you and me were hurt badly in an explosion and move in for the kill, right?" I answered my own question.

"We could then have our own surprise party," Dan said.

"Right on, old pal! Right on!" I said.

I went over my hastily devised plan in detail with Dan.

"I can pull this off with ease, Sarge," Dan assured me.

Vietnam, The Making of a Sniper

I playfully pulled his soft camo boonie cap down over his eyes and eased back toward the river. Soon, I was crawling very slowly, not making a sound trying to reach a place along the river bank where I could observe without being detected. I soon discovered a narrow 3-foot deep runoff ditch that would provide protection and a perfect place to conduct some surveillance. I eased into the ditch and moved to where I had good concealment and the needed view.

It was Dan's time to shine. I hoped he would be convincing enough. All I could do now was wait and see if whoever was out there would take the bait.

"HELP ME!" a voice in pain called out.

It wasn't too loud, and Dan sounded like he was really in pain.

"Help Me!" came the cry again, only this time fainter.

I watched and I waited, but they had not moved. A few minutes later, came an even fainter cry, "help-p-p me-e-e!"

This time they took the bait. Two Viet Cong fighters stood up, just 30 yards away and began easing toward Dan's position.

When they were almost to him, he opened up with his M-14 and wasted both of them. Automatic rifle fire came from near the river's bank. It sounded like an AK-47. A second AK that was closer to me opened up and began firing at Dan's position. Quietly, I moved along the ditch until I could see part of the VC's shoulder and side. I glanced at the position that was firing from near the riverbank. I could not see the shooter, as that person stayed low. I looked back toward the VC closest to me and moved the scope to his side — just below his shoulder, lowered the scope a tad and fired. We were so close the scope was almost totally useless. I just hoped I hit where I wanted the bullet to go. This spot would allow the heavy bullet to enter his chest cavity from his right rib cage area. It was sure to blow his lungs and heart out of his chest.

There was no sound coming from him, just silence. Dan had peppered the bank where the other guy was hiding. I crawled toward the river, staying south of the VC's position. As I eased down the riverbank, I saw one guy laying half in, half out of the water. Dan's firing had done a number on him also. There was now total silence.

I whistled, since all was quiet. I stood up to signal Dan, and a single shot rang out! I spun around, seeing a Viet Cong being spun sideways by the impact of an M-14 bullet from Dan's rifle. He fell into a thicket. Dead! My heart stopped for an instant. My spotter had just saved my butt.

Now, you know why I think he's the best spotter in all of Vietnam. Dan appeared, and came strolling down toward me, at the river's edge.

"I suppose that jerk didn't like my play acting," he joked.

"There is always a party pooper in every army," I responded. "Let's move!"

We located the raft, eased it out into the current, and held onto the raft's sides. Nearly one half mile downstream, we managed to get the raft over to the Vietnam side of the river.

Three hours later, we reached Bug Island to pick up some of our gear. We picked up Gunny's old Thompson, ammo, food, water, and the radio. Everything else stayed. We still had a full day before we would reach our pickup point with the chopper. With 800 ticked-off Viet Cong fighters mad at us, I knew we would have to be ready to fight at any moment. We quickly gobbled down some C-rats before leaving Bug Island.

It was 1420 hours. I wanted to get information to HQI via radio while we had a chance.

"Fire up the PRC-77 radio, and call *'Hotel-Nine-Alpha',*" I told Dan.

"Roger," he replied.

In just a couple of minutes, Dan began transmitting the information I wanted passed on to HQI.

"*'Hotel-Nine-Alpha', this is 'Delta-Two-Foxtrot'. Over,...*"

No answer — so he tried again.

"*'Hotel-Nine-Alpha', this is 'Delta-Two-Foxtrot', Over!*" he spoke with some urgency.

Still no answer; Dan tried a third time, "*'Hotel-Nine-Alpha', this is 'Delta-Two-Foxtrot'.*"

"*'Delta-Two-Foxtrot', welcome back from the party,*" was the reply from HQI operator.

"Capt. Swanson is here, stand by a minute."

Minutes later, Capt. Swanson asked, "*'Delta-Two-Foxtrot', how was your party? Are you both OK? Over,...*"

"*'Hotel-Nine-Alpha', party was wonderful and wild. Rude guest was removed. Request airmail at 0900 hours tomorrow for two at designated site. Over,...*"

"*'Delta-Two-Foxtrot',*" Roger on airmail for two at 0900 hours tomorrow. Over,..."

"*'Delta-Two-Foxtrot', Out!*" Dan signed off and then turned the radio off again.

"Let's move out Marine, we've already worn out our welcome in this area." I said to Dan as he swung the big radio upon his back, ensuring the strap was not twisted. He then began following about 10 yards behind me, as we moved toward the rendezvous with the helicopter at 0900 tomorrow morning.

The route I selected to the rendezvous point is a different route than the one we came in on — this one was more on a direct line through thick jungle. There appeared to be very few trails on this route. We moved very slowly because that's how to stay alive here in Charlie's backyard.

Gunny Davis had made a believer out of me on the fact that it's hard to shoot what one can't see. Your first mistake can be your last. Make the best of what you've got. Out here, that's TIME. Use it wisely. Take your time and don't rush into situations. The end result is what counts out here — and to Sgt. Mitchem, this meant doing whatever was necessary to stay alive and getting this team back to base in one piece.

Moving real slow is the way to survive here in the jungle. By moving ever so slowly, one becomes part of the landscape and harder to detect. This way it's easier for us to spot the VC before they spot us. It's difficult to fight the Viet Cong when we are at a disadvantage. I just found a way to put the advantage in our favor. Moving quietly, deliberate and very slow, and then fighting hard when we have to is the answer.

Two hours later, I stopped to check our back trail. Dan found a place where he could rest against a large tree, and waited for me to return. Twenty minutes later I returned. I had cautiously eased a few hundred yards to our rear and sat, listened, and watched eagle-eyed for anyone trailing us through the jungle.

"Appears quite," was my remark to no one in general as I approached Dan.

"Ready to move out when you are?" Dan stated.

"OK!" I answered, as I walked past Dan and said, "Let me know if you have difficulty with your load?" Then, I eased into that almost non-moving movement called 'slipping'.

Unaware of the passing hours, only aware of every sound and movement in our surroundings, I eased along, knowing each step was one closer to getting us home safely.

Suddenly, I sensed that something was different or foreign in the jungle — it was that gut feeling again! Cold chill bumps were all over my back. I signaled for Dan to stop and get down, slowly. I watch and waited, trying to detect what I sensed.

The normal little sounds from the jungle were not present — which told me, something else was here that didn't belong! *Something was out there. Waiting!* Waiting for us? We would only know that answer if we foolishly jumped up and moved, or made some noise, or scouted the complete area in front of us silently. Still I waited! Unsure!

Thirty-five minutes passed, and I began to doubt my keen senses. Maybe we should move on before the VC from the 514th walked up on our back trail. I was just about to turn and signal Dan when someone coughed about 60 yards out to our left front.

We apparently had come upon troops. Was it a trap? If so, how many were waiting for us? I needed to know their positions and strengths. I motioned for Dan to ease up to my position.

"Did you hear that cough?" I whispered.

"Yes!" Dan whispered in return.

"Remove all your field gear, and leave it here," I murmured. "We've got to find out exactly where they are and how many are out there."

"OK, what do you want me to do?" Dan asked so low I could barely hear him.

Quietly, we discussed a plan. We agreed to meet back at our gear in one hour.

We checked each other's camouflage and crawled off into the jungle.

I had asked Dan to check our right flank to see if anyone was on that side? If he found any VC, he was to get their positions and number of fighters. I would to do the same thing on our left flank, from where I heard the cough.

I eased forward on my stomach very slowly, making no noise to betray my position. I'm glad I'm toting the Thompson submachine gun. It is much better suited for this type of situation. I knew this weapon cut its teeth in the jungles during World II.

The Japanese had great respect for this weapon. They couldn't match its firepower.

I crawled toward the direction I thought the cough had come from, and soon I began to smell the raw fish odor of the VC. I knew I was getting real close to them – a small group of Viet Cong.

I eased to within 20 yards of them, watching from under a large, long green plant. I could see that four VC were sitting and lying around on the ground. Each of them carried an AK-47. Only one appeared to be observant; he was looking out over the area we would have to cross.

Silently, I moved on, looking for others.

Forty yards away, I located three more fighters in another small group. Continuing on, I discovered no one else along this thicket, but I had to find out if there were fighters out in front of us. I continued searching; finding nothing else, I returned to the radio and gear.

Dan was searching for any VC hiding on our right flank. He moved very slowly and made sure he did not make a sound. He began on the right front, crawling out to 80 yards from our position. As he approached the area to his right front, Dan eased as close as 15 yards to two VC fighters manning a machine gun. The VC talked in whispers; both were very keen and alert, keeping an eye on our small trail.

Dan moved further to his right, searching for other VC. After Dan had moved around his entire area and finding no one else, he headed back to meet Mitch at the gear.

Comparing notes, I got a picture in my mind of the VC locations. I began to sketch out their positions on the jungle floor, so Dan could see all the positions. There were two groups to our left *(total seven men)* and a machine gun set up on our right front *(with two men)* – that totaled nine VC fighters.

It appeared someone had sent out ambush patrols, along a certain line of containment, hoping to catch Dan and me as we raced home. This showed they wanted us real bad. We must have really done some kind of damage to that battalion for them to send out ambush parties along every trail leading out of this area, just to knock off a Marine sniper team. They may have gotten these orders straight from Hanoi. At any rate, now, I had to deal with the situation we were facing and still get us safely home.

My plan was for Dan to get close enough to the machine gun to take it out with a grenade. I would be in position and toss two grenades at the four VC that I had spotted, when I heard Dan's grenade explode. No way to surprise those last three VC fighters. It would be an old fashioned shootout once they heard the grenades and knew we were here. I wanted to turn the surprise party on them.

Hopefully, Dan could flank these last three guys after taking out the machine gun. By flanking them, we could throw some lead at them from two angles and soon end this fight. The plan sounded OK! Dan would throw his grenade in exactly 28 minutes. This would allow us time to slip in close to the Viet Cong.

Off we went on our bellies again, ever so cautiously crawling, as we moved nearer the Viet Cong fighters that were unaware of our presence, but waiting in ambush for us on both sides of the trail.

These nine Viet Cong might have thought they had it made, getting dropped out here in the jungle waiting for a couple of U.S. Marines to come blundering through, so they could score an easy kill. What was the chance the Marines would take this route?

Probably slim to none!

The Americans would think they were safe and, therefore, become easy targets. The VC fighters who brought the Marines' bullet-riddled bodies back to camp would get a month's extra pay. This was promised by Col. Dinh.

CHAPTER 6

A lone colonel survived the sniper's deadly volley of bullets at the Battalion conflict. He was untouched. The sniper had somehow overlooked him. The colonel had fallen backwards on the ground, when his stool tipped over, from his sudden reaction to the first shot fired. He was trying to get up when the dead XO fell into him and knocked him back down.

Lying on the ground, Col. Kie Dinh could see the deadly accuracy the Marine sniper possessed.

Commissioner Thayn had most of this head missing; he was beyond recognition, and the general had a large hole through the center of his chest. The XO had been shot through his left chest; and the sniper's bullet exit point showed parts of his insides blown out that were all over Dinh. *I puked my guts out and was afraid of dying that day, Dinh remembered. The XO's blood covered me from my neck to my waist.*

Somehow, he had to get out from under the XO, and get to his hands and knees. Everywhere Col Kie Dinh looked, an officer was going down.

When that killer fired his weapon, an officer died. No one knew where the shots were coming from and the explosions killed a large number of fighters. Col. Dinh noticed that the sniper was targeting mostly officers. He crawled on his belly to where a dead fighter lay close to the kitchen tent, removed the dead man's shirt, and put it on over his. Getting to his feet now, he felt he was safe from the sniper. Col. Dinh began shouting and directing men to fan out from camp and hunt for the sniper.

Some fighters soon located the sniper near the eastern edge of the camp's perimeter. A fierce firefight erupted for nearly six minutes. Many fighters were either dead or injured; but, when his men swept the area where the sniper was thought to be, the sniper was gone. The fighters reported there were two snipers, but Col. Dinh knew that a Marine sniper team usually consisted of two men. Only one was the sniper, the other was his support. The Americans had begun using these teams this year. These two had not left much of a trail. Col Dinh sent for the trackers, ordering them to push the sniper team toward the river, where an ambush was already set.

Two days before, word had come to camp about a sentry's death and a raft missing. The XO had sent trackers and a few fighters out to search the river along both the Vietnam and Cambodian side for the raft. After finding the raft downriver that same day and not knowing who stole the raft, the XO placed five sentries there to watch it.

When the colonel's 20 men arrived at the river, they only found the corpse of their fighters. They also discovered that the raft was gone. Hurriedly, they returned and gave Col. Dinh the news. Dinh knew the Marines were now trying to get back to their base — probably to the American Marine bases near Saigon or the South Vietnamese Army base downriver at Chalon.

Col. Dinh took out his map and studied the routes he thought the sniper team most likely would have taken — *'North along the eastern side of the Hoy River, then turning East; or South down the Mekong River to Chalon, or had they gone straight east, through the jungle to reach a rendezvous point to be picked up by helicopter.'* The route straight through the jungle would be the hardest for his men to trail and locate, so he figured the sniper would take this route. Besides, if they were successful, this was the quickest way out.

The sniper was an intelligent foe, and Col. Dinh would not underestimate his expertise. The Marine sniper team was well versed in survival, but he knew he would get them.

There were three different routes indicated on the map, but Col. Dinh thought the sniper would take the most difficult route, one without many trails. So, he designed a plan to stagger 50 men along two miles of jungle with few trails. This meant Dinh would have to spread his forces thin, but he had a gut feeling the sniper would take this route. He thought about the two Marines — they were true professionals and experts at jungle warfare and very efficient at killing. Never had he witnessed marksmanship like that displayed today. His thoughts returned to *how to kill or capture them.*

He ordered three trucks to meet 50 of his fighters on the Vietnam side of the river near the raft landing. The closest bridge was several miles upstream. He could not wait for the trucks to come by bridge; so he ordered the rafts to pick up his men, and they would meet the trucks near the raft landing. He also had two jeeps at camp; and putting five men in each, one group would cover the Hoy River route, the other the Mekong River route. With 60 men, Col. Dinh thought he could intercept the Marines and stop their escape.

If only his men could locate them, he could surprise them somewhere along their journey.

After what these two had done to the 514th Viet Cong Battalion, if he could show their bullet-riddled bodies to his superiors, he would surely get the CO position for the battalion. *These two had almost totally disrupted the upcoming mission.*

The mission was a major offense against the South Vietnamese Army located just north of Cholan, in the extreme southern delta. But after the attack by the sniper team, it would take months to again train and assign officers, maybe even more time to restock the weapons and ammunition. The hardest task would be replacing the battle-hardened senior officers.

Col. Dinh's military career was now in the hands of his 60 veteran fighters. Trucks got the VC, the 50 men spaced intermittently along the two-mile long line, as close to the jungle as the vehicles could get them. A couple of young officers then led Dinh's men into the jungle, placing them in six different ambush positions along the two-mile trek.

* * * * * * *

The nine fighters that were unlucky enough to have the sniper team come through their area had waited for hours, but no Marines had showed. A sergeant had jokingly said to three of his men, *"The Americans will sound like water buffalo in the jungle."* They all laughed — unknowing that Sgt. Melvin Mitchem had just crawled within 20 yards of their position — Waiting!

Dan had moved into a position about 15 yards from the machine gun's position. Dan had approached them from the side. He didn't want to crawl into that machine gun's firing path. Lying very still, watching the seconds tick by on his watch, Dan took a grenade, held the handle firm, and eased the pin out. Now, he slowly turned on his side and in one fluid motion, released the handle, counted to three, and tossed the grenade toward the two Viet Cong operating the machine gun.

With the explosion, body parts went flying in every direction. A smoldering, tattered bloody arm fell near where Dan lay. He looked at it and crawled slowly toward the three fighters. The explosion was my signal. I quickly tossed two grenades at the position where the four-man VC group lay in wait.

Their screams let me know I had been accurate. One fighter just kept screaming.

I remembered Dan's act back at the river. So I tossed another grenade toward the screaming man and, with the explosion, there was silence from the soldier.

I suddenly began receiving small arms fire from the other position, 40 yards away. They did not know my exact location, so they were just shooting wildly. I decided not to return their fire just yet and give away my position. I wanted to give Dan more time to flank their position.

Bullets begin chewing up the ground five yards in front of me; I either could move quickly or get hit. I swiftly rolled twice to my left and came up firing.

The AKs can sure chew up the real estate. Bushes, small trees, and limbs were falling everywhere the bullets hit. The firing from the VC position stopped, just as suddenly as it had started. I didn't know if they had moved or not. One thing for sure, I had better get my butt to moving before I got it shot off.

Not knowing where they were, I really didn't know which way to move. As I was trying to figure this out in my head, an arm suddenly went around my neck from behind. I instantly moved my right arm up to block the knife that would be coming toward my throat or chest area. As I blocked his first downward thrust of the knife with my forearm, the VC was trying to stab me again. With my left hand, I let go of the Thompson and grabbed his right wrist as it was coming down toward my chest again. Then using my right hand to help, I twisted the knife loose from his hand. He jerked his hand free and with lightning speed was on my back, putting me in a murderous chokehold. I had to escape this somehow — and fast!

The little man was strong, but I managed to get my left hand underneath his arm, between his arm and my neck, thus preventing my neck from popping. My right hand inched its way down my leg trying to reach the K-Bar knife. He now had me gasping for air. I had very little time left. I could feel my strength leaving me.

I touched the knife handle. Desperately I tried to free the K-Bar from its scabbard. I was becoming dizzy and had trouble breathing. There — it's free! I had the K-Bar in my hand and eased my right hand back up my leg; and when it was again at my waist, I plunged the knife backwards toward his stomach. Repeatedly I plunged the K-Bar into him, with every ounce of strength that I had left in my body. I knew in another few seconds this man would have choked me to death. His powerful grip slowly loosened from around my neck.

Slowly, I discovered that I could now breathe again. As my lungs gulped in sweet fresh air, I realized there were two other VC fighters somewhere nearby. Where were they? I knew I couldn't go hand-to-hand with anyone else now. I was too weak. Rifle fire sounded close by; it sounded like Dan's M-14 — no mistaking that familiar sound.

Dan had slipped behind the VC position and spotted one of them crawling toward where I was wrestling his friend. Dan shot the fighter in the back, as the man moved along the jungle floor. Neither of us saw the third man, he either was dead or had run away.

Dan walked over and helped me to my feet. As I stood, Dan could see blood all over my shoulder and back.

He asked, "Are you hit or hurt bad?"

"No!" I answered. "We just need to move out of here fast; others surly heard this firefight and will be here shortly."

Dan located the Thompson and my soft cover hat and handed both to me. He then gathered up all of our equipment and gear. I could see him as he slung the big radio upon his back, and Dan 'eyeballed' me closely to ensure I was really OK as he handed me my gear. Dan and I checked and reloaded our weapons, and then he followed me as we gradually slipped away from the scene.

Looking at my watch, I saw it was 2335 hours; we had been on the move for almost four hours since our run-in with the ambushers back in the jungle. It was now time to stop and take a break. I was starving. I took out a can of pork-n-beans and a candy bar, wolfed them down in a few minutes and sipped on my water. I talked in a low voice to Dan about the rendezvous with the chopper at 0900 hours. A mile east of the rice fields next to the field of cane was the small rectangular clearing where we had debarked.

Dan then doubled-checked our map and compass readings to make sure we had not wandered off course. Our pickup point was nine and one-half miles from Bug Island.

In 20 minutes, we were moving again, slipping as quietly as possible through the jungle. According to the map, we would exit the jungle and have to cross two rice fields. I didn't want to get surprised in the middle of a rice field like I did when we had first started this mission. Crossing the fields at night would provide us a cover of darkness that would be our ally. At 0240 hours we arrived at the rice patties.

Upon reaching the rice fields, I stopped at the jungle's edge, turned, and waited for Dan to approach me. I had been considering skirting the rice patties, but knew we could also walk into another ambush.

"In this vast openness, sounds carry a very long way," I whispered.

Dan acknowledged by just nodding his head. I could not see any dikes, so I just eased into the 2-foot deep water and began heading across. The moon was hiding behind some far off rain clouds; but every few minutes, it would peek out at two weary leathernecks, trying to get back to their base in a far away, war-torn land.

Suddenly, a biting pain raced up my leg. I began to swat at what was eating my leg. I couldn't see very well in the dim moonlight. But very soon, I knew what I had gotten into. A gigantic mass of floating fire ants — thousands of them were on the water, and I was walking through them. Soon, the ferocious fire ants were also biting my torso, both hands and my arms. As I tried to beat the ants off my body, I was aware I was making a lot of noise — slapping and splashing water.

Their bite caused a puss-filled sore, called festers, to appear on your skin within three days at every point of a bite. I was so busy trying to get them off me that I had not noticed that they also were eating Dan alive. They bit me more times than I could count. Some people are allergic to fire ant bites, run a high fever, and even go into a comma. Thank God, neither Dan nor I fell into that category.

We had made way too much noise trying to get away from the fire ants. But when a person gets into a swarm of fire ants, it's impossible to think rationally. You can only think of escaping the pain that the ants are inflicting.

In four minutes, those ants caused the two of us more pain and suffering than any VC had inflicted during this mission. I knew we both would need to get shots when we reached base to help clear up the toxic festers.

I could make out the tree line ahead of us as we continually moved across the rice patty. When we were about 100 yards from the tree line, I heard a 'THUM' and seconds later a Viet Cong mortar round exploded in the water 35 yards behind Dan.

I screamed, "Run Dan!" — And we both took off as fast as we could run in knee-deep rice fields. A second 'THUM' sounded and another mortar exploded 20 yards behind Dan. Here, we were like ducks in a shooting galley; there was nothing to hide behind for protection from those mortar explosions.

"This way," I screamed and moved off to our left flank, as fast as I could run in that water. I could hear Dan right behind me, so I knew we were together. More mortar rounds exploded around us. They had swung the launcher tube around to follow us. It was difficult for the VC to get our exact positions, with us 'hightailing' it for cover.

Small arms fire opened up on us, but I continued running as fast as I could.

I pleaded with God, as I ran for my life, to spare Dan's life, and mine, and I would live a cleaner life. I told God in that rice field that I would start going to church again, if he would spare our lives.

The bullets made a weird sound as they hit the water and skipped across it; those guys with the AK-47s were getting a lot closer to us than the ones shooting the mortars.

I saw a dike, but I was looking beyond that toward another tree line. I did not stop at the dike; we crawled up over it as fast as we could and got back in the water and continued running for those trees. Another hundred clicks, then we would reach the safety of the trees. I veered again, continuously running. I did not want those guys to be able to plot our next move and drop a mortar down our britches; so every 20 yards or so, I would veer off and then next time alternate and veer the other way.

Minutes later, we reached the trees. I kept running until we were about 20 yards inside the tree line. I then stopped and looked back toward the fields; even in the dim moonlight, I could see a large group of Viet Cong in the rice field coming after us. They were still 75 to 80 yards out in the rice field running toward us.

Soon, the ones firing the mortars would move the mortar to within range again. They must have fighters positioned between the taller tree line and us, trying to put us in a squeeze.

"Get on the PRC-77, tell HQI we need immediate air support, we're pinned down by at least a platoon-size VC force with mortars," I spewed.

"Hurry, while I try to slow those guys down some," I reiterated. There wasn't enough moonlight to do much good with either rifle.

But, I knew when the Thompson spoke, they would have to scatter and get down. I had to keep them off us long enough for Dan to use the radio. I fired sparingly, conserving ammo. I had them down in the water; they fired back, their AK-47s had much more accuracy than the .45 caliber. I could not match them in shear firepower, but I could make them get down.

"'Delta-Two-Foxtrot' calling 'Hotel-Nine-Alpha', EMERGENCY! Over!"

A second time he tried, "'Delta-Two-Foxtrot' calling 'Hotel-Nine-Alpha', EMERGENCY! Over!"

"This is 'Hotel-Nine-Alpha'. 'Delta-Two-Foxtrot', what's your situation? Over,..."

"We are under small arms fire from a platoon-size VC force and also receiving mortar fire. Need air assistance ASAP! Our position is 116.37 degrees West by 10.19 degrees North. Over."

"Roger on position, if you move, keep me informed. I'll call Navy air to see if they have anything over your area. Over,..."

"Roger, 'Hotel-Nine-Alpha', we need help from someone quick! We can't hold them off for very long. Over!"

"I'll get back with you soon, 'Delta-Two-Foxtrot'. Over and Out!"

While Dan was on the radio, I did my best to keep the VC pinned down in the rice field. At any minute, they would have their mortars in place again. I needed more moonlight. If I could get a little more moonlight, I could do some hefty damage with the sniper rifle. But until then, I was just happy to have a Mexican standoff with these guys.

The VC fighters in the rice paddies now had only their head and shoulders above the water, not a big target to see in the dark. I kept the Thompson barking at them every now and then. The light was still not enough to use the weapon effectively. Dan couldn't help with the flares until he got off the radio.

I yelled to Dan, "Scout around for heavier cover, fast!"

"OK!" he answered.

Off he went, running here and there. THUM came the familiar sound of the Viet Cong mortar launcher. BOOM! The explosion ripped tree limbs off, sending a shower of splintered wood and mud in all directions.

"Hurry, Dan," I screamed.

The mortar rounds began to hit closer and closer to where I was lying behind a small mound of earth. The fighters in the rice fields had fanned out and were now moving closer.

They were now about 70 yards from my position. Again I fired, making them get down again.

"Hurry, Dan!" I screamed again with even more urgency.

I wanted to put a claymore mine on top of the mound of earth, and set it toward the fighters in the rice patty. But not knowing where I would go next, I couldn't set it. It appeared we might not get back to base; and if this was the case, I wanted to take a lot of these little guys with me.

The next mortar round exploded directly in front of me — less than 20 yards from my position – showering me with mud. I began to ease backward, retreating from the rice field, which gave me less visibility of the rice field and my pursuers. Ten yards further back, I had almost lost sight of the VC in the water and mortars were still coming ever closer.

Suddenly, Dan grabbed my shoulder and screamed, "Come on!"

We turned and ran, with me following him. Forty-five yards straight behind where I had been, Dan had located three good-sized trees lying on the ground, across each other, forming a makeshift barricade. This would provide some protection from the mortars' flying debris, as well as a defense from small arms fire.

As I jumped in behind the tree trunks, Dan turned back and ran to the area we just vacated. He began to set C-4 explosives on trees, and then ran toward the rice field to install more claymores and set them facing the enemy. There was the bright flash of the mortar explosions. I lost sight of Dan momentarily as he was attaching explosives to trees.

Dan soon turned and ran toward our palm tree barricade and me.

We heard the VC fighters screaming as they ran from the rice fields into the thinned-out jungle where we were. As soon as we saw the muzzle flashes from their weapons, Dan flipped the toggle switch on the electrical firing device and a half pound of C-4 exploded, sending its deadly blast hurling toward the unsuspecting fighters.

We heard more screaming in between the exploding mortars. But, still they came at us. They were either very brave or real dumb.

The PRC-77 crackled loud, "'Delta-Two-Foxtrot', this is 'Hotel-Nine-Alpha'. Over,..."

Dan had secured the radio behind the tree trunks earlier. Now, he picked up the head set and answered, "This is 'Delta-Two-Foxtrot'. Over,..."

"Roger, 'Delta-Two-Foxtrot', giving you the frequency band of Navy A4C Skyhawk. Over,..."

"Go ahead on frequency band, ready to copy. Over,..."

"Frequency band, Zorro…setting, 44.8. Code name is 'War Bird'. Over,…"

"Roger on Zorro…44.8. Our position is 65 yards east of rice patties in trees.

Coordinates are 116.36 degrees West by 10.19 degrees North. Over,…"

"Roger on your position, 'Delta-Two-Foxtrot,' give Navy Air a call, they are expecting you. We'll be monitoring your situation closely. 'Hotel-Nine-Alpha', Out!"

With 30 Viet Cong fighters and their mortars bearing down on us, Dan didn't waste any time calling the A-4C pilots. Setting the frequency dial on 44.8, opening, and setting the air channel switch to 'Zorro', Dan gave it a try.

"'Delta-Two-Foxtrot' calling 'War Bird'…'Delta-Two-Foxtrot' calling 'War Bird'. Over,…"

The PRC-77 radio was putting out static, and just as Dan was trying to call the A-4C pilots again, they answered.

"This is 'War Bird' leader, calling 'Delta-Two-Foxtrot'. Give me your exact position, Over,…"

"This is 'Delta-Two-Foxtrot'. Position is 116.36 degrees West by 10.19 degrees North. We're 65 clicks east of rice patties in trees. Over,…"

"Roger on your position, 'Delta-Two-Foxtrot', I have computed your position. Have two A-4Cs in flight, just left carrier, will be arriving at your location near daybreak. Over,…"

"Thanks, 'War Bird' Leader. Hope to still be here when you drop in." Will give 'Red' smoke to mark position on your command. Over!"

"Roger on red smoke. Hang tough Marine, until we get there, Over."

"'War Bird Leader', we have 30-plus VC infantry 50 clicks from our location. They are between us and rice patties. Mortar emplacement is 150 to 200 clicks west of our position and pounding us good. Over,…"

"We copy your situation and should be over you within 8 minutes. Will try and relieve some of your pressure on first strike. Will call 'Delta-Two-Foxtrot' again in 6 minutes. 'War Bird Leader', Out."

The VC fighters were really going all out to make this our last mission. Bullets were chewing away at our position. It was not safe to go sticking one's head up above the tree trunks. Dan would send up flares every few minutes so we could keep track of the VC fighters. If they were near a C-4 plastic explosive, we would set it off. We also spotted a small group of VC fighters sneaking around trying to flank us.

As they reached a small group of banana trees where Dan had put a claymore, I set it off. Those guys would never make it home for breakfast. A hundred or more lead pellets the size of No. 1 buckshot rips a body apart — that's what the claymore brings to the table.

The Viet Cong hated the claymore mines because of the mine's killing radius and the crippling affect it had on their troop morale.

It would be five minutes before the A-4Cs would be here. Dan quickly counted our night flares — only two left! There was not a hint in the sky that daylight would break soon. It had begun to rain harder, and it was a cold rain.

The Viet Cong were trying to ease in closer so that their larger numbers would have a greater effect. If the VC were able to get close enough to lob a few grenades in on us, it would be over real quick. With the dark sky, I wondered if daybreak would indeed come to this small part of Vietnam. Or, had Dan and I already witnessed our last sunrise?

I had given Dan instructions for us to fight with our backs to each other. We both had set out all our ammo, grenades, and flares after Dan got off the horn with the Navy.

BOOM! The explosion was deafening, the mortar round tore a tree apart 12 yards away, sending splinters flying into our position. Fragments from the same exploding tree hit each of us. A piece tore into Dan's left leg seven inches below his knee, and splinters embedded into the back of my right hand and wrist.

I had just finished firing when sharp pain ripped through the back of my right hand and wrist. I looked at my hand, finding small multi-punctures that were bleeding like a stuck hog. My hand suddenly had very little feeling in it. I tried firing my Thompson again and discovered I would be unable to shoot with much accuracy.

When I turned to ask Dan about putting a bandage on my hand, I noticed the large splinter sticking in the calf of his leg. I ripped his trousers' leg open with my K-Bar and applied a torque just above where the one-foot long piece of jagged wood was stuck in his leg. In turn, Dan bandaged my shooting hand; and we continued firing, trying to keep the VC off us.

Things weren't looking very good for 'Delta-Two-Foxtrot'.

* * * * * * *

It would be impossible to run from the VC in this fight. I really needed to get Dan back to base soon, as he was losing a lot of blood. I was determined to keep any VC fighters that survived the air strike off him as long as I could breathe. I owed Dan my life. He saved my butt back at the river. I sure was going to do my best to return the favor.

The VC were becoming aggressive again — whenever a mortar landed close to our position, they would send a team forward to challenge us, checking to see if we lived through the assault. A team had crawled within 30 yards of us before we saw them.

Caught in the open, they crawled forward on their hands and knees. When we opened fire on them, they did the only thing left to do — charge our position and scream as loud as their lungs would allow. One who spoke broken English yelled, *"You die Marines!"*

Dan's M-14, spoke like a true champion, ending the VC's short speech in English. His body piled up in a bloody heap less than 20 yards from our position.

I was lying on my belly, firing at his comrades now with my .45 pistol, shooting with my left hand. My bullets zipped between the tree trunks at the crazy screaming Viet Cong soldiers; this was more a case of point and shoot, hoping to hit anything.

Dan fired at the advancing fighters until his clip was empty. A VC lying on the ground in front of us rose to his knees with a grenade in his hand. As he drew his arm back to throw the grenade, I instantly fired two shots. His body folded backwards, and the grenade exploded near his lifeless body.

The radio crackled, *"'War Bird Leader' calling 'Delta-Two-Foxtrot'. Over,..."*

"What kept you 'War Bird Leader'?" was Dan's loud reply.

"Give me red smoke now, repeat, give me red smoke now?"

"Keep a low profile Marines; we're coming in when I see the right smoke. Over,..."

I popped the red smoke flare and tossed it with my left hand, five yards in front of us.

The firefight had been so intense we had not noticed it was daybreak. Within seconds, we heard the jets — they were just above the treetops. Then the deafening sound of napalm exploded 50 yards away. The intense fireball created by the napalm and the heat were almost unbearable. The jungle burned to a crisp, nothing lived that it touched. The black smoke was so thick it made breathing difficult.

A second explosion and another napalm exploded west of our position. It roasted all life form that was in its path. The mortars were now quiet, forever. If the mortar tubes survived the heat, they would be twisted scrap metal.

A couple of minutes later, our radio was active again.

"'War Bird Leader' to 'Delta-Two-Foxtrot'. Did that eliminate your problems? Or, do we need to put it somewhere else? Over,..."

"'War Bird Leader', this is 'Delta-Two-Foxtrot'. Bad-guys attended a barbeque party.

Negative on additional heat anywhere...and thanks a million Navy!"

"'Delta-Two-Foxtrot, This is 'War Bird Leader'. "Way to hang tough Marines!"

"'War Bird Leader',...Out."

"'Delta-Two-Foxtrot' to 'War Bird Leader'. WE owe you Navy. THANKS! Over and Out."

Dan hurriedly switched back to our HQI frequency 88.63 and placed a call.

"'Delta-Two-Foxtrot' calling 'Hotel-Nine-Alpha', Over,..."

"This is 'Hotel-Nine-Alpha', go ahead 'Delta-Two-Foxtrot'."

"'War Bird Leader' eliminated problem with VC, but we need air taxi ASAP. We have wounded. Over,..."

"Roger on air taxi, Capt. Swanson had already given orders for your pickup. Can you get to the rice field for pickup? Pickup should be arriving in 12 minutes. Over."

"Roger, 'Hotel-Nine-Alpha', we'll be at rice field for pickup in 12 minutes, and thanks, good buddy. 'Delta-Two-Foxtrot' ...Out."

Dan had also taken an AK-47 round in his side. I used the last of our gauze to wrap this wound. It didn't look bad, just bad enough for him to get a short stay in the hospital once we got back. His leg had little feeling in it; but, it would be OK after surgery. My hand and wrist were going to be OK. They would dig the splinters out, and it would be sore for a few weeks. The ant bites were very sore. Our wounds were not the kind that would get us a trip home.

But, maybe we could get rest and relaxation (R&R) for a week.

"Do you want a cigarette, Dan?" I asked.

"Sure, if smoking lamp is lit," he said with a weary smile. Then we both laughed at the smoking comment. It seemed like weeks since we had laughed this much. Our laughter got louder as we got a good look at each other's condition in the daylight. Both wounded by a tree! Wouldn't the guys back at base have a ball with that one?

The rain was still coming down, running down our necks; the dense smoke from the fires was hanging low over the jungle landscape. As we slowly approached the area where the VC fighters had been, the smell of roasted human flesh almost turned our stomachs. As we walked out of a scorched, stinking, smoking jungle, our nostrils filled with the smell of the determined and brave Viet Cong fighters.

Dan was leaning on me as the two of us moved slowly out of the trees to the edge of the rice patties. I had his PRC radio to relieve him of that weight.

Just about the time Dan and I emerged from the smoking jungle, we saw the chopper approaching — that was one more beautiful sight. We began trying to wave our arms. Dan waved one and I waved the arm that was not supporting him. The pilot set the big bird down within 30 yards of us. Instantly, two people jumped from the chopper to assist us. One took the PRC-77 while the other man, a medic, helped me support Dan; and, we all four walked to our waiting air taxi.

I imagined we looked rather ragged. Dan and I looked like walking vegetation, and each of us had bloody bandages wrapped around our tired bodies at one place or another. I noticed the camo paint on Dan's face had started to come off. I knew that my own face must look the same. Most likely, the intense heat from the napalm bomb caused our war paint to run down our face, neck, and hands.

As soon as we aboard the helicopter, the medic began checking and attending Dan's wounds. A machine gunner was overheard, saying, *"Man they look like they've just come from Hell."* I just smiled to nobody in particular and Dan gave the guy a crazy look. *I wondered if Hell really is similar to what we'd just been through.*

Mission Accomplished! 'DeltaTwo-Foxtrot' is going home!

* * * * * * *

After a complete physical evaluation by the hospital staff and spending one and a-half days there, I was released. Dan was not as lucky; after surgery on his leg and side, his hospital stay would be about four or five days according to the Gunny Sergeant.

For the next two days, I was busy with intelligence meetings with our HQI people; plus, there were two other officers, a captain and a major present from Regiment HQI. I guess our little trip into Cambodia was a bigger deal than I had thought.

Intelligence informed me that surveillance aircraft flew into the Cambodian Triangle to gather any pictures they could on the 514th Viet Cong Battalion's whereabouts and activity. I hoped the surveillance aircraft would find the Battalion before they decided to go into hiding until regrouping again. One thing was certain, they would move.

CHAPTER 7

I spent a lot of my recuperation time alone, thinking about my home, back in Florida, where I grew up. I began to walk out to the rifle range and just sat or lay on the grass, thinking about home. Thinking about my mother gave me strength as well as peace. I also spent many hours here remembering what I did growing up back home.

I remembered when I was a very young boy, my mom worked hard to support just the two of us. If mom's sisters hadn't helped us out at times with food, clothing, and shoes, I don't know if we could have made it. Grandmother Williams would take care of me while mom was at work. Mom worked as a food server and later as cashier at the flight line cafeteria on Eglin AFB.

When mom remarried, I guess I was around nine at the time. Her husband's name was Colin Brody. He was a short man with a tree-trunk type build. A staff sergeant in the Air Force stationed at Eglin, he became mean as a snake when he drank whiskey.

For whatever reason, he despised me. Maybe, it was because I wasn't his.

Five months later, mom was pregnant. When my mom had Colin's child, it was a beautiful baby girl that she named Vivian. You would think he would have settled down and straightened out — but, not this guy! He was now getting drunk more often, and he had begun slapping me around and lifting me clean off the floor by my hair.

When I was 10, my stepfather came home — like so many other times — so drunk he could hardly walk. Mother was working the evening shift at the base, and I was babysitting Vivian after I got home from school. I had just given her a bottle and put her in her crib to sleep. It was close to 6:00 P.M. when Colin came home.

Colin was mad because mom wasn't there to have his supper on the table as she usually did. When I tried to explain that she was working, I got punched in the stomach by him. He grabbed me by my throat and slammed me backwards onto the wood floor. My head hit the floor first, and it felt like I had been hit with a baseball bat. He reached down and grabbed me by my arm and snatched me to my feet. Then he began cursing me and slapping me in the face. He then forced me to stand up against the wall, and said if I moved, he would beat me within an inch of my life.

Colin staggered back over to the old couch and sat there cursing me. He then reached into his pocket and took out his pocket knife, opened it, and pretended he was going to throw the knife at me. I was scared to death. I made a mad dash toward the front door, but was knocked down before I got there. Again, he put me against the wall, but this time, he really hit me a hard in my stomach. I couldn't breathe!

He moved back to the couch and threw the pocket knife. I froze! It bounced off the old wooden boards less than a foot from my neck and fell to the floor. Colin came and picked it up, and looked at me with this hatred look in his eyes.

"I can stick this old knife within inches of you. Don't move, or I'll tear your ###****# head off," he slurred.

He staggered back to the couch and sat down and then he threw the knife…..*I closed my eyes.* It stuck in the wall maybe 10 inches from my shoulder. He retrieved the knife so many times I lost count, staggered back over to the couch and threw it again and again. This went on for a long time until finally the last time he reached down to pick up his knife, he just passed out and fell to the floor.

I was shaking all over from fear and hate. Never had I been this angry! I wanted to pick the knife up and ram it into his back. Instead, I went in the bedroom and got my little sister and got out of the house. I walked a little over a mile barefooted to my grandmother's house. I didn't even think about my shoes because I just wanted to get away from Colin as fast as I could.

I had never met anyone as hateful and mean as he was. A few months later, he backhanded me across the face. The only difference was that mom saw him hit me; she was watching through the screen door. Mom had been washing clothes in the dilapidated ringer washing machine out on the back porch, and she ran inside and flew into him like a tiger.

But Colin knocked her down with his fist, grabbed her by her hair, and dragged her back outside to the old washing machine, and yanked her hair until she was in a standing position. He then took her hand and stuck it in the ringer, while it was turning.

Mother screamed in pain. I couldn't take anymore of him beating her, so I ran out on the porch where they were fighting. I saw this old empty coke bottle and picked it up. I knew I had to help my mother, so I really tried to hurt him. I rammed the neck of that old bottle up into his testicles as hard as I could. Immediately, he let go of mother and fell to porch floor in pain, cursing both of us with every breath. She freed her hand from the ringer, and we both ran inside. She scooped up my sister, and we ran over to a neighbor's house. Mom used their phone to call the cops. Colin was arrested. His squadron Commander had him confined to base for two months after he got out of city jail.

When he came back home, he was all meek and humble. He apologized for everything that he had done and then asked mom to take him back, which she did.

My grandmother suggested to mother that I come live with her. Mom finally agreed and I went to live with grandma until I was 15 years old. She was very strict and made me do as she said or I'd get worn out with a persimmon switch. But, the love she showed me was far greater than her sternness.

I also remembered the time when I was in the 11th grade about being on the hit list of a well-known boy whose father was a colonel at Eglin AFB. This guy was Mr. Everything. He was voted Most Popular Boy in our grade, and the girls were crazy about him. He thought he was Mr. Cool. His name was Bob Walker and there were always four or five other guys who hung around with him. Once, during fifth period Physical Education class, we were playing flag football for the school championship.

It so happened that Walker and I were on opposite teams. Our teams had reached the championship game by eliminating other teams we had played. This big game was the result of two weeks of flag football, in which a single elimination tournament was held.

I don't remember every detail about the game. I just remember it was a very close, hard-fought game. Close to mid-way in the game, Walker, who was a running back, was the lead blocker on a quarterback rollout around the end. I was my team's defensive back on defense and a wide receiver on offense. As he came around the end, he threw a forearm to the head of one of our guys. So as I approached him at full speed, I leveled his butt; and, the force of our impact knocked him backwards and flat on his back.

Bob Walker was embarrassed by getting hit that hard. His friends were really ragging him and saying that 'I cleaned his plow'. He was the type who couldn't take a hard hit, disappointment, or embarrassment without retaliation. He took every opportunity he got to take a cheap shot at me. After he had popped me in the nose with a backhand, he apologized and said it was an accident. Later, I was again his victim of a cheap shot, this time a fist to my ribs. He turned and smiled at me as he walked away.

When we had the ball, our quarterback called a pass play, and I was the receiver. Walker also played defensive back on his team. I had caught the pass and was attempting to side step another would-be tackler, when I saw Walker bearing down on me. I suddenly stopped and spun sideways, which caused him to look foolish as he missed me, and I scored the touchdown. Again this caused him embarrassment. Kidding from his friends increased his fury toward me. Again, I received a cheap shot; this time he came up behind me when I was running and intentionally tripped me, causing me to go plowing face first in the dirt. He then said, "Punk, don't _ _ _ _ with me!" That burned my butt.

While wiping sand out of my eyes and face, I decided that I, too, could play his game. So, every time the ball was snapped, regardless of whether he had the ball or not, I tried my best to knock him on his rear end. Soon he and I both had bloody noses. The coach suggested that we put gloves on to settle our differences. But before that could happen, one of the lady coaches approached our large class group of boys and our coach. Our coach told everyone to go take a shower; the game was over.

This incident happened on a Thursday afternoon. I rode the school bus each day, and we had to travel about 14 miles each way. One of Bob Walker's buddies also rode the same bus. On Friday afternoon, this guy informed me that I had *"made a huge mistake by taking on Walker."*

I replied, "During the football game, I discovered that your friend Walker liked to dish it out, but he sure can't take it. You tell him I said that."

Around noontime Saturday, I was sitting at the dinner table with my Grandma Williams when someone knocked on the front screen door. My grandmother went to see who our visitor was. I heard her ask whoever was at the door to come in.

When she came back to the table, she said, "This young friend of yours has come by to see you."

I looked up — Bob Walker was standing beside my grandmother with a sheepish grin on his face.

Being the kind of lady she was, she invited him to eat something with us. He said, "I'm not hungry, I just came here to put a good whipping on Melvin."

"Sonny boy, you sure that's what you want to do?" My grandmother asked.

"That's why I'm here," he replied.

Before I could stand up, grandma said, "Melvin, don't disappoint your friend or he might not come visiting again."

I slowly rose from the table, as grandmother said, "You boys take this fight outside in the yard. No fighting in here."

I looked and saw a smile appear on Walker's face. He had this bold, cockiness attitude. I wondered what else he might do.

Walker turned and walked out on the porch and waited for me. As I approached the front screen door, I could see two cars parked in front of the house. He had brought along his friends, and they were waiting to see him whip me at my home. There was about eight of them standing around the cars looking at us as we emerged from the house.

As I walked past Walker to go down the steps into the yard, he hit me along the side of my head with his fist. His blow knocked me off the porch and into the dirt, flat on my face. I had a loud ringing in my ears. There was loud cheering coming from his friends, as they started toward us.

Quickly, I got to my feet and saw him charging at me, like a mad bull. This time, I was ready. I took his charge and grabbed his head and neck; keeping his head low, twisting it hard, I flipped him over on his back. When he looked up, I was straddle of him and was pounding both of my fists into his pretty face at a rapid pace. I had somehow managed to trap one of his arms underneath my knee. He howled in pain and tried to protect his face, but I kept hitting him.

I could hear his friends nearby cheering him on, encouraging him to get up — and I also clearly heard my grandmother say, "You boys, just stay outside the fence, because if one of you tries to come in, I'll shoot."

"Your friend came here wanting to fight, and now Melvin's giving him what he wanted," she added.

I had put a nice deep cut under his left eye, and blood ran into his mouth whenever he opened it to curse me or scream from pain. I also did a number on his million-dollar nose. It wasn't so pretty now because I had inflicted a lot of blows, which caused swelling and bleeding. I grabbed his ears, one in each of my hands. I pulled real hard and twisted as hard as I could. He screamed like I was killing him. Somehow, while he was squirming and trying to get me off him, he got his head around near my leg and clamped down on my calf flesh with his teeth. I thought he had bit a hunk out of my leg.

As we both got back to our feet, I got another headlock on him and did a reverse pile-driver on him. His head smacked the ground hard with my weight on top of him, and I was trying to drive him into the dirt. I knew he was hurt; his will to fight had left him, and he was just trying to get away from me. Finally, he managed to free himself, ran, and somehow climbed over the old fence, falling to the ground on the other side.

He sure wasn't looking for the gate — just the quickest way out of the yard. His buddies helped him up and dragged him over to their cars. Then they left as quickly as they had come. But, 'Mr. Cool' wasn't cocky anymore, just a bloody mess that Saturday afternoon.

I was so proud of my grandmother. She didn't let his friends come inside the yard; and, she had her .38 caliber police special in her hand to see that they didn't.

"You did good son!" she said as she stuck the pistol back into her apron pocket, and we walked back inside as she put her arm around me. I suppose she had seen the need for the pistol and got it before she came outside.

"Stick this on that big knot behind your right ear" grandma said as she gave me a clean cloth wrapped around an ice cube.

I didn't realize how much my head hurt until I put that ice on it. I had a busted lower lip to boot; but, I sure felt good about how the day had turned out. An hour later, I made a few phone calls to Billy Wayne and three other buddies. Soon, they arrived, all listening intently to Grandma Williams and me telling about the whole episode from Thursday's football game until today's action.

Bob Walker and his friends found out before Monday that I also had friends who would help me if necessary. I believe everyone was glad that the episode was soon over without anymore fighting. I was always on the watch for Walker trying to slip up behind me and take a cheap shot again — but, he never did. Bob Walker's father was transferred from Eglin AFB to some other base during our summer break, and I never saw him again. His close buddies kept their distance and left me alone.

* * * * * * *

I was amazed at how clearly I remembered that episode with Bob Walker. The morning sun was beginning to bear down. I spotted a large shade from a couple of large palm trees and made my way over to it. I lay down on the grass once again at the rifle range; now that I was in another nice shady spot, I thought about home again.

Soon, I was remembering other episodes of my youth. I remembered that mother and grandmother sent me up to my aunt and uncle's large farm in southern Alabama, mostly to keep me out of trouble as a young teenager. I always enjoyed my summers there. Aunt Edith would get up before daybreak and fix a great big breakfast of cured country ham, grits, eggs, fresh homemade biscuits, homemade jelly, coffee, and a large glass of cold milk, fresh from their milk cows the day before.

Uncle Bruce and I would work all day cutting hay with the tractor and then sweep it into long rows so it could dry before being bailed. We bailed hay two days later, from 6:00 A.M. until sundown, and left it in the field until the next morning when the hay was loaded onto two large flatbed trucks. Each bail weighed about 44 pounds on average. These bails had to be picked up and then tossed up to a person stacking the hay on the truck. I walked along side of the truck, picking up bails and tossing them up on the flatbed until both trucks were holding all they could. There were five people gathering the hay — two would toss the bails, two would work on the flatbed truck, and one would drive the truck. When one truck was loaded, the driver got the second truck and we started loading it.

Nobody had to rock me to sleep at night. I loved farm work, from gathering hay to cutting calves and mending fences. Sometimes, my cousin Doug and I would take the horses and ride for hours and then we always usually stopped by the lake on the way home and went swimming — skinny-dipping of course. Here at the farm, I was taught that hard work was good for the mind and body. It was also a lesson about the morals of life that I would forever be grateful for and cherish.

My uncle Robert Phelps who lived in Valparaiso, Florida, taught me about giving, sharing, and love of others. He was a big man who was just a gentle giant — always had a kind word for others. It seemed like he was forever repairing someone's car, boat, or lawnmower. Using his boat to give someone a pleasure ride was his favorite pastime. Anyone who spent any amount of time with Uncle Bob couldn't avoid some of his gentleness and goodness rubbing off on him or her.

So, even without the guidance of a father, I was lucky enough to have three uncles in my young life, and each was a very important role model for me? One taught me how to be an 'outdoorsman', another taught me it required good morals and hard work to succeed in life, and another taught me how to give of yourself for others and about the joy that this brought to one's life.

My mother was my special role model. She borrowed a quote from someone or from something she had read, and one night when I was up late studying, she told me, *"People who never do any more than they get paid for, never get paid for any more than they do."* She had learned that through continuous hard work day in and day out; she was putting herself in a position for a possible pay raise or promotion.

Mother showed love for my sister and me so many times. Once, when mother was sick, and I was laid up with the mumps, we needed some food items for the next morning. Mom put her shoes on her swollen feet, got her sweater and purse, and walked a mile in the dark to a store and back just to get a bottle of milk and corn flakes for breakfast the next morning for us kids. There weren't any street lights on those old dirt roads, either.

We didn't have an automobile. Heck, we never could afford one. I guess you could say we were just too poor. When I went to Niceville Elementary School, I walked from our house to school every day. When I was in the fourth grade, we had moved again, and the distance I walked to school was further. It was over a mile one way.

Mom caught a ride to work each day with a co-worker who had a car. Mom gave her friend money each week for gasoline. Gasoline was 27 cents a gallon down at Mr. Friewall's gas station.

Mom, my sister, and I were living in our 8 foot wide by 45 foot long mobile home that sat in a trailer park overlooking Boggy Bayou along Bayshore Drive. We were almost next door to the Friewall's home.

I recall a very important incident that happened there in 1965, when I came home once on a four day pass, my second trip home after Vietnam. It was late summer, very hot and humid. I had driven down from Camp Lejeune and found the trailer unlocked. When I went in, I saw a couple of notes on the kitchen table. The top note was for me. Mom let me know that *she and Vivian were at my grandmother's house helping her with the pea shelling and Colin had gone off to town.*

The other note was written to mom from Colin, her ex-husband. He was out of the Air Force. Yes, this is the same man who beat me, cursed me, and threw knives at me while I stood against a wooden wall in the rental house where he and mom lived after they got married. The last time we'd seen him, he had choked me and then left my sister and me to starve in Orlando while mom was in the hospital. I was sixteen and Vivian was six at that time.

His note said, *"If you need me, call me at the pool hall, I'll be there."*

A slow smile spread across my face as I decided to call on him, personally. It had been seven years since I last saw him, when he abandoned all of us down in Orlando.

So I got in my '55 Chevy and drove the half mile down Bayshore Drive to Minger's pool hall, still wearing my uniform. As I entered the smoke filled pool hall, I saw Colin playing at one of the tables with another man.

So, I eased over their way and said, *"Excuse me Colin, mother needs you right now. She is very sick. She asked me to come down here and ask you to come home."*

Colin was very suspicious of me coming and asking him to come home. He stated, *"Go back and tell your mom I'll be there in a few hours."* I was ready for his refusal.

So I replied, *"Colin, you left mom a note stating if she needed you, she could call the pool hall. But, you knew it's impossible for her to call you, when she doesn't have a phone."*

The man Colin was playing against threw his pool stick onto the table, and bellowed, *"Man if my wife needed me, I'd be outa' here in a jiffy. We can continue our game some other time. Go take care of your family."*

Colin put his cue stick down on the table and looked at me and said, *"Let's not keep your mother waiting."*

So, I headed for the front door with Colin close behind me. I didn't turn to look at him once outside. I just got into the car and when he was in, I started up the street toward mom's trailer.

"What is wrong with your momma?" Colin asked.

"I don't know, but she's awfully pale and sick looking," I replied. No other words were spoken between us on the drive to the trailer. I held the trailer door open for Colin to go in first. He began calling my mom's name, saying he was home, whenever he entered the front door.

When I stepped into the trailer, I closed and locked the door behind me. Colin heard the *click* sound when it locked.

"Let me out now," he commanded as he spun around.

"It's time for you and me to spend some quality time together, just like we did right after mom had Vivian, when you liked to throw the knife," I replied.

"Notice, I don't have a knife to throw at you, like you did with me when I was ten," I teased.

Colin made a move for the door, but I caught him with a left hook right in his kisser. It dropped him to his knees. I had waited what seemed like a lifetime for this moment, and I was going to enjoy it. Quickly, I stepped in front of him and grabbed his hair, then suddenly brought my left knee up into his face with all the strength I could muster. He screamed in pain. I saw the blood running down onto his shirt and onto the floor. My right foot caught him unexpectedly in the pit of his stomach. He fell forward onto the floor gasping for air. He was still trying to get away from me, but I wouldn't let him go just yet.

As he tried crawling away from me I put my foot on the back of his neck and stomped it with all my power, driving his face once again into the tile flooring. He screamed in pain as his entire body collapsed onto the floor.

I pulled Colin to his feet and hit him as hard as I knew how, sending him flying backwards down the narrow hallway. Blood was pouring freely from a deep cut under his right eye and his nose was fast becoming a pulp. I helped him to his feet and shoved him toward the back door.

He succeeded in opening the door and as he started to step out, I helped him out by giving him a boot in his backside. He fell onto the concrete patio as I stepped outside.

"This isn't over yet, I'm going to kill you, you hear me?" he roared as he got to his feet and pointed his finger at me.

Like a raging bull I went crazy with hate as I hit him over and over again. I grabbed his hair with one hand and his belt with the other and then repeatedly rammed his head into the big solid wooden steps.

Someone was pulling me off of Colin as I tried to inflict more pain on him. I noticed it was two other men that lived in the trailer park.

"STOP! You're killing him," they both shouted. Both of them held me as Colin finally got to his feet again and staggered out the gate, cursing and walking back toward town.

I had to wipe-up and clean Colin's blood from mom's floors before she came home. Later, when mom came home, I told her what I had done to Colin. I told her I would leave if she wanted me to.

"He had that coming son for the way he has treated all of us," she said while giving me a big hug.

Mom said that Colin had come from Tampa up to Niceville just the week before. That was the very last time mom, Vivian, or I ever saw him again. Mom later found out Colin caught a bus going to Los Angeles early the next morning.

CHAPTER 8

My body ached from the encounter with the floating mass of fire ants a few nights ago when Dan and I were crossing that flooded rice patty. A nurse applied salve to the ant bites after I was given a shot in my butt to fight off infection. She assisted the doctor by pulling out pieces of wood splinters from the back of my right hand and wrist. After Doc stitched up my wrist and hand, he applied an antibiotic ointment, then bandaged and put my hand in a sling. Both of my upper thighs, my stomach area, and lower back had festers from the fire ant bites I had received. The shot and ointment helped, but hadn't caused the soreness or the sores to go away yet.

Each morning I had to stop by the hospital and let the doctor change bandages on my hand and get another mini-tube of antibiotic salve to rub on my ant bites. I always looked in on Dan while I was there. He appeared to be getting better each day. We should be back as *'Delta-Two-Foxtrot'* soon.

I walked back to the hut to take a nap or just rest. I was very tired and after lying down on my cot, in the hot Quonset hut, with a couple of pillows under my head, I closed my eyes. I could feel the hot air from the small floor fan that was blowing in my direction. I felt the warm breeze from the fan on my face and arms. My thoughts went back to what seemed like so long ago, when in fact it was just months earlier. I recalled my very first mission soon after completing sniper school — it was in early July.

I was assigned to a two-man scout team with Gunnery Sgt. Davis. Our mission was to locate, observe, and gather information on a company size Viet Cong force operating in the Delta, southwest of Saigon. Aerial photographs by a Navy aircraft had caught a large party of VC crossing a rice patty three days earlier. Battalion Intelligence (BAT-I) wanted us to locate and observe the VC unit — without them knowing we had ever been there. We were to gather information on the routes they traveled, where their headquarters was located, where their weapon and ammunition storage areas were situated, and identify any friendly contacts they had with the local civilian population, plus anything else we could pass on to BAT-I.

We each were issued the standard Marine M-14 rifle with 180 rounds of 7.62 caliber ammo, a .45 caliber Colt M-1911 semi-automatic pistol with 35 rounds, and a K-bar survival knife. If we carried out our mission as planned, there would be no need for our weapons. BAT-I got us a ride out on a chopper that was taking a shipment of M-14 rifles down to the 6th (RVAN) South Vietnamese Army at Chalon.

BAT-I had also arranged for our pickup by one of these choppers when our mission was complete. Our signal for pickup would be a 'green-flare'. No flare, no pickup.

After a short 30-minute ride the pilot looked back at us and said, "This is your stop Gunny!"

As he began to sit the chopper down in a small clearing, we didn't waste any time getting off — Gunny exited one door and me the other. As soon as we stepped off, the chopper was airborne and soon out of sight. There were lots of palm trees in this area; but, they were not very tall, at most maybe 35 feet in height. The natural undergrowth was fairly thick and about three to four feet tall. It seemed that everywhere there were large, wide-leafed plants. They looked almost like a banana tree, but I never saw a banana on the plants.

Gunny motioned for me to move close to him, after I was close enough to smell his bad breath, he leaned closer and whispered, "We've got to move out, so you stay about 10 yards behind me, and keep your eyes peeled and your mouth closed. Only fire your weapon when there is no other option! Got that?"

"Got it," I whispered back.

I tried to maintain the 10-yard interval, but the thick undergrowth hampered my best efforts. A good bit of luck along with proper concealment was going to be the main factor in the success of this mission. But first, we had to find this company, and then slip into their living room without being detected, while watching their every movement.

This sounded quite easy until we landed and I saw how limited our vision would be. The roots and vines on the jungle floor made normal walking difficult. I tried moving quietly about in the jungle following Gunny and soon discovered that Gunny must have thought he was being followed by a wild water buffalo.

In less than 20 minutes, Gunny had had all he could take. He stopped, and as I came into sight, he motioned for me to come to him. I saw a look upon his face that I had never seen. He was furious!

"Corporal Mitchem, you have made me out to be the biggest liar in all Vietnam. I put my reputation and career on the line for the Sniper School, and I've told colonels and generals that our first sniper class showed promises of becoming very good snipers. In only 20 minutes on the ground, you've sounded like some drunk staggering around back there. You might want to commit suicide on this mission, but by God, you are not taking me with you! You take the point, and I'll follow safely behind. Got that Corporal?"

"Sorry, Gunny," I mumbled.

"You try and remember what you learned in my school, and act like the Marine you have shown me you can be," was Gunny's only response.

Gunny's stinging reprimand hurt deeply, but I knew what he had just said was true. I had to get my act together! I had to show him I was ready to be a sniper, and not some goof ball. I wanted to be good! I wanted to be the best I could be. I wanted Gunny to be proud of me and the way he trained every one of us. I just needed to focus all my thoughts and will my entire body to take on the task which now lay before me.

My steps soon began to take on a purpose and my eyes scanned the jungle like radar. My feet seemed to feel what was before them before they hit the jungle floor, and I avoided the noisy stumbling through the thick undergrowth and was super conscious of my surroundings. My muscles even stopped aching.

This whole new process was due simply to basics I knew — DISCIPLINE and WILL POWER! You had to will each part of your body to function as your brain commanded.

Three hours later, the sun was straight overhead, sending down its rays of 120 degrees of stifling heat. Throw in the humidity, and it felt like 140. My throat was like a baked potato and my lungs longed for a fresh cool breath of clean air.

"What's so special about this God-forsaken land that men will fight for it?" I wondered.

There wasn't one dry thread of clothing on my body. In just three hours of quietly slipping through the jungle, I looked like I had been swimming in a river fully clothed. I paused and glanced back at Gunny who was also soaking wet with sweat; but, he just looked at me and smiled.

Another two hours passed, and finally I moved 40 yards off the small trail to a stand of thick banana-like trees; we lay down in their shade for a brief rest. It was a few degrees cooler down here on the ground in the shade, but breathing normally was very difficult. There wasn't any air on the ground level among the soft green undergrowth. I wanted to stand so I could get my lungs filled with oxygen.

"Breathe in small, little sips of air between your teeth. Making any other movement could get both of us killed. Sip on your water a few times — don't drink, or chug it," Gunny whispered as he read my thoughts. I nodded that I understood and did as Gunny instructed.

Twenty minutes later, we were back slipping along the small path. Gunny took the point, and nearly an hour had passed when Gunny suddenly stopped! There were loud sounds coming from someone just ahead of us. Gunny Davis turned and put his finger to his lips to let me know to remain as quite as possible.

We slipped quietly through the thick undergrowth. Soon we were able to see a large open farm field and small rice patty — a Vietnamese family was going about their daily tasks of working a farm.

One young teenage boy was having some difficulty with his water buffalo. The animal would not pull the plow, but instead kept lying down in the dirty muddy water of the small rice field. The youngster was whipping and hollering at the animal, but it would not get up until an old man came to the boy's rescue. The older man was probably the grandfather and appeared to be in his 60s. Two females were busy near their three huts made from elephant grass and bamboo. These people appeared to be just peasant farmers, trying to scratch out a living here in the Delta. My mind began to take in the situation and react.

"Where was the young boy's father? Why wasn't he here? Was he with the South Vietnamese Army? Had he been killed? Could he be a Viet Cong guerrilla?"

Gunny and I laid at the edge of the jungle quietly watching the events before us. Half an hour later, Gunny bumped my arm and when I turned to look, he motion for us to ease back and leave. Our job was to locate the company of VC that had been photographed crossing a rice patty.

The rest of that day we eased further and further south, looking for that company. We were approaching a large rice patty a little after sunset when Gunny stopped and signaled for me to join him?

"According to our map, this is where our aircraft took the photos of the VC crossing the rice patty," Gunny said. "I don't know if we've already gone through their main area yet or not? But, if we have and it was anywhere close to where you sounded like a drunk walking through the jungle, you've already scared them to death."

After saying this, he broke into a huge grin. As darkness was soon approaching, we moved a good ways off the trail and Gunny selected a spot for our dry, cold camp. After a few minutes of resting and rubbing our sore muscles we began to eat our rations. I was so hungry even the lima beans with small pieces of pork tasted OK this time around.

"One of us will be on watch while the other rests," Gunny announced. "Mitch, you take the first watch till 2330 hours, and then wake me and you can sleep till 0430 hours."

I glanced down at my watch — it was now 1905 hours. After Gunny laid down on a small piece of tarp that he had taken out of his backpack and rolled out, I noticed he laid the M-14 across his waist and closed his eyes. He appeared to have gone to sleep with his finger resting near the trigger guard.

I eased about 20 feet away, sat down with my back against a palm tree, and began adjusting my eyesight to everything around us — every bush, every tree trunk, and every limb. I studied everything's shape, filing these things away in my memory bank. I only moved my eyes back and forth, keeping my head and the rest of my body frozen against the palm. I listened to the sound of the many frogs and insects around us in the jungle, became familiar with those noises, and knew they would warn me of any intruders by lapsing into total silence.

My time on watch passed with ease — no intruders; and, after waking Gunny for his watch, I slept like I was sleeping on a king size bed at the Holiday Inn instead of a mat made from moss and large leaves. Even as tired and exhausted as I was, I was awake before 0430 hours. We moved out at 0500 hours to continue our search for the large VC force.

Dawn in the Vietnam delta was a beautiful sight. We had a thick, low fog close to the ground, making us appear ghost-like when slipping very slowly through it. The tops of the palm trees could be plainly seen. I kept a keen eye out for VC snipers sitting up in any of the palms, but none were waiting to pop our heads off. Surely if the company of Viet Cong fighters were in this area, they would have scouts out.

At 1300 hours we moved about 100 yards away from our small trail and took a chow break. Our rations were lima beans and pork again. I studied Gunny Davis's face as I sat a few feet away. He had been nearly frozen to death in Korea with the 1st Marine Division at Inchon. The 1st had to fight off five full Chinese Army Division's frontal assaults. Gunny had said earlier during a training class that "if the Chinese hadn't attacked, we'd all have frozen to death for sure. I only stayed alive because the heat from the barrel of my M-1 rifle kept my blood circulating." His face was pitted with several scars from what appeared to be grenade fragments hitting him.

His chin had a four inch scar starting just below his bottom lip and running down toward his neck. There was a one inch wide burn scar beside his left eye that traveled down to his cheekbone. Gunny also had a two inch scar below his left eye. Man! He was one ugly dude! But he was one tough jarhead who loved his beloved Corps. He was a professional killer who was at his best in combat situations. Gunnery Sgt. Rickard Davis stood 6 feet, 3 inches tall; and, his 204-pound frame was packed with solid muscle.

At dawn the morning of the third day, we were eating our breakfast (you guessed it, lima beans and ham) when Gunny suddenly froze and motioned for me to lay flat and not make a sound. The noise of many men walking close by caused chill bumps to run up and down my spine. Not a word was spoken by these men; they just moved through the morning fog heading northeast. I stayed flat on the floor of the jungle until Gunny whispered, "In an hour, we'll follow them. That will insure we're safely behind the main column's rear guard. Right now, we've got to skedaddle out of their way and let the rear guard pass by. Grab everything and let's get!"

Sure enough, it was nearly 35 minutes later that the rear guard consisting of nearly a dozen men moved silently through the area following the main group.

In one hour, we moved out in the same direction the Viet Cong fighters had gone.

Gunny moved so slow that at times it was almost impossible to determine if he had moved at all. I knew he was being as tactful as a surgeon; he moved like a large cat.

His head hardly moved at all, but his keen eyes were scanning the dense jungle for any sign of the enemy. Way past noon time, he stopped.

"Eat something soft on the way, we're not stopping to eat," he whispered as I approached him. With that said, he broke out some peanut butter, and ate a small can of it, washed that down with water and said, "Ready

Corporal?" Without waiting for my reply, he turned and began slipping through the jungle again, tracking the large group of VC fighters.

About an hour before dusk, Gunny stopped again. Without making a sound or saying a single word, he eased to his left, and I followed. Fifteen minutes later, he stopped and motioned for me to ease out of my pack and gently lay it down. I did as instructed, thinking we must be right on top of the large party of VC. Gunny eased back to my position and whispered, "Mitch, we're close; so let's take turns getting a little rest while we can."

I didn't answer, I just nodded my head, in agreement.

Gunny moved over next to me, and he began talking in a whisper. "I feel we are within a mile of the main column, maybe closer. It's the outer flank patrols we have to avoid so we should be OK from this distance."

I checked my rifle to make sure it was ready in case I had to use it in a firefight. Everything looked OK; magazine was secure in chamber, the safety on, front sights clear of trash. My other ammo magazines were fine; pistol was ready, if needed. Knife was in scabbard just below right knee, strapped to my calf with two leather thongs — one each at top and bottom of the scabbard. When I glanced up I saw a big grin on that ugly face again, and deep down I knew he was OK with my performance in the field, except for that first 20 minutes or so on the first day.

We did our usual watch — me taking the first half, and Gunny taking the last part of the watch. Gunny went through the same procedure as I did on checking his weapons and ammo. He then spread his small tarp, laid down on his back, and rested his M-14 across his waist. Each night I watched him, and each night he seemed to have an on and off switch that his brain commanded. One minute he was awake, the next minute he was asleep. I wish I could train myself to fall asleep and wake up like he does.

Last night when it was time to wake him for his watch, I eased over toward him with my hand down toward his shoulder. But before my hand could touch him, he sat up; it really startled me. I had a little trouble getting to sleep at first, thinking about whether he had been actually asleep or not, or *did his instincts cause him to move before I could touch him.*

I moved some 15 yards away from where Gunny was lying. Sitting very still and listening to the night sounds of the millions of insects nearby. My thoughts drifted back to Gunny's sniper school.

I remember how we were all taken out to the edge of the rifle range the very first afternoon to begin our field training. Gunny had everyone seated on the ground at the edge of the partially cleared jungle; and, he was standing with Staff Sgt. Angelo facing us, his back to the rifle range. We were all listening very intently to each and every word they spoke. I was taking notes on a small pocket-sized pad of paper with a short pencil without an eraser.

"Does anyone know the scientific art of true concealment?" asked Sgt. Angelo. When no one volunteered an answer, he asked everyone to stand, turn and face the jungle.

"Can anyone detect anything unnatural in the trees or undergrowth?" was Sgt. Angelo's next question.

"It looks like the area just recently had a haircut," Cpl. Miller said. The class snickered at his remark!

"Shut up! You bunch of *#**#* dummies," Gunny hollered.

"What do you see that's unnatural out there?" Sgt. Angelo repeated the question to each of us point blank, one at a time. Before my turn to answer, I began scrutinizing the area, scanning the trees and undergrowth for anything out of the ordinary. I had visually examined the thinned out 200-yard deep area piece-by-piece without finding anything unusual. I felt really comfortable that nothing was out of the ordinary out there. I was the last one to be called on.

"Cpl. Mitchem, have you observed anything out of place or unnatural?" Sgt. Angelo said one last time. Everything out there still appeared perfectly natural, so I answered as others had.

"No, Staff Sgt.!" I answered.

Sgt. Angelo moved to our front again and began his lecture on *'concealment being one of the single most important issues to becoming a good sniper'.*

About five minutes into his lecture, the loud unexpected sound of a rifle firing a single shot and Sgt. Angelo fell down face first on the ground. There was a look of total shock and fear on his face as he was falling forward. Three seconds later another loud crack of a rifle fired, and this time Gunny plunged forward while grabbing at his heart as he fell. The entire class jumped to their feet and scrambled for the nearest cover.

We were some scared Marines for about two minutes. We found out Sgt. Angelo wasn't dead when the shrill sound of his whistle permeated the air. He and Sgt. Davis had us return to our seats; and, then on their signal, two fully camouflaged snipers arose not 90 yards away, standing side-by-side. We were led out to their position; we discovered they had lain hidden in a small, narrow fire line cut that was one foot deep and two feet wide. It twisted and turned through the thinned-out undergrowth unseen by us. The two snipers, camouflaged from head to foot with the natural vegetation that was present, melted into the scenery.

"God, I could have stepped on either of them before discovering they were there," I thought!

Neither had too much vegetation attached to their Marine-issued 'tiger striped' uniforms or their M-14s. Just the right amount to blend perfectly into the landscape, the Marines accomplished this by having about 20 strips of camouflaged cloth attached to their clothes — these were three inches wide and 24 inches long and had slits cut in the strips about every six inches.

In the days that followed, Gunny and Staff Sgt. Angelo skillfully taught each of us just how to use the available vegetation perfectly to camouflage our partner in any situation or landscape. We spent more time on properly using the right vegetation and applying the correct amount needed to let us move undetected into our selected shooting locations than any other single issue.

We spent many hours on the techniques of stalking an enemy undetected or slipping into any location quietly and inconspicuously — these and concealment went hand-in-hand.

We all had shot 'expert' on the rifle range, so every Tuesday and Friday for two hours, everyone practiced firing at pop-up targets on a 50-yard range. On Monday, Wednesday and Thursday, everyone (all 12 of us) fired on the 200- and 300-yard range for three hours.

On both Saturday and Sunday, we practiced three hours in the early mornings, two hours at noon and another three hours in the late afternoon. We used the 500-, 600-, and 800-yard range with the snipers shooting at silhouette targets. Each spotter's M-49 spotting scope provided the exact yardage and elevation, along with correct windage needed, for a sure kill at the required distance. Once on target, we strived to shoot tight groups in the four-inch range. I logged all yardage and elevation needed to achieve my shots. Thus, when in the field alone, I only had to get the windage correct.

Daybreak, high noon, and dusk were the usual times Gunny liked. Twice from 600 and 800 yards, sniper teams had to lie in three-foot grass, camouflaged, for three hours in the middle of the day with the temperature hovering near 125 degrees on an open, sun-baked range, and not move a body muscle before being told we could fire at our targets.

Not moving a body muscle meant 'NO' scratching, rubbing, wiping sweat or insects from your face, arms, legs, or body. We could not harm any insect crawling on or biting us. The only movement allowed was the very, very slow progress of our head up to our riflescope, and then slowly back down again. We could not eat or drink anything at all until after completing our firing.

There was always an NCO sitting in a 10-foot high tower with a raised grass roof, 20 yards behind each team. One wrong move and he noted the time and type movement you made. That day, each team had a specific time when they were "to try" to slip undetected, under the ever-watchful eyes of the observers, into a good firing position and make our one shot — a killing shot on our target downrange.

At the end of each yardage-firing event, Gunny Davis collected scorecards. There were different points deducted for each type of unnecessary movement or sounds observed. Just Gunny and a select few sergeants would score us after our time on the range. Movements or sounds most easily detected at greater yardage garnered the highest point value, and so on, down to where the very slow, side movement of a foot acquired the lowest point. Value of movement points were between 12 and 1. Each sniper knew that if he accumulated 30 points, he was out of sniper school. That was THE RULE OF SNIPER SCHOOL!

The most points allowed by any spotter was 35 points, and only that person and Gunny knew. The class only knew when someone failed to show up for classes. My final total point count was 11. Only Gunny and I knew my total. However, I later told Dan when he asked me.

In concealment training, it took on an art appeal. We practiced with our partner repeatedly, taking turns camouflaging each other until Staff Sgt. Angelo was satisfied. We actually spent more time on this one very important lesson than any other single thing taught in sniper in school.

Sergeants Angelo and McKnight and Gunny Davis all had the same thoughts, *if spotted before reaching your objective and the target…YOU LOSE! Your life is over! Finished!*

* * * * * * *

I glanced at my watch; it was 1120 hours. I was supposed to wake Gunny at 1130 hours, and I thought how the time just flew by. It seemed like just minutes ago I eased over here and sat down. As I slipped slowly over to where Gunny still lay on his tarp, I bumped his foot with my rifle barrel. He immediately set up, and in a whisper of voice, asked, "Is everything OK?"

"Everything is quiet, Gunny; it's your watch time," I said in a low voice.

I eased over to where I had made me a bed with moss and big leaves and sacked out until Gunny woke me at 0430.

"You get a good bite to eat; it might be a long, long day for us," Gunny said as he woke me. I found eggs and ham and topped it off with peanut butter and jelly on a cracker. I washed all that down with water, and I was ready to begin a new day. I also said a soft little prayer under my breath. I asked God '*for an all-day rain*'. The rain would drop the temperature by at least 15 to 20 degrees.

Gunny came over to where I was sitting and whispered, "We need to make contact with the main column today, so we can observe them better." Did I hear him right! Was he taking us between the rear and flank guards and the main force?

"Now, we have to bury all gear that is not absolutely necessary, understood?" he whispered. "Take only food and water for three days, along with weapons and ammo; everything else we leave here. Let's get started on the hole!"

The only thing I had to dig with was my knife and hands, so I began softening the ground up by stabbing the blade into the jungle floor; and, when I had it where I could scoop dirt out with my hands, I did that. Gunny was digging right along side of me; and in a short time, our hole was deep enough to bury our excess gear.

We only wanted to take our light packs with us to store our rations and extra ammo in. Next, we used the natural jungle vegetation to camouflage each other. Once, we were satisfied with our new look, Gunny moved us out slowly in the direction of the main column. The difficulty would come trying to penetrate their security perimeter without either the flank or the rear guards spotting us. There would maybe be 15 guards on each flank, plus the dozen in the rear guard. We would have to be precise in every aspect to complete this mission and get back to base camp — alive and in one piece.

After two hours on the move, Gunny stopped! He motioned for me to go to him. When I was along side of him, he said, "Be very careful, watch your every movement, and do it very slowly once we make contact. Remember, once we're inside their security perimeter, the closer we get to the column, the safer we'll be from their flank and rear security patrols."

"OK!" I whispered with my heart really pounding.

It sounded like he was hell bent on slipping into the open mouth of an angry lion. Gunny moved out again, taking us closer and closer to the Viet Cong Company.

Around 1020 hours, when Gunny stopped — I froze! Slowly he moved his arm behind his back, held up five fingers, and pointed off to our right flank. We were standing in four-foot high jungle undergrowth, and I didn't think we would be spotted. Still, I slowly eased my butt toward the floor of the jungle, just in case. I was kneeling on one knee, keeping a sharp eye on the jungle where Gunny had pointed. I was able to see flankers moving slowly, toward our rear in single file, spaced out with nearly 20 yards between them. The flank patrol was wearing the traditional grey uniforms and each had the typical green soft cover on their head.

They moved like cats, lifting each foot up and selecting where to put it down. Within minutes, they had disappeared from sight. They couldn't have been more than 30 yards from our position; and, even though they looked our way, more than once, they saw nothing in the jungle to alarm them. Thanks to the natural camouflage attached to our tiger stripe uniforms, along with the green, brown and black camo paint on our faces, necks, and hands, we were a part of the landscape. Even our M-14s had green and brown burlap cloth wrapped and taped tightly to them.

We slipped closer toward the main column. Gunny wanted to get us within 150 yards. Being this close would make it easier for us to observe from even closer range, and this yardage would keep the patrols away from us. I was going to log this devilish tactic in my memory bank for future use if it worked.

Later that evening when the column stopped for the night, we set up our observation post within 50 yards of their latrine. Gunny said this would be the safest place. It would be the easiest location from which to slip in closer and observe whenever we needed.

"Enjoy it while you can; by tomorrow morning, the smell will knock you down," Gunny whispered.

"I hope we'll be alive then to enjoy it," I whispered back.

Gunny grinned like an opossum, sat down and broke out his rations, and began to eat. I also started to eat while I could enjoy it.

There was very little moon or stars out tonight, but no thunderheads appeared to be close-by. Gunny came over to where I was sitting and sat right next to me. He whispered, "We're going to slip into that camp tonight and get a closer look at their strength. We will move out at 0230 hours; we'll get a few winks of sleep before then.

"I'll take the first watch, and wake you at 2330 hours," Gunny said. "Then, you wake me at 0200 hours," Gunny instructed.

"OK, Gunny!" I whispered back and grinned. Soon, I was relaxed on the jungle floor and knew that I would soon be asleep. I never really went into a sound sleep; it seemed that I was awake every 20 minutes or so.

When Gunny eased over to me to wake me at 2330 hours, I was awake. As his hand eased down to my shoulder, I sat up.

"Everything is quite!" he said lowly. I nodded my head OK. Gunny eased back to where he had his mat laid out and lay down. I moved to where I could see beyond the latrine, but saw nothing in the darkness. If I couldn't see them, then they sure as hell couldn't see me. I could usually tell when a soldier came to the latrine, because he would clear his throat and spit before leaving the latrine area. I guess some men have a few things in common.

Tonight was quite dark and almost impossible to see more than 20 yards in front of you. I glanced down at my watch, it was almost 0115 hours; up until now, there had been maybe half a dozen troops visit the latrine. Now, I heard quite a few troops at the latrine at once, which was surprising. Their low talk seemed to get louder and soon it seemed that another large group was approaching the latrine; the first large group left, and I knew something was in the air.

I eased back to where Gunny slept, only to find his pallet empty. Looking around, I spotted him getting both of our gear together. I eased over to him and whispered, "Guess you heard all the commotion?"

"Yea! Something is about to happen, so let's get our packs on," Gunny said in a low voice. Soon after the third group finished at the latrine, you could hear them digging and throwing dirt, then cutting undergrowth and throwing it onto the latrine.

Within minutes, they were moving back toward their area in a hurry — soon we knew why. The company was moving out, on the march again. I glanced at my watch — 0142 hours. We followed the company, staying close to their rear, but not hanging too far back. I walked right beside Gunny. We managed to stay only a few feet apart in the darkness that morning.

Daybreak found us now moving on a West-Northwest heading. We dared not move too slowly or the rear guard would have our butts roasting over a fire for lunch, so we kept pace with the large column of troops in front of us for hours. We had expanded our distance between each other to about 15 yards just after daybreak.

Gunny spotted a movement in the thick undergrowth just in front of him. He immediately stopped! VC troops lay scattered about on the jungle floor just 20 yards in front of us. Unknown to either of us, the column had simply stopped. What I saw scared the living daylights out of me. Gunny had caught the movement of a few troops getting to their feet and moving from man-to-man, looking for a smoke.

We both froze! Not daring to move even the slightest, for fear of being detected, we stood as we were for what seemed to be an hour, watching them smoke and listening to them talk to one another in low tones.

I really began to sweat, and I knew my body odor must be terrible. I hoped none of these guys had the keen sense of smell to detect either of our body odors. If even one did, we would die like two rabid dogs — shot in our tracks. I just said a prayer, asking God not to let any of them come any closer to us and keep our position concealed.

Some mosquitoes chose this moment to begin biting the side of my face and ear. If they continued biting me with their fierce sword-like muzzle, ever sucking the blood from my skin, my face and ears would swell for days. I dared not move a muscle to stop the agonizing pain. I chose to bear the pain and live.

Soon, I heard the voice of a senior NCO barking out sharp orders. The troops quickly got to their feet with their gear and the formation moved out again. I looked at my watch and saw that we had been standing frozen for only about 12 minutes. When the main column was out of sight, I followed Gunny as he moved directly toward the company's left flank. We stopped and looked for the flank guards when we had moved about 50 yards out on the flank.

Hearing and seeing nothing, we slowly proceeded to move out from within the VC column's perimeter. I felt like we had just escaped from the jaws of a bear! I still had chill bumps on my back from escaping a close encounter with sure death. I shuddered with both fear and relief. The dozen or so VC soldiers lying around in front of Gunny and me all carried Chinese AK-47s, so we knew the company possessed a lot of small arms firepower.

If those smokers had not gotten up to bum smokes, we would have walked right in on them. I shuddered again, and looked skyward and under my breath, I said, *'Thank you Lord!'*

We lay low until we knew that the flank guards had passed us by, and then we fell in behind the flank and followed them. The flank patrol stopped around 1400 hours to eat. We knew that the main column must have also stopped. We moved to where we could observe the patrol and crawled as close as we dared, maybe 30-plus yards. We then watched these guys act the fool, by teasing the youngest one of their ranks who looked all of sixteen. I lay there thinking they were not so different in many ways from American troops.

Their ideology brought the Americans to this part of the world. They wanted South Vietnam's will broken and turned into a communist country. They did not mind cutting the throats of men, women, or even small children. They raped, plundered, and killed at will. Their favorite targets so far had been the poor farmers and fishermen of the Delta region. While the villages were burning, the women were raped in front of their fathers, husbands and children before most males in the village had their heads cut-off. Villagers sympathetic to South Vietnamese troops were always beheaded.

The movements of the patrol going back to guard duty brought my thoughts back to this stinking situation we had encountered. We watched as the two flank patrols split up and went about their duties of keeping intruders away from the main column. Gunny eased up off the jungle floor and began to move slowly in the direction the column was traveling. I followed about 15 yards behind him and to his right.

In mid-afternoon, the main column approached a large village and stopped. We could see the village from our position on the far left flank looking across a large rice patty. The company of VC set up camp along the village's eastern side; but, under the cover of a big grove of palm trees, and out-of-view from any aircraft flying overhead.

Gunny and I ate our first meal of the day only after ensuring the patrols were over at the main campsite near the village. After eating and resting a bit, I put my foot in my mouth, by asking, "Are we going into the village?"

Gunny must have had bad gas or something, because he sure let me have it. "Why in the hell do you think we've followed this company so long? We're going into the village and have us a look-see, if that is OK with you?"

I wondered what I had done to cause this reaction from him. "Sure Gunny, it's OK with me," I replied, letting it go at that.

He walked off a piece and lay down, then said, "Get me up at 2100 hours, and I'll wake you at 0030." He then laid his M-14 across his chest, and I eased away from him and over to the edge of the large rice patty.

I was on the far side of the rice patty about 200 yards from the village with a young cane field at my back. I found a spot where I could see the column's camp from just inside the edge of the cane. I noticed another cane field closer to the village and in front of the encamped Viet Cong Company.

The VC must have felt very secure here at the village because they had the smallest number of security guards posted that I had ever seen them use. Around midnight, we went over the plan for getting in and out of the village. We also discussed the *'what if'*-scenario, then double-checked everything, and slipped off toward the village.

Crawling very slow on our stomachs once we got closer to the village, we inched forward mere millimeters at a time. Keeping a very thin line of trees to buffer our position from the Viet Cong force's encampment on our right, we gradually moved closer toward the nearest hut that was still some 70 yards away. Soon the thin tree line would end, and nothing would provide us concealment except the one and one-half foot high grass that ran from the tree line toward the hut.

When we were within 30 yards to the nearest hut, we could see a few cooking fires burning inside the village. Occasionally a woman would appear from a hut to check the pot hanging over the fire. The village dogs were barking, but their owners had tied them to stakes probably due to the large number of visitors in the village this night. Therefore, the barking dogs were not an alarm to anyone.

Fast-moving thunderheads in our direction showed promise of rain. The night sky revealed a brilliant display of its own firepower as bolts of lightning streaked across the night sky. Soon the air felt a little cooler, but then the rain began and escalated within minutes to a full-fledged downpour as amazing spider-wing lightning bolts lit up the sky. This type weather was certainly to our advantage for there would be less people outside during this storm. Within 20 minutes it was over, the thunderhead had passed by; and, there was movement in the village again.

Steadily we inched toward the hut. Troops began venturing out again, occasionally coming "t-o-o" close to us on their way to and from the village. A few times, we dared not move as some of them walked within 10 feet of us. Each time we resumed our trek, steadily inching closer to the village huts. Glancing at my watch, I saw that it took 75 minutes to crawl within 20 yards of the first hut. We had nothing on us that would rattle, clang, or make any noise.

Before we began this crawling maneuver, we secured our M-14s to our backs in order to make better time and for comfort. I had my .45 caliber pistol strapped to my lower right thigh, and my trusty 13-inch K-bar with its eight-inch razor sharp blade strapped to my chest.

Gunny and I had redone our facial camo before we moved toward the village. Mine ran diagonally down my face from left to right; two inches of brown; three inches of black; and finally, two inches of green down my face. My neck was both a mixture of brown and green; Gunny said that I looked like something out of the grave, which I took as a compliment.

I could smell dog crap very strong, which meant I was properly lying in it. This predicament was sickening, but it actually helped me because the dogs would think I was just part of the landscape, as my human scent was now blocked. Ten minutes later, Gunny was going under the first hut. Soon, I was lying beside him, and I could tell by his facial expressions when he got a good whiff of my new smell. I looked at him and smiled. He motioned for me to keep going; my job was to check out the huts on the western side while Gunny checked the ones along the eastern side. The village layout resembled a big horseshoe. The village had a double row of huts along each side and a number of larger huts in the back at the curve.

I eased past Gunny and slowly made my way around to the first hut on the western side. This took some time, but once there I used my K-bar to open a small hole in the floor about the size of a quarter. With it pitch dark inside and not being able to see anything, I stuck my nose up to the hole and got a good whiff of dirty soiled clothes and a strong odor of dead dried fish, which was probably hanging somewhere in the hut. I crawled on to the next hut and performed the very same process, with the same results.

As I attempted to move to the third hut, I noticed a small light coming from underneath the old bamboo door. As I eased under the hut, my ears let me know what was going on inside. It sounded like a half-dozen or more couples were engaged in sexual activities.

This was only one of several huts on my route that the Viet Cong and their 'lady friends' were using for sexual pleasures. I thought *there couldn't possibly be that many young girls from this village*. Something else must have already happened or will transpire soon, for Charlie Cong to receive this type of a welcoming. It had to cost someone a bundle of money to get 50-plus 'prostitutes' to leave Saigon and come out *'to God only knows where'* in the jungles of Vietnam to provide Viet Cong troops sexual pleasures.

There was more than lust involved in this deal for sure. But, what was it? What would we find?

Checking my watch, I saw it was 0250 and knew it was time to leave and meet Gunny at our predetermined meeting place. As I began crawling slowly away from the village, I heard men laughing and moving toward my position. Lying on my stomach, I eased my head up slowly and looked in the direction of the sounds. I found myself in the path of two VC guards, and both of them had a rifle slung over their shoulders.

They were only 10 steps from me and if I moved, they would discover me; but if I stayed where I was, they would step on me. Suddenly, a young girl appeared in the doorway of the hut just 15 yards away and called to them. They immediately stopped, turned, and walked over to talk with her. I took this opportunity to slide off into the jungle and watched from 30 feet as they turned down her offer this time. Once they were off guard duty, they would be back.

After sensing they were no longer a threat to me, I continued crawling along the edge of the jungle; and upon safely reaching the tree line, I eased my way northward. Finally, after slipping past all the huts along the western side of the village, I turned back toward the northwest to meet with Gunny at the cane field before daybreak.

At the corner of the cane field, where it buttoned up against the jungle, was where Gunny and I had planned to meet-up.

I was lying on my stomach just inside the edge of the jungle facing towards the village, some 200 yards away. I had removed the M-14 from my back and was holding it across my arms, enjoying the comfort and security it gave me. I listened for the sound of human movement. Everything was quiet! Nothing was stirring except a few blood-sucking mosquitoes, biting me on my neck and the back of my hand. Our plan was to meet here at 0430, which would allow enough time for us to safely reach our camp, gather our packs, and move our base camp further away from Charlie's campsite before daybreak arrived.

I looked down at my watch — 0426 hours. I'm thinking that *Gunny better show up soon*. Daybreak was one hour and 22 minutes from now. Our plan was to slip along the side of the sugar cane field toward the VC camp, then cut north to our base camp. There we would pick up maps, packs, extra ammunition, and our gourmet C-rations of lima beans and pork — and maybe even another scramble eggs and ham for me. We had planned to either relocate our camp or slip slowly out of the area and head home before any Cong or their friends from the village were wise about our whereabouts. However, this depended on what we each discovered. *"Come on Gunny!"* I thought to myself.

This was not like him to be late — totally out of his character!

I knew down in my gut that if something had happened to Gunny, I would have to make a go of it alone. I was to get myself back to the helicopter LZ for pickup on my own, if it became necessary. During our pre-trip briefing back at base, the one thing our superiors required was getting any quality information on this Viet Cong Company back to BAT-I. In two days, our Marine choppers would begin flying close enough to see our LZ or our designated smoke color for pickup. The choppers would be flying in close proximity at 0700 hours in the mornings and then check again at 1600 hours each afternoon.

This pattern would then continue for the next four days. Our orders were if one of us was seriously wounded, hide him and get his co-ordinance (GPS) back to Intel for a rescue attempt within two hours.

My gut feeling said, *'Go look for Gunny Davis'*. Nervously, I looked at my watch — 0430, just four minutes since I last checked. I got to my feet and located the small roll of surgical tape that I have made a part of my field gear; it was in my pants bottom leg pocket. Taking the small roll of tape, I took another ammo magazine and taped it upside down to the magazine in the M-14. Preparing two magazines this way assured me of 40 rounds of firepower, if I needed it quickly.

Reaching down and getting a handful of mud, I carefully smeared this over the white tape to change its color. Again, glancing at my watch I saw it was already 0434. I had better get moving if I wanted to reach the small tree line leading back into the village and do some scouting for Gunny before daybreak. I had already decided Gunny's life was more important to me than any intelligence report concerning this company of VC.

I knew if I found him, I was taking him out with me. I thought, *if I don't find him, I'll just lay low and look again tomorrow night*. I was also aware that it would take me two full days to reach the LZ; about every other day, our helicopters carrying supplies and weapons to Chalon regularly flew close to the same small cleaning where we were dropped off for this mission. Gunny and I had looked at the map last night to familiarize ourselves with the direction we would be traveling and the time needed to reach the LZ.

We were now about 20 miles West-Northwest of that LZ. Our present location put us right smack in the middle of Viet Cong Charlie's living room. We had slipped into Charlie's house undetected thanks to the skills of Gunnery Sgt. Davis. Now, I guess the burden was on me to get both of us out and back home.

I reached the small tree line leading into the village without spotting Gunny or anyone else. I had begun crawling on my stomach just before reaching the tree line. But, this time I carried the M-14 across my arms in front of my body as I slowly moved into the eastern side of the village. I had not seen Gunny since we split up at the first hut, about four hours ago, as he crawled off in an eastwardly direction looking for whatever. Now, I really did not know where to begin looking, but I would search all the huts on the eastern side of the village first — then the entire village if it took it, looking for him. My watch showed it was 0458, which gave me just 40 minutes to find him and be out of the village before daybreak.

On my way back to the village, I worked out a two-night search plan in my mind.

'If I couldn't find Gunny before daybreak today, I'd slip back into the jungle and hold up on the western side which is the opposite side of the village from the VC encampment and watch closely during the day for any activity that might identify his possible location. Then at dark, I'd slip back into the village and search for him again. I knew that I had just four days to catch a chopper ride home, so I could spend the next two, if necessary, looking for Gunny. I just hoped that I would be able to get us back in one piece.' I sure needed his compass, which I last saw in his possession. It would be rough trying to get back to that LZ without it.

* * * * * * *

I watched Cpl. Mitchem slip quietly toward the western side of the village to have a look-see; it was now time for me to ease down the seven huts of the inside row first and have a peek inside each hut on this eastern side. At the fourth hut, I could tell by the sounds from inside that several people were having sex. I eased on toward the next hut, and again found it used for sexual purposes. The sixth and seventh hut had nothing but dirty clothes and dead fish smells. I then saw the four larger huts at the bottom of the large horseshoe-shaped village.

A few minutes after I slipped inside the closest big, dark hut, a group of people came through the door with two lit lanterns. I was near the back wall on my stomach, behind a number of wooden boxes. *Great, Gunny*, I thought! Trapped! And, I couldn't move at all for fear of being seen.

Slowly, I peeked from behind the boxes at the people in here. There were two Viet Cong and three villagers. The two VC had weapons. It appeared they were searching for something. One of the villagers began pointing in my direction. Then, they all came toward me. I knew they had not spotted me. My mind was racing — maybe they would stop at some of the crates before getting to me.

The three villagers and the VC sergeant did stop, picked up two crates, and carried them back toward a large table near the doorway. I knew this was my one chance of getting out of here. As they were inspecting the crates, I eased the five feet toward the back wall; slowly cutting my way through the bamboo and grass wall, thinking I would be discovered any moment. Heck, I was afraid these guys would shoot me anytime in the back while I tried to cut my way out.

Finally, I had an opening large enough for me to squeeze through. I eased the M-14 outside first, then I poked my head out, and everything suddenly went black. Sometime the next day, I regained consciousness. My head seemed to be exploding, and I discovered I had been tied and staked to the ground when I tried to rub my aching head. What had happened?

I was lying face down, my hands and arms tied and staked above my head. I had a gag stuffed in my mouth, and a blindfold over my eyes so I could not see. In this spread-eagle position with my ankles tied to stakes, I realized my boots were gone — most likely given to the soldier who gave me this headache.

I knew I had a cut on my head because I could smell my dried blood in my hair. I was not hurt too bad, but being able to only feel pain and smell my own blood didn't do a lot for my ego. I just knew I would get out of this someway at some point in time. I needed to concentrate on breathing only through my nose right now.

I could hear a person breathing close by, but they made no other sound. I knew by the fish smell that it was a VC fighter assigned to guard me. *Was there more than one?*

My brain was thinking *'had they also caught Mitchem? Or, had something worse happened to him?'* I knew I couldn't answer that question now. Just maybe, they think I was working alone as a one-man recon.

Later that day, the guard was changed. The new guard liked to poke me with a stick, and he got a kick out of it if I tried to talk with the gag in my mouth. He would mock my muffled sounds. This guy never stopped his game with me the entire time he was on duty guarding me. If I could get my hands around his skinny neck, I'd break him from laughing at my situation.

That night, two men came in and barked an order to the guard. The guard pulled my blindfold up and removed my gag. One of the men came over and knelt down, grabbed my head, turned it toward him, and poked a metal cup with water to my lips. After allowing me two swallows of water, he removed the cup and ordered the guard to put the gag back in my mouth and pull the blindfold back down over my eyes.

There was no indication that any food would follow. To my knowledge, no VC officer had been in here. But, maybe I'm wrong. Surely, I'll get a visit from their leadership. Getting answers to important questions would be their reason for visiting. I really have to urinate and take a crap bad, but there is no way I can communicate with anyone with me being hog-tied and gagged like this. My guard, whom I'll call *'pokey'* because he constantly poked me with a stick and he didn't care if I had the urge to relieve myself or not.

Soon I discovered that I was unable to hold my urine indefinitely, and when I felt the warmness inside my shorts, I knew that I had just found relief.

The guard awoke me again during the night to drink water — only two sips again. I made a motion with my mouth and pretended to chew. The man holding my head hit me in the mouth with his fist, busting my lip, and then held my head still and spit in my face. My gag was reinserted, my blindfold retied tightly around my eyes, and, just to show their superiority, one of these fighters stomped the back of my neck with his foot as I lay there, tied like a hog, face down on the ground. Then the two walked out, and *'old pokey'* and I were alone again inside the tent.

When I awoke early the next morning, the guard had changed again during the night, because *'old pokey'* was not my guard. This guard left me alone, not bothering with me except to provide two sips of water, remove my blindfold and gag, and return me to the same state.

Sometime around mid-morning, I got the visit I didn't want. A Viet Cong Officer came in to see me. He brought four other men with him. They untied me, lifting me completely off the ground and turning me over so that I now was in a face-up position. Once again, they tied my hands to the stake above my head, and secured my feet back to those stakes that had kept my legs in constant cramps.

With my blindfold removed and tied tightly around my mouth, I was unable to make much noise with the gag still in my mouth. The officer appeared to have the rank of a captain. He spoke to me in very broken English saying, *"Tell me why you come here?"*

For not answering, I was struck in the face and kicked between my legs repeatedly.

* * * * * * *

With my plan developed, I focused mentally on what I had to do, but at the same time scared of what I may find or not find. It was now time to execute that plan. I slithered quietly like a snake underneath the small huts located on the eastern side searching for Gunny.

This was a big village shaped in a large U-design, and at the beginning of each side of the U were a double row of seven small family huts; then, along the bottom part of the U were two rows of two very large huts. All around the village, the space between each row of huts appeared to be about 20 yards apart. The larger huts were also set back closer to the jungle.

Tomorrow night and the following night, if required, I would be searching for Gunny. If I had not found him or his body by midnight of my last night to search, I would have to return to our mini-camp and take the map and only essentials such as ammo, flare, and some food before heading out for the LZ alone.

The eastern sky was beginning to get that pale look about it, and I knew that within a few minutes it would be daybreak. The morning fog was low as usual and very thick, so I moved slowly toward the closest jungle cover, which was the southeastern side. I had to slip very quietly now as the women were slowly trickling out of their huts to begin their daily chores of starting a cook fire for the rice and fishcakes. I had been able to checkout seven of the small village huts on the outside eastern edge of the large 'U'. I had to cross 20 yards of open ground between the outside row of huts and the jungle. I moved very slowly into the jungle, and once again smelled the strong odor of dog crap on me and knew this would work to my advantage, as unpleasant as it was.

Suddenly! Just as I was easing to my feet, I confronted a large sow hog with a litter of young pigs going into the village. The sow stopped 10 yards from me and made a few challenging jesters toward me. I eased away from her route to the village. Once I retreated, she then led her piglets into the village and underneath a nearby hut away from potential harm. Nothing around here would be any more vicious to face than a large mad sow with piglets. In a couple of minutes, she settled down with her young getting their morning meal. It was now safe for me to continue on my way, so I again moved further into the thick heavy protection and security of the jungle. I eased southeast of the village looking for a safe place to lie low.

About 100 yards from the village, I found the perfect place — standing beside a large, tall tree at the edge of a swamp, I looked up to see it was close to 40 feet tall and had good foliage cover toward its upper branches. The large tree was climbable, but presented a challenge.

Twenty minutes later, I had reached the upper parts where some large limbs provided adequate camouflage. After leaning back against the trunk of the large tree and getting comfortable on a large limb, I listened for sounds from Gunny. I heard only the normal sounds of a village.

I could smell the fish cakes as they cooked. Last night was the last time I had eaten anything. As my stomach began to growl, I located a couple of candy bars in my inside jacket pocket and began eating a coconut bar. With the natural foliage camouflage attached to my jacket and pants, it would appear to anyone looking up that a vine and bush was just part of the tall tree here at the edge of the swamp. I hung the M-14 from a smaller limb just above my shoulder. This provided me with the freedom of movement of both hands; yet, it put the rifle easily in reach.

As the sun rose higher in the bright morning sky, sweat begin running down my body. I kept a keen eye out for any sign of Gunny in the village. I saw plenty of VC troops entering and leaving the village before noon, but no sign of Gunny. Toward late afternoon with still no sign of Gunny or his whereabouts, I really started to worry. My mind played tricks on me when I thought about Gunny. At times, I would start shaking all over just from the fearful thoughts. I knew I had to get a grip on my thinking like that. I needed a clear head to do what I had to do.

Just before darkness fell, I begin my slow descent down the big tree. I knew just one wrong move would fatally plunge me 40-plus feet to the ground — ever so carefully, I eased down the tree one foot at a time. Fifteen minutes passed before my feet touched the jungle floor. I felt like getting on my hands and knees and kissing the ground; I was so thankful to be back down on the jungle floor. I was shaking like a leaf in a windstorm. I sat at the base of the big old tree massaging the cramps in my legs; still I waited until my breathing became normal before attempting to move toward the village.

Once at the jungle's edge, looking again upon the horseshoe shaped outline of the huts, I slipped very, very slowly toward the hut where I had ended my search before daybreak. Once there, I inched my way ever so slightly toward the next hut, and the next, until I had searched both rows of the small huts along the eastern side of the village. Now, as I moved a few inches at a time toward the first large hut, a VC officer walked briskly toward the entrance of that same hut. The officer was maybe 30 yards from me, but did not look in my direction, as he was intent on entering the lighted doorway, and I was heading toward the side of the building. I wanted to get to the back of the big hut and peek inside, if possible.

After reaching the back corner of the hut, there — not even five yards from my position — stood two VC soldiers, both with rifles slung over their shoulders. I immediately assumed they were on guard duty. Could Gunny be the hostage? Maybe, they were guarding the weapons cache.

I couldn't move around the back corner of the hut with the guards right there. It was best if I just waited them out, see what developed, and take my chance when the opportunity was available. So I positioned myself up against the wall of the large hut, waiting and watching.

Every 15 minutes or so, I eased my head to the back edge and peeked around the backside at the two guards. They stayed together whispering and laughing softly at each other's jokes and remarks, for another two hours, until just minutes before they were relieved. They split up when one moved off toward the next large hut. The new guards were staying on their assigned posts, which was the opportunity I needed to move around the building and get a peek into the large hut. With the closest guard 25 yards from me, I opened a small hole in the thatched hut with my knife and peeked inside.

From my angle, I could see the entire dimly lit room. There were five men inside; two were VC, and three were villagers. The large floor was the storage site for numerous crates with Chinese markings on them according to the boxes closest to my peek hole. There were weapons and ammo inside the wooden crates of assorted sizes and shapes. The five men appeared to be performing a count of each type of weapon; the VC officer and one of the village men appeared to be in charge of the counting.

I eased my head back and saw that the guard was still standing in the same spot, so I moved off into the edge of the jungle and ever so slowly made my way toward the second large hut — hoping that I would find Gunny. I knew that I would have to pass right in front of the other guard, so I was being extra careful not to make any noise. The last thing I wanted now was to have to kill one or both of these guards. This would just make my job of finding Gunny even more dangerous. Killing now would be like stirring up a hornets' nest. The VC get really nasty when one of their troops is killed. I like it when Charlie doesn't know I am around; it makes my job much easier that way.

If they had Gunny, I knew he wouldn't talk and give me away. But, I also knew this was probably why the guards were posted around the large huts. The Viet Cong were keeping an eye out for any other jarheads wandering about their village. I just hoped to find Gunny alive. My mind was racing and most thoughts were not pleasant.

Upon arriving at the second large hut, I found it impossible to approach the hut from the rear. This guard was sitting with his back against the rear wall, looking back and forth, scanning the area for unwanted intruders as he should be doing. His weapon wasn't on the ground next to him, nor leaning against the hut, but in his hands and across his lap. My only chance of getting a peek was to take him out with a com-pound bow and arrow. But this was not to be for I did not have one with me, so I eased backwards into the jungle again and made my way toward the further side of the hut.

Once there I scanned the immediate area for signs of any more guards; seeing none, I crept slowly to the back corner of the structure and lying up against the base of the hut, I cut a hole only large enough for me to peek through. With my heart beating faster and faster, I looked through the small hole. My eyes saw just a dark room, and I could not make out any form in the darkness. I thought about going inside, but then thought, if my entrance way was discovered, my goose would also be cooked and it could make things worse for Gunny if he were alive. So, I eased back toward the safety of the jungle; once there, I was lying low and watching for anything to give me hope.

My brain and my heart were in a constant battle as I looked at the rear of the large hut. One part wanted to do the safest thing and the other wanted to be a hero of sorts. I kept the hero heart from emerging as long as I could; but, finally my body surrendered to my heart, and I found myself moving again toward the back corner of the hut where I had seen nothing but darkness.

Glancing toward the guard again, I saw he hadn't moved, so as I approached the peep-hole, I pulled out the K-bar to cut out a two-foot wide opening and slipped quietly inside. Once inside, I moved away from my entrance point and along the back wall a few feet and stopped, waiting for my eyes to adjust to the darkness. I knew the guard was just on the opposite side of the thin wall, and the last thing I wanted was to alert him.

Once my eyes were accustomed to the darkness, I saw that there were many boxes stored here. I moved slowly towards the nearest boxes and moved in and around almost every bundle and box in that large room and all of them were too small to hold Gunny. I then glanced at my watch, and it showed 2310 hours. So I made my way back toward my entrance point; and, after stopping and peeking outside, I eased myself out. Once outside, I again flattened myself against the base of the side wall while checking the area for any activity of villagers or guards. Finding none, I moved back into the jungle and headed toward the third large hut, intent on finding Gunny.

Arriving at the third large hut almost 40 minutes later, I discovered a guard at the rear of the hut. I assumed that a guard was posted at the front of each of the large huts, as I was sure that there was a guard posted at the first hut where I saw the VC officer enter to take inventory of the weapons from China.

Again I made my way to the far corner of the hut after making sure I could do so without being spotted. Upon making myself a peep-hole again, I strained to see inside the dark room; but unlike the last time confronted with this situation, I wasted no time opening an entrance to slide through. Once this was completed, I entered the darkness of the room, moved away from the entrance and immediately began getting my eyes adjusted to the near total darkness.

As soon as I was able to safely move about the room, I began searching for Gunny. Even though there were some large boxes scattered about near the center of the room; only two were large enough to hold a man, but they were just empty boxes — so again, I did not find Gunny.

The fourth large hut was a carbon copy of the others, Gunny wasn't there. After exiting from the fourth hut, I eased back further into the jungle, and headed toward the western double roll of small huts which consisted of 14 huts. These were the only huts I had not inspected after Gunny failed to show up at our meeting place.

I spent the remainder of my time carefully looking inside every hut, hoping to see my friend and comrade in arms. The eastern sky was beginning to get that familiar grayish hue to it, so I knew I had to lie low another day and search again after dark.

I again located a safe place to eat and get some much needed sleep before beginning my final search for Gunny. This spot was not up a 40-foot tree! I waded out into a nearby swamp and found a piece of high ground maybe 30 feet long and 20 feet wide surrounded by swamp water on all sides. Here I could rest. I didn't even think about gathering moss, large leaves, etc., for a bed, I just got down on my hands and knees and removed the sticks and such that would make sleep impossible. This done, I lay down, shut my eyes, and passed out. I don't know when I had ever been so tensed and bone tired.

The sun was well up in the sky as I was suddenly awakened! I could hear someone or something walking in the water close to my bedding area. Rolling onto my stomach, I slithered toward the edge of the water with the M-14 across my forearms to where the noise was coming from. My worst fear was that villagers had picked up my trail and was leading Charlie to me.

I was prepared for the worst as I begin to ease my head up to look. I knew that I would fight and run, and continue to fight and run until either I got away or they found me dead. My heart was about to blow out of chest, as I raised my head to look around.

There, not more than 50 feet away was the sow hog and her litter of pigs wading toward another small island a short distance from me. Spasms of relief washed over me. Soon after that, I felt OK again. I ate a breakfast of scrambled eggs and chopped ham. I wanted a smoke so bad I could almost taste the tobacco. I knew deep down that would lead to certain detection. I decided to look for something to lie on besides the wet sand. I found enough bedding materials to keep myself comfortable and hopefully dry while I rested my eyes again.

As night fell upon the village, I circled around it and the VC encampment, maneuvering to the east side. During my tenure inside the fourth hut I made up my mind that if the VC had captured Gunny, the only other place they might have him was in their camp.

One hour later I was positioned some 15 yards from the communication tent; yet, concealed in the safety of the jungle. Twenty yards away was a second tent and there were just five tents total in the encampment. I saw this when Gunny and I first arrived at the village. I was on first watch when I saw the troops putting up these five tents from my advantage point.

Nothing special was happening at the communication tent; no officers were going in or out, and just the operator remained inside manning the radio. So I moved off toward the next tent. Moving in real close I saw no troops close by, so I eased up to the rear and peeked under the rear flap.

Lying spread eagled, hog-tied, and staked to the floor was Gunny Davis. One guard sitting cross-legged on the floor was throwing a pair of dice about six feet from where Gunny lay. The AK was on the ground by his side. He was facing toward Gunny, but concentrating more on his dice than on his prisoner in the light of a single small candle.

I glanced again at Gunny; he had a black cloth tied about his eyes, his hands were tied together and staked to the ground above his head, and his feet were spread with each staked to the ground near his ankles. His boots and socks were missing, and he was barefooted. I looked around the tent trying to locate his boots, but didn't spot them.

I could tell that he was breathing, but even that appeared difficult. I didn't know he had a gag in his mouth because the blindfold over his eyes also covered much of his face. I moved my head back outside the tent and scanned the area; seeing minimal activity nearby, I decided to take advantage of the moment and get Gunny out.

Quickly, once again scanning the area, I then crawled toward the front of the tent. Seeing that the way was clear, I eased right up to the edge of the opening and slowly eased my hand down to the trusty K-bar strapped across my chest. Once it was firmly in my right hand, I slowly got to my feet and swiftly entered the tent. The guard didn't look up quickly enough. I grabbed him, immediately covered his mouth with my left hand, and stuck the eight-inch blade clean through his neck, causing just a weak whimper to escape his lips. Without hesitation, I brought the razor sharp blade forward to sever his juggler vein. His warm blood rapidly covered my left palm. Dropping his lifeless body to the dirt floor, I turned my attention to Gunny.

I removed his ropes from his feet and then his hands; Gunny sat up and removed his blindfold and gag. He looked at me, smiled, and whispered one word, 'Thanks!'

He removed the sandals from the dead sentry and slid them on his big feet, then he picked up the sentry's AK-47 from the floor, and I relieved the dead sentry of his bandolier of ammo. Soon, we were ready to split. I knew when Gunny's escape was discovered, along with the dead guard, old Charlie would really be mad.

I whispered to Gunny, "I have to take care of the radio before we leave." He replied in a whisper, "Go!"

I sliced a long slit in the rear of the tent for our exit. Once outside, we crawled over to the radio tent. There inside sitting at a small table which held the company's main radio was a single operator on duty. Again, I moved to the front of the tent entrance and quickly slipped inside the tent.

Moving swiftly toward the radio operator got me within five feet of him. Quickly sizing up the situation, I sprang toward his back with the K-bar in my right hand. He did not know anything was wrong until the knife went deep under his left shoulder blade. The only sound coming from his lips was a death gasp! I then did as much damage to the radio as I could without making much noise, cutting wires, etc. Exiting the back of the tent, I saw that Gunny was ready to go.

He asked, "Business completed?"

I whispered, "Sure is Gunny."

"OK, let's move out!" he said, and off we went into the dense jungle with him hobbling along behind me.

We slipped back to get our grub, extra ammo and Gunny picked up his map and compass. As soon as we put our light packs on, Gunny had us heading toward the LZ on an East Southeast direction at a smooth walking pace. We had not walked but maybe 200 yards after picking up our gear when loud shouting could be heard across the fields. It had taken the VC only 20 minutes to discover the dead bodies and Gunny's escape. It sounded like the whole camp woke-up.

There was angry shouting and a lot of noise, which I assumed was coming from the VC Officers and senior NCOs. Once we had moved passed the village, I quickened our tempo a little. I knew Gunny would be trying his best to keep pace with me.

Gunny seemed to also get the message of what was about to take place, when he noticed I had picked up speed. I knew it would be almost impossible for them to track us until first light. Right now, they really didn't know there was anyone other than Gunny to capture. They probably assumed he had gotten loose and killed the guard and radio operator. They might try sweeping certain areas around the village to see if they could flush him out. But come daybreak, it wouldn't take them long to discover that there were two of us. I'm sure we had left enough sign to tell them that. One of Gunny's remarks during sniper school was foremost in my thoughts at this moment. *"The Viet Cong are some of the best trackers in the entire world."*

I glanced at my watch, it was now 0304 hours. Two and one-half hours till daybreak. We had less than three hours to put some distance between us and Charlie. We had to make the most of this opportunity now. Maybe we could put two to three miles between us and the enemy. Gunny must have been thinking along these same thoughts.

He asked me to stop, and then said, "We've got to go faster. But, before I can stay up with you, I need some assistance with these sandals. Can we modify them some way?"

I said, "Let's look at what we have in our packs." Between the two of us, we found tape. I cut off about six inches of each of his sleeves, doubled the cloth, and placed it in each sandal. Then Gunny put his foot in each sandal, and we taped each foot to the sandal and cloth. He stood, flexed his feet and said, "Let's do it!"

Off we went with him following close behind me at a quick trot. He was actually close enough to me to put his hand on my back pack at times. We must have sounded like two buffaloes running through the underbrush; but, we both knew all the VC fighters were back there with the company and none were out here now. There was a thunderstorm rumbling off in the distance. Maybe, just maybe it would rain. Rain! How this one thing is so hated in South Vietnam by us Americans. Now, here I am praying for it to rain, to come a downpour so hard it would be difficult for Charlie to see three feet in front of his nose. I just wanted the rain to blot out our tracks so the Viet Cong couldn't track us down and kill us.

I kept leading Gunnery Sgt. Davis through the dark morning hours, along a trail

that was almost non-existent in the dense jungle. I found myself praying quietly and asking God to help us escape the horrors of what the Viet Cong had in mind for us. Even though I was brought up as a youngster in the church and knew the value of prayer, I had found it increasingly difficult to really pray since I was about 18 years old.

So really, I was surprised to find myself uttering prayers, but it really helped me find a little peace in our situation.

* * * * * * *

Capt. Hyuo, the Viet Cong infantry company commander, was outraged that two of his men had been murdered and the American prisoner who was captured in the village had somehow managed to escape. Capt. Hyuo had first thought that the American had bribed his way to freedom, but there was nothing pointing to that. One of the company lieutenants stated someone had to have helped, because the American prisoner's knife was not used to kill the sentry, both his knife and his rifle were still in the lieutenants' tent.

Once Capt. Hyuo saw the knife and rifle for himself, he knew that possibly another American or more were involved in the killings and escape. As hard as his men tried, the trail of the American escaped them. Too many of his men had been moving about the campsite and nearby areas. Glancing at his watch, Hyuo saw that it was now 2:41 a.m. This meant at least three more hours before they could begin trying to find the Americans' trail.

Hyuo decided to spend his time wisely. Back at his tent, he took out a map of the delta area and began studying the map. He wanted to visualize the many options that were available to the Americans. With assistance from their helicopters, the Americans could go about any place and get picked up. Or they could head out for one of their many base camps. The captain asked himself, *"What would he do if he were the Americans?"* Answering his own question, he mused, *"Take the quickest way out by helicopter! That's how he would try escaping. But where would they meet their helicopter?"*

Hyuo knew that the Americans were using helicopters to fly in supplies four days a week to the South Vietnamese Army down at Chalon. They were flying in from a base north of Saigon. So these Americans could get picked up somewhere along that route. *But, where would this take place? Maybe helicopters would come here to get them.*

This 'where' appeared to be a very large question? Hyuo knew that his trackers must find their trail at daylight, and his soldiers must quickly locate and kill the Americans before they reached their rendezvous with the helicopter. He decided to send 20 of his best soldiers along with two of his best trackers and put one of his top sergeants in charge. He would demand the heads of the Americans be brought to him for the killing of his two soldiers and the humiliation that was brought upon him as the commander.

Capt. Hyuo had his orderly find Top Sgt. Luu Min and escort the sergeant to his tent. In less than five minutes, the small rock hard form of Sgt. Luu Min entered the captain's tent. He snapped to attention and saluted his superior. Capt. Hyuo returned his salute, and then asked him to come over by the lantern so they could sit and talk and study the maps. After discussing the mission in detail for 20 minutes, Hyuo considered which personnel Min would take to find the escaped Americans. Sgt. Luu Min stood as the Capt. Hyuo rose to his feet; they shook hands, and the sergeant promised him the Americans' heads.

Sgt. Luu Min walked out into the dark morning air, allowing a faint smile to appear upon his hardened face. He was honored the Capt. Hyuo thought highly of his skills as a leader to give him this important mission. His father would have been proud of him if he had survived the fighting with the French. His father was killed in a big battle four years earlier. His family had always fought the enemies of his beloved country. Luu Min had killed many French soldiers and now it was the South Vietnamese rebels who had divided his country that he was now killing.

The Americans had come to his country to equip and train these rebels of South Vietnam. Sgt. Luu Min had not seen the captured American Marine, but he heard the talk going around camp about how filthy and ugly he was. Min walked on until he reached his platoon's area. He called for Sgt. Hoa Lia Myun and together they chose two top trackers and selected the other 20 men for this important mission.

At 5:15 A.M., the 20 soldiers and two trackers — each carrying the Chinese AK-47 —had drawn extra ammunition and fragmentation grenades. Sgt. Min also picked up three dozen illuminating flares. The 22 soldiers assembled outside the ammunition tent awaiting orders to begin their hunt. All were battle-proven soldiers who knew how to fight and kill the enemy.

* * * * * * *

Gunny and I stopped just one more time before daylight. We quickly ate a bite and washed it down with some water — but, only a little water since we had to keep moving at a rapid pace. Drinking too much water would be bad for us. The quick meal provided needed energy that our bodies demanded and allowed us to keep going.

We only had a few minutes to put even more distance between Charlie and ourselves. Every second wasted would put the VC closer and closer to us. After checking the compass, Gunny estimated we were about 17 miles West Northwest from the recovery LZ. Again I had us moving out at a rapid walking pace heading East Southeast. I noticed a limp in Gunny Davis' steps as we had moved along through the undergrowth.

The storm clouds passed; we would not get any rain from that system of clouds. Now, it was entirely up to us to evade the Viet Cong party and their trackers. God had chosen to stay out of our desperate situation, or He would have let it rain and helped us escape. I was really mad at God right then, we were civilized people who went to church on Sunday and loved Him. Now, He decided not to help us. I was mad at God! How could He turn away from Gunny and me now? He had answered some of my other prayers, but not this important one. The angrier I became with God, the faster I was able to walk. I'm sure that Gunny also realized that the Viet Cong were probably already gaining on us. This thought made me quicken my steps.

I began to quicken our pace until we were doing the Apache Indian style slow jog, maintaining a steady rhythm that really covers a lot of ground. For some reason, this pace was easy on the heart and lungs. My concern was *whether Gunny could keep up?*

At this pace, I thought we could increase the distance between Charlie and us — 100 yards every 15 minutes. This would increase our lead a quarter of a mile every hour.

From what I had learned at Sniper School, the Viet Cong could move about at a rapid pace whenever they wanted to do so. This was going to be some race. Survival of the fittest was what it was going to boil down to — so, I had to keep a sharp eye on Gunny and not let him lag behind because of the limp.

* * * * * * *

Sgt. Luu Min left the *Kai Huu* village camp at daybreak. It took about 20 minutes before the trackers picked up the trail of two people, with one wearing boots. The tracks led them northeast for a few hundred yards; then, the Americans changed direction and headed southeast, skirting the village. Their trail was lost for a short time, but the experienced trackers picked it up again beyond the village. Here the two Americans turned East Southeast; within another hour, Min's trackers had found where the Marines had stopped to rest.

He pushed his men on, he was confident they would soon find the two Marines. The

American Marines would be captured or killed very soon.

Another hour passed and still they had not caught the Marines. Min could see his men also needed to rest; some were wheezing for breath with each step they took. They had been moving at a very fast-paced walk since daybreak this morning. So, reluctantly Min then signaled and called for his squad to halt. He gave them a 15 minute break, which was enough time to eat a bite of fish cakes, get a drink of water, or just rest.

Once back on the Marines' trail, Min quickly gave the order to increase the pace. He was very confident they would soon be finding the Americans. Two more hours passed and still his trackers followed the enemy's trail through the jungle. One thing was foremost in Sgt. Min's mind. Both, he and the Capt. Hyuo had vastly underestimated the Americans' ability to outrun his Viet Cong pursuers. The Marines pace seemed unrelenting.

Once again Min saw that he had to give his men a break. They were not in a tight line of two's, but, rather were becoming strung-out trying to keep pace with him. Min reluctantly gave them another 15 minute break.

As Sgt. Min and his men were trying to close the distance between the two American Marines and themselves in a long distance race across the South Vietnam delta region, the hot 120-degree humid temperature was taking its toll on everyone and was fast winning the race for survival.

As Sgt. Min looked at his men sprawled out upon the jungle floor, he could see that they were not going to catch the Marines if this turned into a long distance race. His men were good for sustaining short bursts of speed over a few hours at the maximum.

Min knew that he had better contact Capt. Hyuo by radio for assistance in the capture. Unless he could convince the Hyuo to ask for another company of brothers to the east to assist him, catching the two Marines was out of the question with the large head start they were given.

Back at the village, Capt. Hyuo had received an urgent radio message from Sgt. Min at 1020 hours that was delivered by the radio operator. He was requesting assistance from other Cong brothers that may be 10 to15 miles east of the village. Sgt. Min stated he regrettably was unable to overtake the Marines because they had too great of a head start on him and his men.

Capt. Hyuo took a small brown notepad from his front shirt pocket and, after a few minutes of reviewing the pages, found the call sign for the company that would be asked to assist in the capture or killing of the Marines. Capt. Hyuo turned toward the radio operator and ordered an urgent message by sent to Capt Wyng Di, who was company commander of a well-trained company of Cong. Di's operating area was just to the east of Hyuo's own operating area.

While the operator was sending his message, Capt. Hyuo hurried back to his tent, picked up his map, and returned to the radio tent before the operator could get Capt. Di on the radio.

Soon, with a smooth voice, Capt. Di answered, "Sir, Capt. Di speaking."

Then Di heard the thunderous voice of his close friend, Capt. Lei Hyuo, "Capt. Di, I urgently need your help in the capture or killing of two American Marines who have spied on our weapons operations at the large village of *Kai Huu*."

Capt. Di replied, "We would be most honored in assisting my friend Capt. Hyuo. How can I help you?"

Hyuo said, "Can you spare about 20 seasoned fighters?"

"I can send even more if necessary?" Capt. Di replied.

"Twenty will be enough my friend. Twenty of my own men and two trackers with Top Sgt. Min in charge are now pursuing the Marines along coordinates W-106.880 by S-16.21 degrees. They are about eight miles east of *Kai Huu* village moving west to east. Can you have your men intercept them? Over," Hyuo stated.

"My soldiers will intercept them for you Capt. Hyuo. Do you have a plan in place for their capture?" Di questioned.

Hyuo had formulated a plan to capture the Americans, but he was afraid if it too failed, he would be humiliated and stripped of rank or worse, shot! His own superiors would see to that.

So, he told Capt. Di "Let's, you and I, trust our senior men leading the chase to come up with the best plan to stop the Americans."

"Great strategy, captain," Capt. Di quickly replied.

Sgt. Quo Mi Loa was in the small village of Qua Li — about 14 miles to the east of the large village of *Kai Huu* — with about 10 of his soldiers, when he received orders via radio from Capt. Di. Di instructed him to take 20 men and intercept two Americans being pursued by another group of 22 Cong soldiers from Capt. Hyuo's company, led by Top Sgt. Min.

Sgt. Loa quickly sent a village runner to the next village a couple of miles away to get the rest of his men to join him. Then Sgt. Loa instructed his men that were with him to begin checking their AKs to ensure they were operational and ready for fighting. He also ordered them to find enough food to take with them that would last 20 men at least three days. His final order was to ensure that there was enough ammunition to last his entire group for five days of fighting. He was going to take his radio with him so he could communicate with Top Sgt. Min.

When Capt. Hyuo radioed Sgt. Min and informed him of the plan to squeeze the Americans between the two groups of Cong soldiers, he informed Top Sgt. Min that how the plan was executed was up to him and Sgt. Ming Loa of Capt. Di's company, who was now leading 20 seasoned fighters to intercept the Americans. Now, Capt. Hyuo believed that the Marines would be killed or captured before sunrise tomorrow. He returned to his tent and spread out his map again and sat down in his chair and smiled to no one in particular. Maybe, just maybe, he could save his career.

He had underestimated the American Marines once, and he would not let that happen again. These two Marines had to be in top physical shape to outrun his seasoned soldiers as they did today. But, maybe tonight would bring good news and the two Americans would pay dearly.

* * * * * * *

Sgt. Davis and Cpl. Mitchem were desperately trying to maintain the two and one half-hour head start they had gained at the large village this morning at 0230 when they slowly slipped away from the Viet Cong village and soldiers. They had seen the many boxes of military weapons that were still in their shipping crates with its Chinese markings on them. These two Americans now knew where these weapons were being stored for the lower delta region Viet Cong forces.

Once past the village, Cpl. Mitchem began moving toward the nearest American helicopter route to Chalon from the helicopter base just north of Saigon. Helicopters usually did not use the same route each day. But, if they decided to do so, they would fly at a higher attitude. All pilots were made aware that there were American marines on 'covert' operations in that area, and to watch for a *green smoke* flare, which would signal *'ready for pickup'*.

With Cpl. Mitchem leading the way to the nearest helicopter flight path, he and Gunny Davis were actually increasing the distance between themselves and their Viet Cong pursuers. The pace Mitchem had set for them was an easy, old Apache Indian gate. It was really just a very easy jog. It was a pace that one could maintain for hours at a time.

Mitch was glancing back to check on Gunny quite frequently; since they had been running from the VC, Gunny had begun to show a slight limp in his walking and even when jogging. Mitch thought this could be from Gunny being staked to the ground by his ankles so tightly for many long hours that it almost cut the circulation off from his feet. Mitch thought the limping was due to his circulation being restricted for so long and/or the makeshift way they had taped Gunny's feet to those sandals.

Soon, Gunny would have to stop and rest; it was obvious by looking at him laboring with his pain, yet, so determined to escape the Viet Cong.

At 1300 hours Gunny signaled to Cpl. Mitchem that he needed to stop and rest. When Mitch slowed to a walk and then stopped, he saw that Gunny was already leaning against a tree, trying to get his breath back. Gunny suggested they eat some crackers and peanut butter for quick energy and eat a piece of candy. Together these foods would provide much needed energy to hopefully stay ahead of the VC. They both took their salt tablets and swallowed only small amounts of water from their canteens.

Mitch moved over to where Gunny was sitting with his back against a tree and sat down in front of him. Looking at the tape job on the sandals, Mitch begin to make some minor changes to the taping. They were just a mere foot apart and Gunny asked, "How much time distance is between the VC that's chasing us?"

"Maybe three hours now," Cpl. Mitchem quickly replied. "We should have increased our distance by about 30 minutes during the past four hours."

"Is that all?" Gunny asked. "You've about killed me yourself, with me just trying to stay up with you." Then, he broke into that famous grin of his, and Mitch knew he was just kidding with him.

It was time to move out again after rechecking the map and his compass, but this time Gunny wanted the lead. He was accustomed to the slow trot that Cpl. Mitchem had set and really like it. It was very easy on the body and actually ate up huge chunks of real estate in a short period of time. Gunny wished for his boots, but knew he would have to make the best with what he had — and, that was a pair of VC sandals that were at least three sizes too small taped to his big feet.

They had gotten off course a little, and now Gunny made the adjustment that would put them back on track to get picked up by a chopper sometime tomorrow afternoon, if all went well.

The pace that Gunny now set was about the same as Cpl. Mitchem had used. It was indeed easier on the body's lungs, legs, and feet than trying to walk at a rapid pace. Gunny had to remind himself that they were running from an intelligent adversary who was more than capable of turning the tables on two jarheads.

What Gunny didn't know and it worried him was *'did the pursuing cong soldiers have a radio?'* That one item could be the leading role in Mitch's and his apprehension or freedom. There wasn't any way to know for sure at this time, and only time would let him know if Charlie had a radio at their disposal.

Gunny had himself and Mitch still traveling South Southeast. They had been on this new heading for more than two hours without slowing down. It was at least 120 degrees and really felt like much more. There was not a dry piece of clothing on either Marine. However, the salt pills they took regularly were keeping them in fairly good shape. Gunny now slowed to a walk and soon stopped to take another compass reading and make any adjustment necessary.

Mitch moved up alongside Gunny. Gunny Davis looked at Cpl. Mitchem and said, "I owe you my life for getting me out of that situation back there at the village. I've wanted to say, 'Thanks Mitch', since we left the village, but there just wasn't time. So now that I said my little piece, it's time to run again." Glancing down at his watch, Mitch saw it was 1322 hours. Soon both of them were back up to the easy gate that Gunny had set before they stopped, with the corporal following the sergeant through the jungle.

* * * * * * *

Sgt. Loa had the radio call letters for communicating with Top Sgt. Min. He would now plot on his own map the course that the Americans and Min's fighters were taking as soon as he contacted Sgt. Min. As a precaution, Sgt. Loa wrote Min's call letters at the bottom of his map. He was not one to leave things to memory or chance.

Within a few minutes, he was talking with Sgt. Min and getting the coordinates he needed to intercept the two Americans. Top Sgt. Min said he would call back in about 30 minutes when he allowed his men to stop for a quick breather. Min looked down at the watch that his father had left him. The watch was old, but still kept good time. It showed the time to be 1:43P.M. His father had taken this watch from a French officer he had killed in hand-to-hand combat some years before.

* * * * * * *

Luu Min went home to see his mother in the summer of 1963 for four days. All his travel papers prepared by the Cong high command would ensure that South Vietnamese soldiers who would check the people on the busses for IDs did not detain him. The trip took two days riding on three different old rusty busses. There was bamboo baskets on top of the bus filled with their owners' personal belongings. A teenage boy riding atop the bus tossed the owners their baskets as they exited the bus.

When Min first arrived, a pig was killed for a feast — and a feast it was as many relatives had come to wish Min well. Luu Min noticed there were a number of his male kin that did not show up. Later that day, Luu Min asked his sisters about this. One said solemnly, "The male cousins who had not come had died fighting the South Vietnamese Army."

Later that evening as the sun was setting behind the hills, Luu Min handed his mother a present that he had gotten her about four months ago when he was in Saigon. It was a piece of blue fabric for a dress, along with five large buttons for use as decoration or closure. When Luu's mother opened the brown paper bundle that was hand tied, her face lit up with a smile as she saw the blue fabric. A small brown bag had been tucked inside the fabric by Min a few moments before without her knowing it.

Like women always do, she set the little brown bag to the side and picked up the beautiful blue material and the pretty buttons again. She was so proud of this gift. It was only the third piece of new fabric she had ever owned. She would make herself a new dress — something she had not worn in more than 10 years. Finally, she picked up the little brown bag, turned toward Luu and asked, "Is this from you also my son?" Luu Min assured her it was a second gift for her. When she opened the small bag and emptied it upon the small table, she could not believe her eyes — money, more than she had seen at one time in her entire lifetime.

Luu Min had been putting aside money for his family every time he was paid. When they plundered the dead soldiers, which they had killed, he always took their money. This had been going on for years now. He really could not remember when he started. He just wanted to help provide for his family who were one of the millions of poor families in South Vietnam trying to scratch out a living and survive any way they could.

Luu Min advised his mother to keep this money hidden from everyone, including his sisters by selecting a place on their small piece of land and burying it in a glass jar to help preserve the money from rotting. He also told his mother to only take a little bit of money with her when she went into the cities. His mother said she would think about where the safest place could be, and she and Luu would go together to bury it.

On Luu's second day at home, he wanted to just look around the place where he had grown up and so he asked his oldest sister, Mim So Min, to accompany him. Mim So was happy and felt honored to be seen with her brother. They walked around the small farm and then went shopping in a small town nearby. Here, Luu found more fabric and purchased two colors from the same design with Mim So's help. He purchased enough of the fabric to make two more dresses, one each for his sisters.

Luu made sure not to raise suspicion among the town people, so he had carried along his father's old home made wooden crutch, and he had purposely dressed in an old pair of his father's worn out pants and shirt. If he and Mim So saw any South Vietnamese soldiers, Luu would fake a crippling injury and they should be allowed to continue on.

The evening before Min left, his mother took a small box from under the belongings at the head of her small bed. In the box was a handwritten note from his father stating that if he should die, then this watch would belong to his son Luu Min. He wanted Min to know how proud he was of him and knew he would be a better fighter for his beloved country than his father had been. He charged him to take care of his two sisters and his mother.

* * * * * * *

Sgt. Min signaled for the column of fighters to stop. He could see they were tired; but, he knew that they must press on in order to catch the Americans, who appeared to run fast as a fox. Min looked at his watch again, and told his men to take a 20 minute break and eat.

Top Sgt. Min walked among his handpicked fighters, asking them what they would do with the vast amount of bounty given for the killing or capture of these two Americans.

This seemed to lift their spirits so he continued this tactic with each man as they ate a quick meal of precooked rice and dried fish. Min told his fighters to think about killing the Marines and not about trying to capture them. He also told them, "Sgt. Loa, with a sister company to our east, is coming toward us with 20 more top fighters who will help trap the Americans between our fighting groups."

Min looked down at his watch again and saw it was now 2:32 P.M. — 10 more minutes to rest. "Check your weapon to make sure the safety is on, and the weapon is ready to fire," Min ordered his men. When everyone had quickly done as instructed, Min knew it was time to move out again. "Move out faster!" he instructed the two trackers.

Sgt. Loa and his 20-man team had a good information meeting about what it was they were to do; but, he informed them that Top Sgt. Min would let him know how the plan to capture or kill the Americans would take place. Loa had his men draw enough ammo to last each fighter five full days. Food issuance was only enough for three days. If things worked in their favor, they could be home in two days.

Sgt. Loa had plotted the route the Americans were using on his map with a series of dots — this he showed his men. They would squeeze the Americans between themselves and Top Sgt. Min's fighters. Loa did not know how close Sgt. Min's fighters were to the Americans. The distance between them would have a bearing on whose fighters made contact with these Americans first. Loa knew that if the Americans were two hours or more ahead of Sgt. Min's men, the odds were that his fighters would make contact first.

* * * * * * *

Gunny Sgt. Davis had set the same pace that Cpl. Mitchem had used. This style of a jog was refreshingly easy on the lungs and their legs' calf muscles. One's lungs did not feel like they were on fire, nor did your legs cramp up. This was easier on the human body, and it covered a good bit of distance over a short period of time. The biggest plus that he had discovered for him in this Indian style gate was that stopping to rest was not required as often. Gunny decided he would teach all his students in future sniper schools to employ this method when necessary for eluding or escaping the enemy.

Gunny's thoughts went back to a previous thought, *'did the pursuing Viet Cong fighters have a radio?'* He would assume the worst and that they did have a radio with which they could communicate with their own forces.

This one item plays such a large part in the success of any mission. Gunny was thinking what he would do to stop the Marines, if he were the enemy. If radio communications were possible, then he would ask for assistance by having a second or maybe even a third group of fighters help in corralling the Marines with some type of trap or ambush before they were able to reach their helicopter rescue location.

Gunny stopped and motioned for Mitchem to come to where he was. When Mitchem reached Gunny's side, he asked, "Is there anything wrong?"

"Maybe!" Gunny answered.

Then he began sharing with Mitch his hunch that *if the pursuing VC had a radio and were smart enough to use it to their advantage, they could plot our movements through the jungle and set up an ambush.*

As Gunny took the map out and spread it on the floor of the jungle, he began to plot their present location. Once he had decided where they were, he circled that location on the map and then plotted the distance to the chopper pickup point. They were less than seven miles from LZ#1.

Studying the map again, Gunny noted a cleared, large square area that would be an excellent ambush area for the VC. Here, there was about a mile of sparse vegetation that the Marines would either have to cross the open space or skirt around it. Our Navy Seabees and the South Vietnamese soldiers had cleared this area for a future base a year ago, and still there was no sign of construction.

Gunny pointed out this area to Mitchem. "This would be an ideal place to set up an ambush for us. They would be able to see you and me when we stepped into that sparsely grownup field. They could set up people here and here," he indicated with his finger moving to two locations on the map as he spoke. "Corporal, what would you do, knowing this?" he asked Mitchem.

After a few minutes of studying the map, Mitch stated, "Gunny, I would change the direction we're heading and head South and set a course to intersect the helicopters at this location." I showed that position with my finger on the map.

Gunny studied the map again and said, "You are absolutely right Marine — let me get a new bearing and we'll be off and running again soon. Since this is your brain child, you lead for awhile. Right now we'll take a quick 10 minute break before we leave."

At 1610 hours, we began our trek through the jungle again. We started by moving down the original route and took turns moving lightly off the old trail to retrieve some large limbs and leaf plants. Then we circled back to where we took our break and began walking backwards, sweeping away our tracks as we went for maybe 40 yards or so. This little trick should give us another 30 minutes of lead-time on our pursuers, if we were lucky. We discarded the plants in a manner so that they would blend in with other similar vegetation in the area.

"Keep the same pace," Gunny ordered, and soon I was back on that Apache-style gate. We moved swiftly and quietly toward a hopeful reunion with one of our helicopters coming back from the South Vietnamese Army base at Chalon. As darkness began to settle over the landscape, Gunny said he wanted to get another reading before the sky turned black, so I slowed down, and we stopped while Gunny checked out our heading. Still on course and with Mitchem in the lead, we continued our trek into a jungle that was growing dark fast. When Gunny was checking our bearings, he used his tiny red lens flashlight that was in his pack. He now gave it to Mitch to find the way through the jungle.

* * * * * * *

The trackers lost the Marines' trail. They saw where the two had stopped for a break, and then they proceeded on the same way they had been going. Then about 100 yards from where they took their break, the trail just stopped. There was no more sign to show where they might have gone. It was as if something had lifted them from the earth. One tracker stayed and tried to find some kind of sign, even if just a broken twig, that would help track these two Marines who run like wild pigs through the jungle. The second tracker returned to where Top Sgt. Min and his men had stopped and advised him of their situation. Sgt. Min had taken this time to give his men another well-deserved break while the trackers were trying to locate the Americans' trail.

When Min's fighters had reached the spot where the two Marines had stopped to rest, the Americans had been long gone for close to two and one-half hours. It was now dark; the cloudy skies moving in indicated a chance of rain.

Sgt. Min signaled for his radioman to come to him and instructed the radioman to contact Sgt. Loa for him. When Sgt. Loa was on the radio, Min's radioman handed the headset to him, who informed Sgt. Loa of their location and their situation. He told him that as soon as they had rediscovered the Marines' trail, he would have his radioman contact him and provide the new route. Sgt. Loa said that would be satisfactory. Min asked Sgt. Loa what was his and his fighters' location.

Sgt. Loa gave Top Sgt. Min his location and saw on his own map that they were about six miles apart now. He relayed the distance between them to Sgt. Min who again said he would keep Sgt. Loa posted as soon as he learned something. Sgt. Loa acknowledged and signed off.

He then commanded his fighters to halt. They, too, deserved a needed break. Sgt. Loa decided he would not move his men out again until he heard by radio from Top Sgt. Min.

The trackers had been trying to pick up the trail again for almost 15 minutes in the darkness without any success. They had agreed that finding the Marines' trail would require them to have some sort of light to see any markings or disturbances in the jungle floor. The two trackers began gathering any dried sticks that were less than a couple of feet long. Once they had the small wood sticks, they then tore a piece of their shirtsleeve off, wrapped this around the sticks, and lit it with their matches. These makeshift torches would provide light for about five minutes at most.

The trackers had used up two sleeves when they found where the Marines had moved off the trail for good and doubled back a short piece, and then they lost the trail a second time. After gathering more sticks and cutting another sleeve off, they were now able to see that the two American Marines had changed direction and moved off in a South by Southeast direction.

Sgt. Min was angry that the trackers had lost the trail, but glad they found it before the rains came. He ordered the radioman to give Sgt. Loa the new direction, which the two Marines and his fighters were now taking. Top Sgt. Min estimated he had lost almost 20 more minutes on the Marines.

Top Sgt. Min had his radioman call Capt. Hyuo, who was still back at the village, and provide the him with the new heading the two Americans had taken. When Capt. Hyuo received this message, a big grin broke upon his face. He was thinking that very soon now the Americans would die, their bullet-riddled bodies severed at the neck, and their heads would be his.

When Sgt. Loa got the new directions the Marines were now traveling, he looked at his map and studied it for a few minutes. A grin moved across the young rugged face of this battle-hardened Viet Cong sergeant. Sgt. Loa thought the two Marines changed direction to make their final run toward where their helicopters fly regularly. He and his fighters were miles closer to that location than the Marines were. Sgt. Loa knew he and his fighters could get there before the Marines. He did not wait for orders from Top Sgt. Min before he moved his fighters out, traveling southwest. He had gathered his fighters around him and told them they would be racing the two American Marines to the area where the U.S. helicopters flew almost every day carrying supplies back and forth to the South Vietnamese Army near Chalon.

Within 15 minutes after Sgt. Loa's fighters had begun their race with the Marines, he received a second communication from Sgt. Min, asking him to try to stop the Marines from reaching their new destination further south. Sgt. Loa advised his radioman to tell Min that he understood and would do his best. Sgt. Loa looked at his watch. It was 7:17 P.M. His fighters were well rested after their last break; so he stepped up the pace, racing to cut off the Americans.

Sgt. Loa now had his 20 fighters moving to the southwest and they would reach the lower helicopter fly area maybe an hour before the Americans did. Loa and his VC fighters had almost five miles less to travel than the Marines. He would surprise the Americans tomorrow as they tried to signal the helicopters. There were only two small clearings maybe four miles apart that the helicopters could land on in this area, which he knew so well. He would set traps that the Americans would not see, and he would kill them. If the Americans were lucky, they would die a quick death. If they were not so lucky, he would see that they died a slow, painful death over a fire pit. He would slowly roast them alive and personally cut out both their tongues and feed them to his best fighters, who would feast on the enemies' flesh.

Sgt. Loa's fighters were very seasoned soldiers with most every one of them having been fighting for over two years. They were very good at beating their enemy in combat. Creating ambushes was something that came natural for these fighters. Sgt. Loa hated the South Vietnamese soldiers and the lazy Americans who came here to help them. His hatred ran deep, for South Vietnamese soldiers two years earlier had killed his girlfriend. He did the only thing he could do to avenge her death by joining the Viet Cong fighters. He became enraged each time he went into battle against them and satisfied his vengeance by cutting off one of their ears. He kept his collection of ears in his home village and now had 30 or more. He would love to add two ears of these Americans to his collection.

Sgt. Loa could not understand how two lazy American Marines could outrun VC fighters for over 18 hours through the jungles of Vietnam. The only movie he saw of America showed how lazy and overweight these people were.

His fighters would run all night if Sgt. Loa asked them. These soldiers were itching for a good fight and did not care if it was Americans or the South Vietnamese soldiers. He looked back to check on his fighters, and they were keeping a close, two-abreast formation.

Looking at his map, Loa reasoned they had traveled nearly seven miles southwest. He was near where the American helicopters flew past, shuttling supplies. There were two places he could fix the perfect ambush. He would scout those two places come daylight. Staying on the eastern side of the river, Sgt. Loa's fighters had raced southwest to the usual flight path of the American helicopters.

He slowed his men down, not wanting to race into the arms of any South Vietnamese army patrols. He would bed his men down near the first clearing, which he would inspect at the first sign of daylight. Glancing at his watch, Sgt. Loa saw that it was 9:50 P.M. He guessed they should be close to the first clearing in maybe another 20 minutes.

* * * * * * *

Cpl. Mitchem maintained that Apache Indian pace wherever the terrain allowed.

When Mitch ran into thickets or denser vegetation, he would slow the pace down to a walk. The last thing either he or Gunny wanted was to get either of them hurt bad enough that it would affect the outcome of their race for survival.

Trying to stay within a few yards of Mitch was a challenge at times. The landscape would play a major part in this. But, Gunny Davis knew the man moving along in front of him was one smooth jarhead. A Marine that had been quiet around the other snipers and men in school recently was now a silent stalker, who knew how to kill swiftly when he had to with his big knife. Gunny was amazed at how quietly Mitch moved now.

Gunny knew that Mitch displayed coolness in rescuing him; but, he really saw it by the single lamp burning in the communication tent when he witnessed Mitch silently stalk and kill that VC with his knife. Gunny remembered he had looked at the throat of the VC guard who had been guarding him, after Mitch had almost severed the man's head from his shoulders with that big razor sharp knife he carried. Gunny witnessed one cool killing machine in action. Yep! Gunny sure was proud of Cpl. Mitchem for the Marine sniper he had now become.

They had been moving steady for over three hours; the watch on Mitch's wrist showed it was 2043 hours. Mitch glanced back at Gunny and saw that he was just a few feet behind him, seemingly moving without much pain. Mitch slowed and finally stopped.

He turned and asked Gunny about how much farther till they reached LZ#2? Gunny broke out the map and asked Mitch for his little red light. It only took a few minutes for Gunny to say, "We are two and one-half miles from LZ#2."

Mitch felt around in his pack until he touched the smoke canister that he had carried since they had packed their belongings back at base. This was their way of signaling the choppers during daylight. Mitch knew that they could be at LZ#2 by 2200 hours tonight, but when they slipped in there would be the call of his Gunny Sergeant.

"What do you think we should do Gunny?" Mitch inquired.

Gunny took his time before delivering an answer. He thought about every possible situation they would face that could pop-up. He also knew that they were still two to three hours ahead of the VC fighters from the village. *He worried about the other VC he did not know about, but suspected.*

Gunny thought that Charlie would have fighters strung out along the helicopters fly route trying to stop them — but exactly where, he didn't know. These last few miles to LZ#2 could be a game of cat and mouse. He definitely was not going to lead the Viet Cong right to the LZ. That would be suicidal. *He wasn't aware that Sgt. Hoa's fighters were already very close to that LZ.*

Gunny knew that it was now time to make another course change.

"We must lose the VC following us," he finally answered Mitch. Leaving no tracks or sign of which direction we have taken, we must slip back up to LZ#1. We have all night to get back up there. That is the last place I would look for us." Mitch thought, *"Wow, great idea, but, how do we throw them off our trail?"*

With both of them looking at the map, Gunny remarked, "Mitch, when we reach this small river here *(pointing at the map)*, we'll try to find a spot where we can wade across, turn and head north, staying in the river for maybe a mile. There, we'll exit the river and head off to the Northeast. We'll stop somewhere close to LZ#1 before daybreak. Making sure it's secure, we will slip in and wait on the chopper to come flying by to take us home. We do have a green smoke flare, don't we?"

"Yeah, we have a green smoke," I answered. Gunny suggested we should each eat a couple of small cans of peanut butter, for quick energy, and I agreed by saying, "OK."

Moving along the old trail again traveling South Southeast, Cpl. Mitchem and Gunny within the hour stepped off into the black waters of the small river. They soon found a crossing spot where the river was shallow and the water was no more than waist deep. They eased slowly across the river's soft bottom to the other side, staying in knee-deep water and turning up-river heading north. One and one-half hours later found them moving very quietly out of the river and into the adjoining swamp. They then turned northeast and quietly moved away from the river swamp. Entering a big hardwood forest, both Marines were extra cautious because they knew they were still deep in the heart of VC territory. They were about 20 miles from their Marine base and maybe 10 miles from the South Vietnamese military base further south at Chalon.

* * * * * * *

The fighters and trackers of Top Sgt. Min could not close the two and one-half hours time difference between themselves and the Marines. Sgt. Min saw how crafty the Americans were when they tried to throw him off their trail. He had spoken with Sgt. Loa once since they had last changed directions. Min gave his worn-out men another break. It was now 9:23 P.M. He knew that he had pushed them too hard yesterday morning when the race had just started. But, he was so confident that he would catch the Americans before noontime that he ran his men into the ground trying to overcome a deficit of two hour and one-half hours' head start by the Americans.

Sgt. Min now had great respect for these two American Marines. Everyone had to earn his respect, and these two did just that. Min saw these two as great and superbly conditioned warriors. He was sure that they could more then hold their own in a fight. He wondered how long had they been on his company's tail. He would guess two days or more before they had reached the village.

He knew that the Marines must be good fighters. They carried the black rifle in 7.62 caliber, possibly equal to the Russian AK-47 which also was in 7.62 caliber. Min had neither seen this Marine weapon, nor heard any reports on its accuracy and firepower. He knew the captured Marine had a black rifle; they took it from him at the time of his capture. However, he was well aware of the military's advance technology the Americans possessed.

Top Sgt. Min gave the order to stop and after looking at his map knew that he and his fighters were about five miles from the helicopters' flight path down to Chalon. He decided he would rest his men here until 4:00 A.M. His men would be fresh when they had to fight the Americans come tomorrow morning.

* * * * * * *

Gunnery Sgt. Davis and Cpl. Mitchem were slowly slipping toward LZ#1 and had been traveling NE now for four hours. Gunny knew it was time to rest as both of his feet were hurting like crazy — 0235 hours. They stopped to rest and ate their 'C' rations, and then moved ever closer to the LZ.

When Gunny sat down, he took his K-bar out, cut everything off from the old VC sandal, and felt his swollen feet. His body ached from his head to toe. He had been dirty and beaten down when he was a prisoner back at the village. His head was cut from the whack he received from the butt of a VC rifle. And, he was dirty after urinating on himself several times. He was so tired now that all those feelings came rushing back to his memory and his body.

Cpl. Mitchem eased over near Gunny and asked, "Are we close?"

"Within a mile of it," Gunny answered. Then he pulled out the map and spread it out on the ground. "Here is our approximate position. Here is LZ#1. You can see how close we are now." Knowing that Gunny and I were almost there lifted my spirits. I wanted to get closer.

I wanted us to get a ride on the first chopper, coming or going didn't make any difference to me. I just wanted airlifted out of here. I wanted to get out of this stinking jungle. We had run when we thought we could go no further and reached deep down inside to outrace a group of VC fighters across the Delta for 20-plus miles. Running through the jungle trying to avoid getting our butts shot off by Viet Cong fighters is not an easy task.

Gunny took his pack off and lay his head on it. He only needed to do this for a few minutes, and his body would stop screaming for rest. Within minutes, he was sound asleep. His breathing was fast at times, and then it settled down to a normal rhythm.

Mitch looked at his sergeant and great pride swelled up inside. This man was a legend. He also knew that if he had been the one captured, Gunny would have moved heaven and earth to get him out.

The young corporal stayed alert and watched over his friend while he slept and rested. When it was 0500 hours, Mitch eased over to where Gunny slept and bumped his leg with the M-14. Gunny opened his eyes and sat up. "It's time to get some breakfast into our stomachs." Mitch said. He then sat down next to Gunny and opened a can of ham and egg from his C-rations. "Want ham and egg or something else?" Mitch asked the sleepy Gunny Sgt.

"Ham and eggs is fine." Gunny replied. Mitch handed him the can of ham and eggs to eat, and then got himself the same breakfast.

Daybreak found these two Marines slowly slipping closer to LZ#1 where they had gotten out of the helicopter upon the start of this mission many days before. Gunny was keenly aware of the possibility of finding some of the VC fighters here. He sent Mitchem to the west and to the north of the clearing looking for signs of VC hiding in wait for them, while he went around the south and east sides scouting for the same things.

Mitch slowly eased around the western and north sides of the clearing without spotting any sign of VC. I was lying low on the north side and waiting for Gunny or his signal when I heard him whistle, then I waited a minute then returned his whistle. Gunny had pinpointed Mitch's position and slipped slowly towards him.

"It's time to go home Marine," Gunny said as they met. "This area is all clear and our ride should be here shortly."

They moved to where they had a visual of the flight path. Mitch took the green flare out of his pack to signal that they were ready for pickup when they spotted a chopper. At 0716 hours, they heard sweet the sound of a helicopter as it approached from Chalon.

Mitch popped the flare and threw it out into the open clearing when they saw the helicopter flying high, at nearly 1000 feet. Within seconds the smoke was clearly visible above the tree line, and the chopper circled the LZ, turned, and came in low just over the trees to pick up the two Marine snipers that were waiting in this LZ.

Thirty minutes later the chopper sat down on the helicopter runway at our base. The pilot had already radioed that he had picked up two healthy hitchhikers. So, BAT-I had their jeep meet us to take us to headquarters.

The intelligence that we provided was way above what they had expected. A group of three Navy fighter-bombers wasted the village and VC munitions it had hidden. The company of VC was not at the village, nor could they be located.

We both got a hot shower, a change of clothes, and some hot food.

Three days later on Thursday, I was called into the Major's office at 1020 hours. As I stood at attention in front of the Major's desk, I saw Gunny Davis and the Colonel were also present. I didn't know what to expect. Then the Major came around his desk and handed something to Gunny; then the Colonel and Gunny approached me and stopped right in front of me.

"Cpl. Melvin Mitchem, you have been promoted to the rank of Sergeant for showing valor in extraordinary situations," the Colonel said.

"Gunny, you have the honor of pinning these stripes on his sleeves. Congratulations, Sgt. Mitchem," the Major added.

Gunny's face broke into a huge grin as he said, "Wanna go back again, Sarge?"

"Maybe!" I replied.

There was a lot of hand shaking and back slapping going on for the next few minutes.

The Major then said, "Sgt. Mitchem, you are to report to Gunny Davis at 0530 hours Saturday as a sniper school instructor until you get your spotter or unless orders change."

"Thank you, sir," I responded.

"The Major and I are in agreement to let you two sergeants have the remainder of the day and tomorrow off," the Colonel added.

"Thank you, Colonel," Gunny and I responded in unison.

The remainder of that day and Friday, our time off, we spent cleaning our weapons thoroughly. We had our clothes washed by the Vietnamese women who regularly do our laundry.

Then at 0700 hours, Saturday morning, Gunny started another sniper training school. My assignment as an instructor and a sniper meant I would get the best spotter from this graduating class. I was to instruct on the techniques of *Escape and Evasion* (E&E).

CHAPTER 9

On a rainy Saturday morning at 0645 hours on December 6, 1964, Sgt. Mitchem and Lance Cpl. Dan Gibson were in a briefing with Capt. Swanson, the company Intelligence Officer, and Gunny Sgt. Davis about an upcoming mission. The mission's location was about 30 miles northeast of our base of operation.

Sgt. Mitchem and Lance Cpl. Gibson make up one of four Marine sniper teams operating out of this base. Two companies of U.S. Marines at base have the job of being military advisors and weapon instructors for the South Vietnamese Army and Marines.

Everyone at base except the sniper teams is fully involved in providing training for the South Vietnamese forces in American battle tactics, equipment, and weapons use.

Capt. Swanson and Gunny Davis were providing details on a unit of Viet Cong fighters who were terrorizing villagers that were friendly to South Vietnamese forces. Our recon reports indicated that more than 80 villagers suffered rape or murder in a month. These VC would hit hard and fast, and then disappear into the jungle.

Reports said that this same group was responsible for recent attacks on the South Vietnamese Army at night, slipping into the Army's bases and blowing up supplies. Other times, they set up ambush points or a series of booby traps in the jungle within a 30-mile radius of Saigon. Our orders came down from the top brass to eliminate this group.

Capt. Swanson was not cutting any corners. He was flat out telling us this mission was going to be extremely dangerous and not easy to accomplish. We would be up against a well-trained and highly-disciplined group of about 60 heavily-armed regular VC fighters.

Vietnam, The Making of a Sniper

"This group uses battle tactics similar to ours," Gunny offered.

Both Gunny and Capt. Swanson repeatedly stated that they wished they had more information on this unit. Very little info was available about this band, other than the bloody trail of death they were leaving behind wherever they attacked.

We were to jump off at 1340 hours this afternoon. A chopper would carry us to their last victims' village, just 17 miles northeast of our base. The attack on that village came late yesterday afternoon just before dark. Our first order for the mission — "Before dark, pick up the Viet Cong trail leading away from the village."

"We had better be on our toes, this time," I said to Dan as we walked back to our area.

"We always are," Dan replied.

Then, we both got lost in the job that lay ahead, thinking about what to carry on the trip. We were told to expect an extended stay of up to 15 days in the field. This meant we would get an airdrop of supplies. I preferred this did not happen, but we had no control over it unless the mission was successful sooner than expected. A chopper coming in low to a DDZ (designated drop zone) would alert any enemy force in the area of our presence. This part worried me. The VC would know these dropped supplies designated for American or South Vietnamese soldiers indicated their enemy was located near the DDZ.

So far, we had been successful on missions by staying undetected. Only when we strike a target would we expose our presence in an area. The Viet Cong are worthy opponents on the battlefield. They are good fighters and excellent trackers, and if either Dan or I became careless, our butts would get shot off.

My method is to fight them on my terms, not theirs; and, in doing that, we just might be lucky enough to survive and live to tell about it.

At 1330 hours, Dan and I were sitting in the chopper with our gear. The rain began to subside. This would be a short 20-minute ride, and the chopper would set us down within 100 yards of the village. Hopefully, this would allow us a little time to find their trail before dark.

Dan and I began slipping into the village from opposite directions. The rain clouds had turned the sky a grayish color, and evening shadows showed the ugly work of the Viet Cong in the village. There were burned huts and dead bodies of six village leaders — each was tied and hanging upside down from three palm trees. Their heads severed from their bodies lay in a neat row at the foot of the trees for the villagers to see.

There were also six naked corpses of the leaders' wives or daughters, each repeatedly raped and then shot in the head. The VC had left a clear message for this village. Swift punishment and death would be the cost for anyone collaborating against them. I saw only a small handful of villagers, and none would approach the village or us. They remained hidden in the jungle. Dan and I split up again to begin searching for any sign that showed which way the VC had gone.

It took another 30 minutes to locate the direction the VC had taken when they left the village. It appeared that about a dozen fighters had raided the village. The only sign that we found was a few broken plants lying on the jungle floor by a group of people in a hurry heading west. The tracks were from sandals, and the villagers were barefooted.

Shortly, Dan and I were slipping along very slowly on this small trail in the jungle. I was on the point, watching for booby traps and any additional sign that the VC might have left behind. We had traveled about 300 yards west from the village when I spotted the second sign — a single cartridge from an AK-47 rifle was lying in the middle of the path. Possibly, one of the VC had been trying to reload his weapon, after their attack on the village and had accidentally dropped the cartridge.

Daylight was fading and I knew we would be taking undue risks if we continued following them now. I eased away from the trail some 40 yards and found a small clearing where we could get some rest. Tomorrow morning at first light, we would resume tracking the fighters. Dan and I slept in shifts. I took the first watch and woke him at midnight. I told him to rouse me at 0445 hours.

After eating a hearty meal of cold ham and eggs, I was ready to resume our task of tracking the fighters who raided the village. Easing back onto the trail at daybreak, I was eager to begin trying to catch up to the village raiders. About 500 yards later, we noted the fighters had entered a field of elephant grass. Their trail, still leading westward, was not too difficult to follow. A half mile later, they exited the grass and turned north. I estimated they had a 20-plus hour head start on us.

Suddenly, I froze! *"Booby trap!"* my brain screamed.

Three inches in front of my foot, a thin trip wire stretched across the trail. My eyes followed the wire slowly to a thicket just four yards away.

"Booby trap," I whispered as I pointed to the wire. Dan froze. Slowly, I backed up two steps, then got down on my knees, and eased toward the thicket and peeked into it. There, tied to a stake, was an American made fragmentation grenade rigged to explode if anyone tripped the wire.

Slowly, I eased my right hand into the thicket and touched the grenade's pin, which was almost all the way out.

"Cut the trip wire," I said to Dan as I held the pin safely in place.

After the wire was cut, I pushed the pin all the way back into the grenade, rendering it harmless for now. Dan then cut the grenade loose from the stake and dropped it in his front jacket pocket for the time being.

I again moved forward slowly, hoping not to miss any other crafty traps. The fighters had left a surprise for anyone attempting to follow them — a gift from a dead South Vietnamese soldier no doubt. I was just lucky I saw the wire at my feet. We were also lucky the terrain had changed from elephant grass to low flatlands because less than 200 yards later, I discovered another trip wire on the trail. I signaled for Dan to ease up to my position.

"Look here," I said to Dan as I exposed the wire partially covered with moss, just a few inches above the ground. "I want you to carefully check it out," I said to Dan.

He eased his field pack off and put it on the ground behind him, and then he stepped carefully over the wire. Dan moved slowly, stopping 10 yards away. I could see him looking into the dense jungle growth very carefully.

Dan looked back at me and said, "Move back about 10 yards, Sarge."

When he saw that I had moved back the required 10 yards, Dan pulled his wire snips out and cut the wire holding the tension on the deadly trap.

"WHOOOM!" From nowhere a board propelled by a small tree trunk passed by me. It was moving so fast it was hard to see it clearly. But, if I had remained standing near the moss covered wire, I would have been impaled by three 2-foot sharpened sticks rammed through my guts. The board had been securely tied to a 4-inch tree trunk, which was pulled around and tied to a large stake in the ground. The trip wire would set the tree in motion like an arrow being released from a bow. The three 2-foot long bamboo spikes were tightly fitted into small holes carved into the board, and it would kill whoever it hit.

Two booby traps planted within 200 yards of each other — unusual and alarming. This second trick would disembowel any followers for sure. The design was crude, but deadly.

This group of fighters sure was trying to discourage anyone from following them. One more booby trap and I might look for another route myself. The bobby traps had now caused my body to really begin sweating. I was sweating hard now; and, my heart was really beating fast, making breathing difficult.

In a few minutes, I was OK and we were back on their trail. At 1400 hours, I signaled for us to stop. It was time to eat; my stomach was pleading for food. As Dan and I ate, we talked about the guys we were trailing. Both of us admitted these fighters were very professional.

Dan had asked if he could take the point, but I told him that was not necessary. Shortly, we were back on their trail. About an hour later, I saw we were approaching a large swamp. The trail led into the water. Several people had left footprints in the mud as they entered the swamp.

The further the fighters traveled away from the village, the more sign they were leaving. I knew there was only one sure way to follow their trail now. We would split up and take different routes around the swamp. It was so large that seeing across it was impossible.

I instructed Dan to meet me around on the far side. According to the map, this swamp was one-third of a mile wide and a mile in length. Setting our compasses, we moved out in different directions. I had instructed Dan to kill only if he had to — but 'no noise' was our best ticket to a successful mission.

One and one-half hours later, Dan met up with me on the opposite side of the swamp. I had not seen any sign where anyone had exited from the swamp. Dan said he had found their trail, about 100 yards back. After locating the trail, we followed it again north. The tracks suddenly disappeared; but after some backtracking, I saw that the fighters had moved off the trail and had made a dry camp in a small clearing.

This is where they had rested and slept last night. I looked at my watch; it was now 1610 hours. We had gained one hour on them today. I felt sure they had left at first light, just as we had this morning. There was still good light left, and I wanted to use it to gain more time on them.

At 1745 hours, I found a safe spot for us to rest near an intersection of trails. There had been no booby traps since this morning. If none were discovered by mid-morning tomorrow, maybe I could pick up the pace and close the distance. After eating and discussing tomorrow's options, I instructed Dan to take the first watch and wake me at 2400 hours. I would be waking him at 0445 hours in the morning if everything went as planned. I was so tired, I didn't want to eat anything — I only wanted rest.

The booby traps had put a tremendous amount of mental stress on me today. I had to really focus mentally, looking for the traps. After 12 hours of searching for booby traps, my brain was fried. Within 15 minutes, I was asleep.

* * * * * * *

Suddenly, I was awakened when a rough hand was clamped over my mouth. Startled, I tried to sit up but another strong hand kept me pinned to the ground. When my eyes focused, I saw that Dan was kneeling beside me, holding me down. He removed a hand from my chest and put it to his lips, signaling for me to remain quite. When I nodded my head that I understood, Dan removed his hand from my mouth.

Putting his face next to my head, he whispered, "A small party of VC fighters is sitting on the trail 40 yards away, taking a break or maybe bedding down for the night."

As I eased up from the ground, I whispered to Dan, "Let's get our gear and ease out the back door, now." In minutes, we were crawling, moving further away from the trail. Thirty minutes later, we had managed to crawl 100 yards. I stopped and waited for Dan who was 10 yards behind me.

"Now, let's walk slowly out of here," I said softly, just above a whisper.

By 0120 hours, I had circled and re-entered the trail a mile from where we had been camped. I decided to continue moving slowly west on the trail for an hour longer. At 0225 hours, I moved off the path and stopped.

"Let's try this place for a few hours," I said.

"Do you want to get some shut-eye, Sarge?" Dan asked.

"No!" I replied, "You get a few hours rest, I'll be OK."

I then settled down into a comfortable position and watched for other unwanted visitors. None showed — so at 0430 hours, I woke Dan.

At first light, we were again tracking the village raiders. When 0900 hours arrived without sighting a booby trap, I began to pick up the pace. I knew we would be getting close to the fighters by late afternoon if I kept up this pace.

I used the Apache Indians' pace — a rapid stride that was short of a run, yet much faster than a walk. I had taught Dan how to effortlessly glide over the ground using this method. We now used this smooth gate to cover distances quickly, while at the same time conserving energy and moving quietly.

Over a long distance, the Apache would outrun a horse in the desert southwest areas. Here in Vietnam, using this gate after making a hit on a designated target had saved Dan and me a few times already from capture by the Viet Cong.

At 1400 hours, I stopped for just the second time since setting the pace to relax our legs and let our lungs get a break. It was time to feed our stomachs. I packed energy foods into my mouth — peanut butter and a candy bar. This gave me a quick energy boost, which I needed to continue this fast pace. Also, I opened and ate a meal, then drank a small amount of water.

Looking over at Dan, I saw he too had eaten two small cans of peanut butter and two candy bars. He was now sipping on water. We buried our food cans and papers.

"Ready to go?" I asked Dan.

"Whenever you are," he answered.

So I began to get my gear back on, picked up my Weatherby, and eased back to the path. Once again I began to pick up the pace until I had reached the desired stride that would close the distance between the squad of VC fighters and us, possibly within a few hours.

One thing I had to prevent was coming upon them too suddenly. I did not want to give our position away. The last thing I wanted was for that squad to know that Dan and I were on their trail.

At 1600 hours, I stopped to discuss our options with Dan. We settled upon a plan. I suggested that we put on natural camouflage, plus paint our face, neck, and hands before we started back on their trail. Forty minutes later, we were ready.

We began tracking the squad again. We had not gone much more than a mile when I saw the remains of their mid-afternoon campsite. Still visible on the jungle floor were about a dozen imprints where men had sat down and rested.

This proved they were a few hours ahead of us, and we would have to quicken the pace again to catch up to them before nightfall. If I set the same gate as earlier, we would catch up with them soon — but, this could get tricky!

If I were the VC squad leader, I would have a rear guard a few hundred yards behind the main column. The rear guard would be a good man, who would detect anyone trying to approach the column from the rear. I also would set out sentries on my flanks, thereby providing protection from surprises from these directions as well. But, I'm not him, and all I know is that Gunny Davis said they used tactics similar to ours.

The sun was beginning to set on the horizon, and I had not seen hide or hair of them yet. Their trail was still visible upon the ground — just a footprint here and there, and sometimes it was broken twigs on the ground or a broken plant leaf. I had stopped to study the surrounding ground when I heard something up ahead of us. I froze! Whatever it was, it was just about 40 yards or so away.

Signaling to Dan, I motioned for him to move 20 yards to my right and stay there. When Dan was in position, I moved off very slowly toward whatever was up ahead. My heart was beginning to beat faster. It usually does this whenever I'm trying to slip up on an unsuspecting target or enemy fighter, or when unknown things promise excitement and adventure.

I moved like a lizard, very quietly, watching my every movement to ensure that I made no noise to give my position away. Closer and closer I crawled toward the sound. I stopped when I realized it had been a few minutes since I had last heard the sound.

After waiting 10 minutes without hearing a sound again, I decided to ease closer.

I moved another 10 yards and stopped again. Again I was listening for any sound that might give me a clue to where it was located. Absolutely nothing! No sound!

I decided to stay where I was for the time being. I eased my head up to see through a large leaf plant. I was now trying to spot any movement. I saw nothing and eased my head back down very slowly; so if someone were watching the back trail, they wouldn't spot my movement.

Another 15 minutes passed without hearing a sound. I decided to move ahead again.

Whoever had made the noise was close by, unless they had already left the area. I had to find out who was out there without getting Dan and me shot up in the process.

This time I moved more to my left, slowly inching my way through the jungle. I had moved another 20 yards when I spotted a slight movement up in a large tree just ahead. I froze! Then I began dissecting that tree, inch by inch, until I saw the sentry about 25 feet up a big old palm tree. He was closely watching the trail that Dan and I were using. He was armed with an AK-47 and had a large knife on his side. There was some camouflage on him, but not much. He had put a clump of small palm leaves on his back. His clothes blended in well with the bark on the tree's trunk, and the growth of leaves made it hard to spot him. But he had moved, and I saw the slight movement of him relocating his leg.

The sound I had heard was probably him climbing the tree. The guard had climbed up into the large tree so he could see a greater distance. I looked at all the other trees large enough to hold a man in this area. I knew the person I saw was the only one up a tree. Now, I began to question what my next actions would be. *How was I going to take him out without making any noise. Was I going to attempt it alone?*

Dust was beginning to settle upon the jungle, and I knew it would be dark soon. I would wait for darkness. Shortly, it was pitch black. I knew the sentry would not be able to see me now, so I slowly eased back the way I had come.

As I approached Dan's position, I gave a low native bird whistle. This would keep me from getting my butt shot off by my partner. Dan returned the call to let me know I could safely come into the small area where he was hiding. I sat near Dan and in a soft voice relayed to him the position of the palm tree VC sentry.

We discussed ways to take out the sentry, and then after a few minutes decided on the best option available to us that posed the least amount of risk. Working as a team, tomorrow morning at first light we would take out the sentry in the tree.

We eased further away from the sentry, going deeper back into the jungle. Later, we ate a good meal from our C-rations and again buried our trash. Dan and I took turns resting for a couple of hours, and then we checked our gear again to make sure only what was absolutely needed would be taken along. Nothing that could make noise was taken, except our weapons.

One hour before daylight, Dan and I were easing toward the rear guard. We moved slowly toward the large tree where the sentry was posted. I just hoped he was still in the tree. As dark as it is, Dan and I could crawl within 10 feet of him and neither of us would know the other was there.

In 30 minutes, both Dan and I were within a dozen yards of the tree. Waiting!

This would be a perfect situation in which a crossbow could be the weapon of choice. It's quiet, quick, accurate, and yet very deadly. The crossbow is something I want to ask the Gunny about after I returned from this mission.

It still was so very dark that I could not see Dan who was lying within 10 yards of me. Soon daylight would come, and then we would take the rear guard out. As soon as light began breaking the eastern sky, I was looking up into the big palm, trying to locate the sentry. As it got lighter, I discovered the sentry was not in the tree.

I moved over to Dan's position and said, "The hen has flown the henhouse."

"Where do you think he is?" Dan asked.

"He's gone! So, let's go back and get our gear," I replied.

One hour later, we discovered the squad of VC had left sometime after midnight, moving on west. They had a large base camp somewhere around here, and just maybe they would lead us to it.

As I gave Dan the signal to move out and once again follow their trail, I surmised our targets were five to six hours ahead of us again.

Around 1330 hours, I stopped at the edge of a large swamp. The VC tracks showed they had entered the swamp here. I did not think it safe for both Dan and me to be in the swamp at the same time, so I instructed him to ease around the swamp and meet me on the other side with our packs. Dan was entrusted with the care of my gear until we met up again on the other side of the swamp.

After Dan began moving off toward the southwest, trying to skirt around the swamp, I eased myself into the murky waist deep waters. There was a lot of slime on top of the water, and the bottom had a lot of silt and rotted fallen trees, which made walking almost impossible at times. I tripped and went under a few times in the first hundred yards, and was glad now that Dan was carrying my heavy pack. I was aware that I was an easy target here in the waist-to-chest deep swamp.

I moved very slowly, keeping the Weatherby resting upon my shoulder and my finger near the trigger at all times — just in case.

Deep down inside I knew that if I was ambushed out here in the swamp, most likely I wouldn't make it out alive because in this situation one's mobility is greatly reduced. There are few places to hide except under water, which is not always the best hiding place unless one can swim like a fish with about 20 pounds of clothing, weapon, and ammo attached to you.

Twenty-five yards ahead of me was a group of trees large enough to provide some concealment and cover in case of a sudden ambush. My body wanted to hurry and get to the trees, but my brain would not let my body rush forward. Slow and safe was what my brain kept repeating. Slowly I sunk down lower into the dark murky waters, allowing only my neck and head to be exposed above the water surface. My rifle was held just above the surface in my right hand. My finger was still close to the trigger, but not touching it. I was hoping not to stumble on debris on the bottom and make a lot of noise. This would let any Viet Cong nearby know that someone was trailing them.

Suddenly, as a loud splashing noise came from my left, I moved quickly bringing my weapon to my shoulder as I eased upward and turned in one graceful motion. There, standing just back in the trees in belly deep slimy water was a water buffalo. It had become startled by my presence. My heart was beating so wildly, it had almost come out of my chest. I looked at my hand, and it was still shaking.

I reached the security of the trees without further incident. Once in the trees, it became apparent that there was a trail or old roadbed that twisted through the cluster of trees growing out in the water.

More than an hour later, I exited the swamp — my clothes covered with the yellowish green slime. I eased away from the swamp and found a spot where I could see Dan when he came by; so I sat down and rested. I removed my green sneakers and green socks, and then poured the water out of the shoes and turned them upside down to finish draining. I then turned my attention to my wet socks. Holding them together, I squeezed as much water as I could from my socks, then I laid them out in the grass to dry.

A small sound behind me made me reach for the rifle, but before my hand could grab it, a foot kicked my weapon away. I turned to see a Viet Cong with his rifle pointed at my head. He motioned for me to lie down on my stomach. I eased over on my stomach and was now lying face down. He wanted my hands behind my back. I didn't respond as quickly as he wished, so he rammed the barrel of the rifle into my ribs, causing intense pain in that area. He quickly tied my hands behind my back, and then motioned for me to stand up. As soon as I stood he hit me in the chest with the butt of his rifle, knocking me back to the ground. Grabbing me by my hair, he yanked me to my feet. He took my knife strapped to my leg and then picked up my Weatherby and motioned for me to move off toward the northeast with him following close behind me.

For the first time since he surprised me, I had time to think as I walked ahead of this warrior from Vietnam. My first thoughts were on Dan. *What was his fate? Was he also captured? Or worst yet, was he dead?* My captor kept poking me in the back with his rifle.

I looked down at my feet and realized I wasn't wearing any shoes. I turned to glance back at my captor to see if he had my shoes, but all I got for my effort was another hard jab in my ribs from his rifle barrel.

We had walked for about an hour when suddenly we entered a clearing and a village. My Viet Cong captor now began to shout, and the villagers came out to see him and his captive. A suddenly sharp pain hit me between my shoulder blades as my captor hit me viciously with the butt of his rifle, causing me to go sprawling face first into a mud puddle. I was dragged through the mud over to a one-room hut near the center of the village. An old woman held open a bamboo door for us to enter. As I got to my feet and stooped to go through the doorway, my captor shoved me headlong into the dirt floor. He quickly tossed a grass rope over a large bamboo beam located overhead. My body was subjected to immediate pain as my hands were pulled up high behind my back toward the beam. He checked his knots; and satisfied he had me hog-tied, left the hut.

* * * * * * *

Dan had completely circled the swamp without seeing the Sergeant. He began to really get worried. Sgt. Mitchem would have been waiting unless something or someone kept him from it. Dan began easing back around the swamp for the second time. Now he would begin searching for sign of a struggle. Moving very slowly, Dan eased through the jungle toward where the Sergeant should have exited the swamp. Three quarters of an hour later, Dan found Mitch's shoes and socks, but there was no sign of the Sergeant anywhere. Dan knew that Mitch had exited from the swamp at this point, but what happened after that was the mystery.

Dan began studying the terrain very carefully, the way he had been taught to do by Sgt. Mitchem. He was looking for anything that could give him a clue as to what happened here. Dan could tell that there had been a scuffle close to where he found the shoes. Moving 10 yards, then 20 yards out and covering a complete circle, Dan began analyzing the landscape — piece by piece — trying to decipher what had happened to the Sergeant.

He was some 20 yards from where the shoes were found when he came across a couple of footprints. One had the traditional sandal shape, and the other had to be the Sergeant's because it was a partial barefoot print in the dirt. The tracks led off toward the northeast. Dan returned to Mitch's shoes and socks, picked them up, tied them to his belt, and headed off in a northeastern direction, following the tracks.

Dan still kept his composure and kept his pace slow and easy, even though he knew the Sergeant was in trouble.

There were times when Dan thought the Sergeant was leaving him signs to follow. He would find dirt kicked up by the barefooted tracks every once in a while. Dan slowly moved toward the northeast, intent on finding any sign left for him to follow.

It would be dark within the hour, but Dan had to keep tracking as long as he could see any sign. Soon, it was hopeless; darkness settled upon the jungle.

Dan located a good thicket to bed down for the night, just a short ways from the trail he was following. He had stuck only a few candy bars, some crackers and a small container of peanut butter in his pockets when he began searching for the Sergeant. Now, knowing this small amount of food may have to last him another day or two, he just ate one candy bar and curled up into a tight ball and dosed, while waiting for daylight and a chance to find Sgt. Mitchem.

* * * * * * *

As I hung from the bamboo rafter, with just my toes touching the dirt floor of the hut, I began to evaluate my situation carefully. Here I was strung up like a hog for slaughter and no way to get loose. I had tested the ropes that secured me to the bamboo pole by letting my entire weight swing on it briefly. The rope was strong, and the bamboo would not give an inch. I would have to find another way out of this predicament.

Shortly the door opened, and my captor and two other VC entered the hut. I could tell they were all drunk, and there was a lot of talk and bragging on their part. The younger VC grabbed my hair and jerked my head around toward him. Then the young VC hit me in the face and laughed real loud. The open-handed blow busted my lip, and I could taste my blood. One of them left the hut, then re-entered a few minutes later with a piece of bamboo about as big as my arm and maybe three feet in length. The bamboo was stuck behind my arms and my biceps were tied to the bamboo rod. The rope was then tied to the bamboo, and the three of them hoisted my body off the floor.

As I spun around and around, they repeatedly hit me again and again. For the better part of an hour, these three VC poked and slapped me around and drank rice wine. They boasted and bragged to each other until they each passed out from the wine.

My shoulder blades felt as if they had been pulled out of my back. Hanging suspended a few inches above the dirt floor put a tremendous amount of pressure on my shoulders and arms. My mouth tasted of dried blood, and my left eye was almost swollen shut from the beating; yet, I knew I was lucky to be alive.

As hard as I tried, I could not budge these knots. I was hurting and tired, but I couldn't let myself fall asleep. I had to figure a way out. *Think! Think!* I told myself. There has to be a way out, and I have to find it before these three awaken from their drunken sleep. Dawn was peeking through the grass roof, and everything was quite in the village. The whole village was asleep. I was the only person who had not slept at all last night.

A dog barked, and then it too was quite. I looked around the hut — there were no windows, and the only way in and out was through the one door I had been shoved through yesterday afternoon. There was absolutely nothing in this one-room hut but the three drunken Viet Cong fighters and me. I was helpless to do anything except hang there and wait for them to wake up.

Around midmorning my captor and his two buddies staggered to their feet and went outside. Maybe an hour later, the door opened and the older VC came in and brought me a bowl of rice with a small piece of meat in it. He held the bowl up to my face, and I gulped the food down as best as I could. He made no effort to feed me, other than holding the bowl at an angle for me to get my mouth into it and eat the rice. Before I finished eating the rice, he just dropped the bowl and smiled, then kicked the bowl against the wall and went outside.

* * * * * * *

Dan had found the village that the tracks led to — now, he must find a vantage point from where he could locate the Sergeant. Easing up into a large tree, Dan found that he would be able to see almost every building. Two hours after climbing the tree, Dan saw three men dressed in the traditional black pants and shirt exit from a hut in the center of the village. None carried weapons, and all three appeared to be in a drunken state. They would stagger and laugh loudly; then they entered another hut. An hour later, one of the men came out of the hut carrying a small object in his hand. He had gone back into the hut that he and the other men had first exited.

Dan watched the Viet Cong come back outside and move off toward the larger hut where his buddies were. Dan hoped the hut the VC had just visited would be the one where the Sergeant was being held. He stayed in the tree and watched and waited for the chance to find Sgt. Mitchem. He believed the Sergeant was still alive and was a captive in one of these huts. But he couldn't go asking if anyone had seen an American. He would have to know more before he ventured into the village after dark.

When the three Viet Cong came out of the large hut just before noon, they each had their weapons; the taller one had Mitch's Weatherby slung around his shoulders. The other two left the village, moving north into the jungle. The taller man picked up a gourd and poured water into it then he re-entered the same hut the three had just exited — the same hut the lone VC had visited earlier this morning. That had to be where the Sergeant was held captive.

Now, that Dan was certain he knew where Mitch was, he begin to formulate a plan for getting him out of the village.

* * * * * * *

I spun around on my ropes as my captor entered the room. He walked toward me holding something in his hand. Stopping five feet from me, he poured some of the water onto the floor, then moved closer and held the gourd up to my busted mouth for me to drink. As I strained to drink the water, I noticed he was carrying my Weatherby around his shoulders and my K-Bar was strapped to his waist. I wanted to cut his throat or choke him to death with my bare hands, but all I could do was wait for my chance.

He left the hut again, but soon returned with three of the village men. They tied a larger piece of bamboo pole up under my armpits, then tied my upper arms, still behind my back, to this pole, and cut my hands loose. They removed the smaller bamboo pole that had been stuck between my arms yesterday and then the three village men hoisted me up off the floor again. I found myself again dangling close to six inches above the dirt floor. The rope was tied to the larger pole under my armpits. This position put tremendous strain on my shoulders and upper arm muscles, which supported my entire weight as I hung there.

After making sure the knots were tight, they left the hut. I felt lost and knew I was in a tough situation. I'm not very good at praying, but this was a time to ask for help. I could do nothing to free myself, so, I had to gather some inner strength and pray, and then I kept praying for a miracle.

* * * * * * *

The three Viet Cong fighters were from this village. Capturing the American was very big for Hoa Min Ghan, the middle brother of the three. The American would bring a great reward for Ghan and the entire village. He would get a whole year's salary for the capture and would be promoted to a leadership position in his unit. This morning while eating after the three had left the American in the hut, they began to talk about how to collect the reward offered by the NVA. The soldiers from North Vietnam had visited their village two months ago. They had come dressed as Viet Cong fighters and were offering big rewards for the capture of South Vietnamese or American soldiers.

Hoa Min Ghan sent his brothers to a large Viet Cong camp 11 miles north of the village to return with many fighters so the American could be turned over to them.

* * * * * * *

Dan stayed in the tree until it was dark and then slowly made his way toward the hut that he was sure held Sgt. Mitchem. Staying close to the grass huts as he moved into the village, Dan moved like a panther stalking its prey. Slowly he moved toward the hut, stopping at times to allow villagers to pass by without seeing him.

Upon reaching the rear of the hut, Dan lay along its grass and bamboo wall, peeking inside after opening a small hole in the side of the hut with his knife. Dan saw the Sergeant suspended above the dirt floor. The Sergeant was the only person in the room. The taller VC was outside drinking rice wine with some of the villagers. They were maybe 30 yards from this hut. Dan had carefully slipped around them.

As I was dangling from the bamboo pole, I heard a noise behind me and twisted my body so I could see what was happening. I saw a knife cutting the ties on a couple of poles, then in English came a low whisper, "Sarge, it's me!"

Minutes later, Dan stepped through the opening he'd just made. Moving swiftly to my side, he cut the rope that had me dangling above the floor. He lowered me to the ground and cut my arms free. Dan then helped me to my feet and led me to the opening he had cut in the rear wall.

I could hardly move because my body was numb from my waist down. But, with Dan's help, both of us made it outside. Once outside, we both began to crawl toward the jungle some 50 yards away. We had to get past three more huts before reaching the safety of the jungle.

The feeling was slowly coming back into my feet and legs. If we could just reach the jungle before I was discovered missing, we would have a fighting chance. The last two huts showed no life signs, so Dan and I eased to our feet and safely slipped past them into the jungle. Once there, we continued moving with Dan helping me along.

"Sarge, let me know when you can walk on your own," Dan said.

"You'll be the first to know, good buddy," I replied.

Dan supported most of my weight and helped me stay on my feet by having me lean on him. We had moved about 200 yards into the jungle, when suddenly, rifle shots were heard from the direction of the village.

"They know I'm missing," I exclaimed.

"Sounds like they might be a little upset," Dan wryly replied.

We continued moving toward the southwest as fast as I was able to walk with Dan's help. The Viet Cong fighter, Hoa Min Ghan, gathered 10 men from the village that could track and promised them part of his reward, if they helped him recapture the American.

Hoa Min Ghan thought the American had found a way to free himself and escaped. He was also sure the American couldn't be very far away.

Daylight found Dan and the Sergeant still moving southwest. They were now more than three miles from the village. Checking the map and compass, Dan knew they were about two miles from the swamp where the Sergeant was captured. He also knew that their supplies and gear were hidden back there. Dan knew he would have to leave the Sergeant long enough for him to return to the swamp for their gear and the rest of their weapons.

After securing the Sergeant in a good thicket and leaving him a .45 caliber pistol, Dan left.

It took Dan three hours to reach the swamp. Dan eased toward the western edge of the swamp, where earlier he had stashed their gear before searching for Mitch. Dan knew that the VC may have already found the gear or they might have someone watching it. Either way, he was playing it safe. He would expect the worst, and hope for the best. When Dan was within 50 yards of where he had hid their gear, he stopped to listen for any unusual sounds in the jungle that might provide a clue to anyone being there.

Hearing nothing unusual, Dan slowly eased forward. Once he was at the stashed gear, he realized it could also be booby-trapped; so very slowly, he inspected the gear. Half an hour later, Dan was satisfied that it wasn't bobby-trapped, and he gathered it up and headed back.

Four hours later, Dan was back with the Sergeant, and he had brought all their gear. When Dan saw that I was moving around like my old self, he asked, "Which way do we go from here?"

"We'll angle west, and try to pick up the squad's trail again — that's the general direction the VC squad was headed when I was surprised back at the swamp," I replied.

After eating a nice meal and washing it down with good clean water, I laid back for a few moments in the tall grass, thinking about the past 24 hours, feeling very lucky to be alive. Thankfully, I had a partner who had risked his life to save my butt — again!

* * * * * *

The afternoon shadows were beginning to appear. It would be pitch dark within the hour. There was a large thunderstorm moving our way, and the rain would be coming shortly. We had to get moving now. I took the lead, and Dan followed about 10 yards behind me, carrying the PRC-77 radio, along with other gear.

When darkness made it impossible to move quietly, we stopped and made a cold camp. As lightning danced across the darkening skies, I suggested that we erect a sturdy lean-to type shelter that would provide some protection from the coming wind and rain. In a short time, Dan and I had cut some wood from a nearby group of trees to build our frame for the lean-to. We gathered palm leaves and large looking banana leaves and overlaid them to try and make the shelter as dry as possible. We had kept the front of the lean-to low in order to provide greater protection from the rain and wind.

We had just put our ponchos on, stored the equipment and radio, and crawled under the lean-to when the rain began coming down hard, with a vicious wind kicking up. We lay under the shelter looking out at the jungle, waiting for the storm to pass, but this storm was here to stay — it seemed personal. It didn't want to go away, just here to cause more misery for us.

Both Dan and I were soaked to the bone within two hours. Nothing was dry!

But, the storm became both our friend and our enemy. As our friend, it washed out our tracks and erased any sign we might have left that the VC trackers might follow.

As our enemy, it was likewise washing away any sign and tracks of the VC squad we had hoped to locate. This storm was a bad one with high winds, lightning, and heavy rains. A Monsoon! It pounded us for 15 straight hours.

I knew that the only sensible thing we could do was request a chopper to pick us up and return to base and just wait for the VC squad to attack again. We couldn't possibly raise anyone on the radio during this storm. But, we had to try! All Dan got was static on every frequency he tried, so calling headquarters would have to wait until the weather cleared.

Hours later, I glanced over at Dan's large sleeping form. He was the best friend I ever had. Someday, after we both left Vietnam, I wanted to go visit with him and his family, and tell them what a great son they had, and let them know what kind of a Marine and personal friend he was.

After the storm passed, Dan managed to raise headquarters on the radio. Capt. Swanson agreed about canceling the mission, and we selected a designated time and pickup point; three miles further south of our present position, the chopper would pick us up and fly us back to base.

We carefully slipped out of the area, first by moving southwest, then turning southeast, and finally south to our pickup point. We arrived one hour before the chopper was due; and after carefully searching the surrounding area for VC and finding none, we hunkered down to wait for the helicopter.

* * * * * * *

Nearly two weeks after Dan and I returned to base, the VC squad we had hunted attacked again — this time a South Vietnamese Army supply unit. Capt. Swanson assigned the mission to another sniper team, so Dan and I took a few days of R&R in Hong Kong with Gunnery Sgt. Davis and several other Marines.

I had to get assigned the other Weatherby 300 and another K-bar knife. It took nearly two whole days to get the new rifle shooting the way I wanted it to — like a comfortable friend.

In mid-December, Gunny Davis informed me that Dan and I would soon have an intelligence meeting with the brass. Gunny would not say much about the upcoming meeting, except that it would be another long field trip — this time a lot farther north.

CHAPTER 10

At 0412 hours on the morning of December 20, 1964, Lance Cpl. Gibson and Sgt. Mitchem were being airlifted by helicopter to an area where northern Cambodia and southern Laos meet South Vietnam. This area was another hotbed for Viet Cong activity. The triangle of countries provided the North Vietnamese Communists with a major route with which to transport supply shipments. Supplies were being transported down the Ho Chi Minh Trail for the Viet Cong Communists fighting in the south. This route has kept them supplied with weapons, ammunition, food, clothing, and medical supplies since the fighting began.

Neither Dan nor I spoke on our nearly two-hour chopper flight from base to a location northwest of the city of Pleiku. Pleiku is west-southwest of Da Nang. From there, we would head out on foot for the mountains and the Ho Chi Minh Trail. We both were very quiet and our thoughts were personal.

* * * * * *

My thoughts were on our last two missions, when Dan and I went into Cambodia after Commissioner Thayn and we took on the Viet Cong 514th Battalion. Dan was hospitalized for a week with his wounds. He received the Purple Heart for wounds received during that mission and was promoted to Lance Cpl.

Me — I spent less than two days in the hospital and I got light duty for a week. My right hand and wrist healed up nice. I received treatment as an outpatient since my wounds were not that serious. Upon Dan's release from the hospital, he and I flew to Clark AFB in the Philippines for a week of R&R. Dan spent a happy week with Kathy, who flew over from the States. They were married the day after we arrived by the base Chaplain.

Me, I got lost; they didn't need me around! I spent a lot of time sightseeing and lounging around the pool at a first class hotel in Manila — soaking up the sun, catching up on my sleep, and eyeballing the cute girls in their bikinis. Eyeballing is all I did. I was scared to death of having sex with these girls. I guess you could say I was more scared of them than any Viet Cong back in the jungles of Nam. My fear was catching some dreadful venereal disease that the doctors could not cure.

Shortly after our return from R&R, we were given the assignment to track and eliminate a Viet Cong terrorist squad. On this mission, I managed to get myself captured, and rescued, and we never even fired a shot at those guys before having to return to base.

Now, we would be engaging the enemy to derail the supply lines to the Communist Viet Cong fighters along the Ho Chi Minh Trail.

On this mission we each brought along our choice of C-rats, water purification tablets, five M-26 grenades, four bandoleers of claymore mines, 20 half-pound sticks of C-4 plastic explosives, plus blasting caps, timer detonators, and one M-57 electrical firing device, our weapons, and plenty of ammo, plus a waterproof bag for 10 flares and launcher.

I carry my .300 caliber Weatherby Magnum bolt-action sniper rifle with a Redfield special 9X scope. The Weatherby has a special built flash suppresser and fires a 173-grain soft point bullet. I also carry a .45 caliber semi-auto pistol, colt model 1911A. To finish out my personal arsenal, I strap K-Bar knife with an 8-inch razor sharp blade to my thigh. I lost my old trusty K-Bar knife and rifle when I was captured. But, I'll make do with the new Weatherby just fine.

Dan also carried an M-49 spotting scope, M-79 grenade launcher, 10 rounds each of white phosphorus (WP) and high explosive (HE), plus our PRC-77 radio. In addition, he carried his M-14 rifle, 200 rounds of ammo, and a K-Bar knife while in the field.

Each of us is generally loaded with 75 to 85 pounds of gear on our trips, which doesn't include the food necessary for long stays in the boonies in the weight total. I usually have the lighter load, while Dan is saddled with the remainder of the heavy equipment. Dan and I train hard for our missions, so taking this amount of equipment into the field becomes natural for us. These tools that we use each time we are in the field increase the chances for a successful mission and our survival.

* * * * * * *

When Dan first arrived in Vietnam, he was assigned to Company M as a weapons instructor. I was one of the sniper school instructors. As a weapons instructor, his personal training included a live fire range that new Marines and Army instructors had to traverse. Upon completion, these personnel would become instructors that taught and trained South Vietnamese troops how to use U.S. weapons. Dan's attention to details was outstanding. He was an expert rifleman, had a high IQ, and was willing to follow orders.

I asked Gunny Sgt. Davis, our senior NCO instructor for sniper training exercises, to check out Pfc. Daniel Gibson and consider him as a possible member of our special team. Gunny found Dan to be an excellent candidate and called Col. Bowers to request Dan's transfer into HQI. Gunny Davis got the word three days later that Pfc. Daniel Gibson was officially our man. Gunny asked me to drop by his office at 0730 hours the next morning and sit in on the meeting with Pfc. Gibson.

Gunny and I were having a cup of coffee when Pfc. Gibson reported. Gunny told Dan to just relax and said he wanted to ask him a few questions.

"Do you want to make a real difference in this war?" Gunny asked his first question.

"Yes, Gunny Sergeant," Gibson responded.

"Would you like to get off of guard duty and mess duty for the rest of your tour?" Gunny asked.

"Yes! I would," Dan answered enthusiastically.

Gunny then explained that both he and I thought Dan would make an excellent candidate as a spotter on a future sniper/recon team. Gunny explained in detail how the spotter's mission should work and stated, although there was great risk at times, the rewards were just as great. Dan jumped at the chance. After Dan completed our Sniper School, he and I became one of the four Marine sniper teams selected.

* * * * * * *

My thoughts were jerked back to the present when I heard someone yelling at me above the roar of the engines.

"Three minutes till debarkation, Sergeant," the pilot barked.

I checked my watch; it showed 0547 hours. Daybreak was greeting us!

Dan and I began putting our gear on and checking our weapons. We exited through different side doors as soon as the chopper sat down. It was airborne again in seconds, leaving us lying in a field of tall grass that was surrounded by palm forests. Off to the west, we could see the mountain range and knew somewhere up there lay Laos and the Ho Chi Min Trail. To the east, the morning sun had not yet rose above the tree line.

Doing a slow crawl in single file through the tall grass for 10 minutes, we finally reached the cover the jungle provided. It was now time to camouflage our clothing with the natural undergrowth. We tried to blend into the landscape like a salamander. Our tiger strip fatigues blended in great, so we painted our face, neck, and hands black and green — and by adding natural moss and vines with leaves to our clothing, we became part of the jungle's landscape.

The easiest and best way to have success against a quality foe like the Viet Cong is to not let them know that you are in their area. Always, always move s-l-o-w and appear to be a part of the landscape to increase your chances of survival.

I instructed Dan to remember that we are in the VC's backyard, and they are the real experts on fighting a guerrilla war here in Vietnam. Our only hope of succeeding on a mission is completely surprising the Viet Cong. In order to do this, we have to become invisible, be quiet, and move very s-l-o-w when moving about their territory.

It should take at least three minutes to move 10 yards. There will be times when five minutes is required for moving 10 yards in order to remain undetected by the enemy. Our orders were to remove a North Vietnamese Army Captain and his staff, which would suspend their directing the flow of supplies down the Ho Chi Minh Trail for the Viet Cong. Two companies of VC fighters guard supplies that come out of Laos. Capt. Ngo Van Nhu, a North Vietnamese Army quartermaster, ordered, received, and distributed weapons and supplies to the Viet Cong 42nd Battalion operating in the northern sector of South Vietnam. Capt. Nhu's staff consisted of four NVA personnel trained in issuing and handling of military supplies. There is a small NVA guard attachment responsible for their security — no more than two dozen men and an officer.

The terrain for our mission is mostly mountains and jungle. We must get to our target unannounced, eliminate Capt. Nhu and his staff, destroy the supply warehouses, and make it back to base in one piece. Then, and only then, will we be able to determine if our mission is a success.

I checked and double-checked the natural camouflage we were putting on our fatigues. Finally, I was satisfied that we both looked as near to being part of the jungle as we could.

After finishing our camouflaging, I said to Dan, "Inform HQI of our location, and tell them we'll check in again at 2100 hours tonight."

"OK!" Dan said as he called HQI on the radio.

"'Delta-Two- Foxtrot' calling 'Hotel-Nine-Alpha'. Over,..."

"'Delta-Two-Foxtrot', this is 'Hotel-Nine-Alpha'. Over,..." the radio crackled.

"Our position is grid square Zulu-four 7135-4820. Will make contact again at 2100 hours. Over!" Dan spoke into the mouthpiece.

"'Delta-Two-Foxtrot', Roger on location and contact at 2100 hours. Good hunting guys."

"'Hotel-Nine-Alpha' signing off."

After getting our position to HQI, we saddled up and eased westward toward the mountains on the horizon. Skirting fields, I stayed in the jungle and moved ever so slowly toward our objective, bypassing villages and farms to avoid all Vietnamese contact. This is the only way to surprise the Viet Cong. It is most likely that a small percentage of the VC in this area is from these very villages and farms.

We had been moving steadily for nearly three hours when I spotted three VC fighters to our left, coming toward us. They were moving through a field of elephant grass, about 40 yards from the edge of the thin strip of jungle that we were using. If they turned in our direction once they reached the jungle, their travel path would be within just yards of us. We had skirted a village about an hour ago; and, more than likely, these three were going there.

The farmers or owners of the land in this area had left only 50 yards of jungle, with the remainder cleared on either side. This thin strip of jungle was what I was using to avoid detection. Now suddenly, we would have to share it with three VC fighters.

I signaled for Dan to remain silent and to follow me as I eased farther away from the elephant grass field and toward the far side of the jungle strip.

When the three fighters reached the jungle and turned toward the village, they were only 30 yards from our hiding place. With our weapons ready, we watched as they entered the jungle and started our way. They would almost have to stumble over us to know we were here. But, just in case, our weapons followed them until they were out of sight. I waited another 10 minutes without seeing or hearing anyone else; then we again began our slow trek toward the mountains.

By late afternoon, around 1645 hours, we had reached the mountains. I began looking for a safe place for us to rest — *avoid the trails, find something remote,* I silently thought, not wanting the worry of unexpected company dropping in on us. After a 20-minute rest in a secured area, we trudged deeper into the mountains while there was still light, searching for a safe place to bed down.

Before dark, I discovered the perfect place — a small winding cut back into the mountain measuring maybe 200 yards long and 75 yards wide with large boulders strewn along the floor for most of its length. One of the best features was a small opening at the very back, where we could slip through — quietly, if needed.

We made a cold camp — which is no fires or smoking to give our position away. After shedding our gear, we ate a healthy meal of C-rats and buried our trash, as we always do. Just before 2100 hours, I asked Dan to again call HQI with our position and get any updates they might have for us.

Dan turned the PRC-77 on, set his volume low, and began his calling.

"'Hotel-Nine-Alpha', this is 'Delta-Two-Foxtrot'. Over,..."

No response!

"'Hotel-Nine-Alpha', this is 'Delta-Two-Foxtrot'. Over," he tried again.

Still, no response!

Dan checked the radio to verify it was on 88.6 and he continued calling.

"'Hotel-Nine-Alpha', this is 'Delta-Two-Foxtrot'. Over,..."

This time, the radio sputtered.

"'Delta-Two-Foxtrot, go ahead, this is 'Hotel-Nine-Alpha'. Over,..."

Dan gave them our location coordinates and asked for any new info.

With no new updates, Dan informed HQI we would try to contact them each evening around 2100 hours. A radio receiver and transmitter located somewhere near Pleiku was assisting in getting our radio messages through.

We took turns sleeping four-hour shifts, with Dan taking the first watch, and then he would get some shut-eye whenever I took over at shift change. At 0200 hours, Dan touched my shoulder to wake me and said everything was peaceful and quite; we talked in whispers for a few minutes, then Dan sacked out.

After sitting and leaning against a boulder for about an hour, looking out into the night fog, my mind began to wander. I began thinking about home. It had been a long time since I had been home — the last time was just after I received my transfer from sea duty on the USS Constellation to Camp Lejeune, North Carolina.

* * * * * * *

I had gotten married in California. While in New York City, I had met a very nice girl named Peggy, and we saw a lot of each other. When the USS Constellation left New York City for its new homeport of San Diego, California, Peggy then moved out of the New York apartment she shared with her sister and brother-in-law and took a bus to Los Angles and stayed with relatives living there. Three months later, the ship arrived in San Diego and we soon began seeing each other again.

We got married after knowing each other for 13 months. We were married in Burbank, California, and moved into a nice small upstairs apartment. I would fly or drive up to Burbank every time the ship was back in port, and I could get a weekend pass. This was usually every other weekend because I had to pull guard duty twice a month when the carrier was in port.

A Marine friend from Florida, Peggy, and I drove from Sacramento, California, to Florida in 34 hours when I was transferred to Camp Lejeune, North Carolina. I took 10 days of leave time, and that was my last time home. My kid sister was still a little girl of eight when I enlisted. She is now 11, developing and growing up quick. Mom is still working at the BX cafeteria on Eglin AFB and living with grandmother in her house.

I do not think mom has ever been on more than two vacations in her life. She has always had to work to support herself and us two kids.

* * * * * * *

I was 15 and in the ninth grade when Colin received orders for transfer to a new duty station at Orlando AFB, right there in Orlando, Florida. My little sister was five years old. Mother gave up her civil service job at Eglin AFB hoping to get work at Orlando AFB once we were down there.

That went south in a hurry. Colin began drinking more and more. He was becoming almost unbearable at times. I was going to a junior high school, whose buildings were located in the middle of a huge orange grove, just outside the base. The government paid transportation/relocation costs for our mobile home from Niceville, Florida, to Orlando AFB, and set up our home in the base trailer park.

It really was pretty down there — beautiful large oaks and pine trees and palm trees growing wild around the trailer park. We were on the very last lot in the trailer park.

I walked out our front door, and down a single lane paved street for 100 yards to the back fence or property line for the Air Force Base. Someone had built steps up and over the fence for students to use to get safely to school.

About when I was finishing the ninth grade, Colin was really raving when he would come home drunk. Often, he would not make it home until maybe nine or ten o'clock at night. He would get off duty at 4P.M. and head to a bar just off base to get tanked up.

Once, I was sitting on the sofa doing some homework because mother was using the table to roll out cookies that she was baking. Colin came in thoroughly smashed! He could hardly stand on his feet. He looked at me with a cold hateful stare and said, *"What in the hell are you doing?"*

I said something like, *"I was trying to do homework until you came in."*

This set him into a wild rage, and he quickly grabbed me by my hair and said, *"When I speak to you, you say sir to me, you understand me."* Then he backhanded me across my face.

I was angry and afraid, but I stated, *"When you are drunk you think you can come home and beat up on us, but not anymore."*

He rushed me and caught me by surprise, pulling my head over to the end of the sofa. Colin had my neck in a death grip. There was maybe a foot between the wall and the end of the sofa. He pushed my head down between the sofa and wall and didn't stop until my head was against the floor. His fingers begin to squeeze my throat so hard that I found I couldn't breathe. He suddenly yelled and got off me. He was cussing mother, and he caught her and beat her because she had stuck the hot cookie sheet to his back, trying to get him off me.

He left within a few minutes and didn't come back home for two weeks. We were almost out of groceries, and mother came down with a severe infection and had to be hospitalized. For over a week, my sister and I ate oranges, grapefruits, and whatever food we could steal, beg, or borrow from the groves or our neighbors in the park.

We lived with my grandmother at her house in Niceville after returning from our episode with Colin down in Orlando. Months later, our trailer arrived, and we rented it out.

My grandmother raised four of us grandchildren. She was more like a mother to me than a grandparent. She raised my sister Vivian, my cousin Darlene, her brother Linton and me, while our moms worked. Grandmother had five daughters who she had raised by herself as a single parent.

* * * * * * *

My mind switched back to the present. I had been in Vietnam for nearly eight months.

I have four months until my DERSO from Vietnam. The <u>D</u>ate of my <u>E</u>stimated <u>R</u>eturn from <u>S</u>ervice <u>O</u>verseas is April 29, 1965. Once back in the States, I would probably be stationed at Lejeune again. I'm due to get out of the Marine Corps in September 1965.

Less than a year and I didn't know if leaving the Corps was really what I wanted to do.

Daybreak arrived and the heavy fog remained with us in this mountainous part of western Vietnam, so I knew it was not going to rain this morning. I glanced over at the sleeping form of Dan Gibson and surmised he must be dreaming about Kathy, for there was a faint smile upon his face as he slept.

I looked back toward the boulders in the middle of the cut, about 45 yards from where we had bedded down. I thought I saw movement, but your eyes can play tricks on you in a heavy fog. There! Another movement! They were like shadows, moving so quietly and yet so fast. Viet Cong! A dozen or more were moving in single file through this cut, slipping down toward its entrance.

I crawled toward Dan's sleeping form, not wanting him to awake suddenly and say something. I planned to gently put my hand over his mouth and whisper into his ear that VC was present. But before I could reach him, Dan sat up, and asked, "What time is it?"

A Viet Cong, out on the column's flank, heard Dan speak, and opened fire with his AK-47. Luckily, for Dan, the thick fog probably saved his butt. The VC on the flank misjudged the distance and his bullets ate chunks of granite from the boulders near Dan's leg. Had that VC raised his rifle barrel a tad more, Dan would have been history. As soon as the main force heard the shooting, they all took cover behind boulders and began showering our position with a huge amount of firepower.

With our concealment blown, we returned fire and began fighting for our lives. For maybe 10 minutes, we exchanged fire with the enemy. I was worried that they might try sending someone to flank us. If they were successful in cutting us off to the south, our goose would be pretty well cooked.

"Get the M-79 grenade launcher and use three WP rounds and concentrate on the main force," I ordered Dan.

I hoped that they would be content to escape this firefight without suffering heavy losses and leave us alone. They really did not know who we were or how large of a force we had, so I hoped they might just choose to depart. The first WP round fell just short of their position.

"Add 10 meters!" I said sharply.

The second round was just beyond their position. "Subtract five!" I shouted over the shooting. That third round exploded right on target.

Everything became quite, except for our own weapons firing. We stopped firing and a few minutes later, I eased toward the area where the main force had been and discovered they were gone. There were no bodies of wounded or dead. They had left, not making a sound, just ghosts in this morning fog. One minute they were there, the next minute they vanished into the fog. We hurriedly gathered our gear, slipped quickly up the cut, and exited through the "backdoor" entrance I noticed before selecting our campsite yesterday afternoon.

We had slowly slipped about 400 yards beyond the back entrance when I discovered where the VC had come from — they had spent at least part of the night just above our camp. We found a few freshly emptied food cans of fish were lying around the ground, as well as some cigarette butts they had left behind.

We continued on, keeping off the trails. The fog stayed until 0915 hours, then it burned off, and the sun actually tried to come out. The sun only stayed for an hour, then hid itself for the rest of the day. Rain began falling around noon. Within another hour, it was coming down in sheets — a hard, cold rain that made you shiver. I tried to keep the Weatherby under my poncho as much as possible.

Easing deeper into the mountainous jungle, I mused that each step put us farther from base; yet with each step, we were getting closer to getting home.

By 1500 hours, we had found what I thought was the Ho Chi Minh Trail. Through my field glasses, I could see across this deep gorge about 250 yards away what resembled a road through the mountains. Our position was a good bit higher than the road, so I settled in to watch for any movement along the passage. If any vehicle tried using it, we could surely hear it. As dark closed in, the rain let up.

Tonight, Dan and I would take turns watching the road. If this were the Ho Chi Minh Trail, somewhere up above us on the mountain or on another mountain we would find Capt. Nhu and his staff. I decided to sack out first tonight, so I turned in early.

****

I dreamed that Dan and I were both back stateside. Kathy, Dan, and I were going places and having fun. We had formed a business partnership and ventured into private business together. We had bought a real estate company and business was great. Kathy and Dan were expecting a baby, and they were on cloud nine. They asked me to be the baby's godfather. I was helping them paint and prepare the baby's bedroom. I could see how large Kathy was and knew it would not be much longer before the baby was born. Dan and I both were trying to satisfy her with the colors and decorations for the room. We were good friends working together to make that room and our business excel.

****

About 1040 hours, Dan woke me from my dream, saying he heard what he thought were troops marching on the muddy mountain road. As hard as we tried, we were unable to see anything through the glasses. The night was almost pitch black, too dark to see anything in these mountains even though the rain had stopped.

Come daylight, I intended to take a look around. I decided to leave Dan at camp to provide any backup cover I might need. I would go down through the gorge and up to the road; if there were troops last night, there would be tracks. At 0530 hours, I roused Dan, told him my plan as we ate a breakfast of ham and eggs, and was soon on my way. It took over an hour just to get into the gorge and almost another hour to climb back up to the road.

When I saw the road surface, it was muddy from the heavy rain yesterday; and, sure enough, the tracks indicated a large number of people had walked down the winding road during the night. There were footprints in the mud — lots of them. Dan had called this one right.

While here, I decided to look around a bit. Crossing the road and climbing up into the jungle above it, then slipping around slowly, I scoured the mountainside for signs of any enemy camps. Finding none and feeling I had covered it all, I worked my way back to Dan to tell him we would be climbing further up the mountain. We climbed for two hours in an effort to reach the top. I had hoped that vantage point would provide a better view of the road and the surrounding area. I thought we might be close to Laos; but here in the mountainous jungle, it is hard to tell exactly where you are.

At the top, we discovered three Viet Cong sentries occupying a small base camp located in a clearing. One was busy cooking some sort of brew over an open fire in a small pot. The other two were sitting on the ground not far away, their AK-47 rifle parts laid out in front of them on a shirt, awaiting cleaning. None of them was aware of us. I whispered to Dan that we would have to eliminate them. Dan was to take the cook and I would dispense with the other two.

Slowly, we crawled closer until we were at the edge of the clearing. They were still 20 yards away. On my signal, we both rushed toward the three surprised sentries.

The two who were cleaning their rifles, jumped to their feet as I rushed toward them. One turned and tried to locate a machete lying near his feet. The other sentry was trying to get his rifle together. I had the trusty K-Bar knife in my right hand. I knew I had to eliminate the sentry reaching for the machete first; otherwise, I could end up as their dinner. As I reached him, I took him down to the ground fast. The force of our bodies colliding caused him to miss the machete he had reached for at his feet. I made sure I did not miss, as I rammed the big knife deep into his chest as we collided. Hearing his muffled screams of pain in my ears assured me I had won the struggle with him.

Quickly, I rolled away from him and located the other sentry. He was frantically trying to get his rifle pieced together. As I moved toward him, he used the weapon as a ball bat, swinging wildly at me as he backed away. His eyes were wild with fear. Unknowingly, he backed toward Dan, who was standing close behind him. The sentry crumbled to the ground as the butt of Dan's M-14 crushed the back of his skull.

Looking beyond Dan, I saw the cook's dead body lying on the ground, his throat slashed. This brief fight had taken less than three minutes. I knew we had to hide the sentries' bodies because other VC would be arriving soon to relieve their watch. The mission would be compromised if their bodies were discovered before we located our targets.

I discovered that instead of seeing the road better at the top, our view from the mountaintop was actually hampered by large trees near where the road should have been. We must go back down the mountain and find a location to observe the road and any movement on it.

By late afternoon, we had not reached a position where we could view the roadway, so I began looking for a place to get a little rest. I found a small cave about a quarter of the way down from the top. Situated not far from the face of the mountain and about 20 yards from the edge of the cliff, it was large enough for us to sleep inside — about eight by six feet with a ceiling height of about four feet. The best part was it was dry, and it would keep us dry tonight.

From the cave opening, Dan radioed HQI to inform them of our skirmish with the sentries and the troop traffic on the road last night. He also reported we had not made contact with our target. HQI informed us of a suspected large build-up of troops for a major push called the 'TET' offensive. Although our intelligence didn't know just exactly when, the event was to be sometime soon. HQI said the supply route would play a primary role in 'TET'. They asked if we could take out a bridge or two to slow them down.

I told Dan that any bridges blown would have to be part of our business with Capt. Ngo Dinh Nhu and his staff — our primary target! The elimination of Capt. Nhu and staff would disrupt the flow of supplies for a little while. Blowing bridges would disrupt the supply line for a lot longer.

We just needed to find them — and fast, before the discovery of the three sentries' bodies. We dumped the three bodies into a deep crevice about 100 yards from the campsite. The location made it rather difficult to see the bodies from the top. Hopefully, this might grant us a little extra time. Again, we went over our mission and then got some much-needed rest.

As daybreak was lighting the eastern skies, I was kneeling at the cave entrance, listening to the sounds of nature. They were telling me everything around us was OK. I woke Dan up and we ate our usual feast of 'ham and eggs' for breakfast.

By late midmorning, we both were on the other side of the road where I had scouted briefly a few days before and found nothing. Following my plan that we discussed last night, we followed the road up over the mountains while staying concealed in the jungle.

By nightfall, we could see a faint light through the jungle vegetation. This had to be some sort of building.

The light could not be from a campfire, for there was no smell of smoke. Being careful and knowing there could possibly be guards positioned nearby, I crawled slowly toward the light. I left Dan behind to provide cover fire in case I needed to make a hasty exit. It had been raining since around noon, and the noise of the rain falling on the jungle drowned out any noise I might make.

I moved slowly, making little noise; I was almost like a giant lizard moving quietly through the wet jungle. Movement! I had seen something move off to my left. I stopped! Waiting to see if I could see what it was. Again, I saw the movement; so, I slowly moved toward that position.

Fifteen yards to my left, I found a sentry sitting with his back against a tree, an AK-47 laying across his lap. I watched him from less than 12 feet away. Every few minutes, he would raise his arm and slash his hand against an insect that was eating at his flesh on the back of his neck — the movement that had first caught my attention. I looked at my watch — 1940 hours. He was guarding the front door of a hut, from which the light shone.

Very quietly, I backed away from the sentry and headed toward the other side of the building to check for other posted guards. On the backside of the building, I found the second guard sitting, facing toward the rear of the hut. As I continued my journey around the area, I found no other sentries.

I eased slowly up to the side of the hut and peeked inside through a small opening. There sitting on a stool was a young Vietnamese woman, her hands tied behind her back. Her shirt lay opened and her black bra was plainly visible. Standing close by was a man in an officer's uniform of the North Vietnamese Army. As he questioned the woman, he grabbed a handful of her black hair and yanked her head backwards as she attempted to answer him. There was a small crate used as a desk in the middle of the room; no other furnishings were present. A single kerosene lantern sitting on the crate was supplying the dim light.

There appeared to be another room off to the side, but only blackness showed through the doorway to that room — probably where the woman slept.

I moved back to Dan's position, and we left the area. Once we were about 40 yards away, I told him what I saw. Somewhere close by, there had to be other buildings. This was probably one of many scattered around the area. I could not play hero and rescue the woman now, but I was hopeful she was smart enough to stay alive until I could intervene.

Dan and I moved on, following the road up the mountain. About 60 yards from where we saw the light stood three other buildings. There were no lights, but the outline of the buildings was visible through the rain. We continued up the road to discern if there were yet more buildings and to find the place where Capt. Nhu had his supply warehouse.

Moving very slowly along the road for about 50 yards, we located a large wooden bridge capable of supporting large trucks. It was nearly 125 yards long and spanned a deep gorge. Fifty yards on the other side of the deep gorge was a large house and another large building.

There was a dim light on in the house, and the large building was dark; so, I chose to look in on the large house first. I needed to check out the security guards and find their locations tonight, if possible, so that tomorrow we could begin keeping tabs on security routines, troop movement, number of soldiers, etc. I suspected this had to be Nhu's supply depot.

Under the cover of the rain and darkness, we slipped across the bridge. Somewhere close, there would be the security barracks containing about 18 regular North Vietnamese soldiers that was providing the security for the Capt. Nhu and his staff. Two companies of Viet Cong troops would be providing security for the supplies coming down the Ho Chi Minh Trail in this section of the triangle.

After we eased across the bridge and made our way to the back of the large house, we searched for other guards possibly posted nearby. When I found no other posted guards, I eased up to the window where the light was located; peeping inside, I saw that it was empty.

There were two doors leading from the room, with a large lock securing each door. I knew that something important must be in those rooms!

Making a mental note of the two locked rooms, I returned to the rear of the house where Dan waited. We then slipped over to the larger building that was dark. Again, we looked for guards and discovered none posted nearby. Dan and I discovered the only entrance was through a pair of large locked double doors. There were no windows. I needed to find a way to get inside, other than the double doors. This surely had to be the warehouse where supplies were stored until shipment.

Dan and I got back to the road by staying in the edge of the jungle; we moved up the road, looking for the troop barracks. Around a sharp bend, we saw the barracks. There were four buildings, which could probably house forty people each. Resting against the jungle was a 15-foot high guard's tower located between the buildings.

A lone guard was sitting in the tower smoking a cigarette. There also was a small storage hut to the left of the guard tower. The rain began letting up and soon stopped.

I took out a pencil and a small notepad and sketched out what we had seen since finding the woman locked in that room a quarter mile back down the mountain. In a moment, we were ready to leave. Wanting to stay above this encampment, we found a spot within an hour that I felt was secure. It wasn't much — no shelter from the rain, but it provided security from the enemy.

It was a six-foot wide cut that extended 10 feet back into the mountainside. Not much at all — but with a little American housekeeping, we could have this place fit to live in for a three- or four-night stay. Concealing the entrance with brush and vegetation was our first priority, and then we constructed a roof. By 0300 hours, we were finished. Dan even fashioned us each a bed made of large banana leaves, moss, and palm leaves.

Taking turns at watch, we managed to get close to four hours' sleep. It was now almost noon, and after eating our razzle-dazzle breakfast of ham-n-eggs, it was time to do some distance scouting. We took the M-49 spotting scope further up the mountain to get a closer look at the buildings and their occupants. If this were indeed the supply depot, we would begin taking serious notes on the entire encampment.

Soon we reached a position that would allow us to observe the large house and large building with the locked double doors. We saw activity at the house where five soldiers were busy working. They were probably Capt. Nhu's supply staff, keeping inventory of supplies. Three NVA soldiers moved about the buildings' compound area, changing out the guards at 1300 hours.

Whenever the supply staff left the building, they were either going to the 'outhouse' located along the side of the house, or they would take a bicycle and cross the bridge and head down the road toward where the three buildings were located. Just before dark, they all came out together, locked the door, walked across the bridge, and headed down the road.

The guards marched off going up the road toward their barracks just before darkness fell. It appeared the entire place shut down at dark, except for a few guards here and there. We had counted 12 guards on watch around the entire encampment that day.

I wanted to get inside that warehouse for a closer look. Although Capt. Nhu was not present this afternoon, he could have been at the house this morning before we began observing. It was time to find out if this was the depot or not. If this turned out not to be the depot, we would move on, continuing our quest for it. If this turned out to be the depot, we would begin compiling information and then locate Capt. Nhu.

I slipped quietly along the backside of the warehouse looking for a way inside; then Dan found planks that we could pry out enough for me to slip inside the building. Once inside, I turned on a small red lens pen flashlight. The warehouse was large, and the northeast corner housed some large wooden crates stacked about six high. Each crate was about three-feet square, and I could see that the writing on the wooden crates was Chinese.

I took my K-Bar knife and opened a crate, finding black baggy pants and shirts. Opening four other crates, I found more clothing — these were grey and light brown uniforms!

I secured each crate back and stacked them back the way they had been. Once I was back outside, we eased toward the bridge. Dan had checked out the bridge while I was inside the warehouse. There were no sentries posted, so we quickly crossed the bridge and headed toward the three buildings just below us.

Upon reaching the buildings, I positioned myself to provide cover fire in case Dan needed it. I quickly explained what I wanted him to do, and then Dan eased toward the bamboo hut buildings to find out why the staff workers came and went as often as we had observed them do earlier this afternoon. Shortly, Dan returned and I learned what was inside.

One of the buildings was their sleeping quarters, another was the kitchen, and the third was a jewel — 'the radio shack'. Here was the Hanoi contact. This confirmed to me that we had found Capt. Nhu's supply depot.

Checking my watch, I saw it was already 2010 hours — time to return to our camp and get some shut-eye. Upon safely reaching our little campsite, Dan and I discussed the things we had seen since finding the depot and other buildings last night. The one thing that kept popping into my mind was, *'Where were the two companies of missing Viet Cong troops?'*

Were they further up the Ho Chin Minh Trail, escorting a large shipment down to this depot, or had they already left the camp with a shipment bound for the 42nd Viet Cong Battalion? Maybe we would find out the answer to these questions in the next few days.

Tomorrow, we would split up to get a closer look at the barracks, the hut where the woman was being held, and also the large house used by Capt. Nhu and his staff. It would be a day for head counts, as well as types of weapons used by the enemy and their locations. Knowing that the scouting would take all day to complete, we would meet up tomorrow night at a selected site 100 yards from our campsite.

After going over how we were to accomplish all this tomorrow, Dan radioed in, we ate, and then Dan turned in while I took the first watch. I did not want to take the chance of getting surprised with both of us asleep.

At 0130 hours, I woke Dan. After telling him that everything was quite and asking that he wake me before daylight, I crawled into my bedding to get some sleep. I had become accustomed to sleeping about four hours a night while out in the field.

Dan shook my shoulder; I opened my eyes, and it was still dark. Looking at my watch, I saw it was 0510 hours — daylight would come soon. We ate our usual breakfast and washed it down with water. Before we left camp to do our scouting, we made sure that each other's camouflage was still looking good. It only required a few little touchups.

Once this task was completed, we slipped back toward the encampment. Upon reaching the road, we found there was already activity on it. Six guards were walking down to the depot buildings as they smoked their morning cigarettes and made light conversation as they made their way down the hill.

We let them pass by, then Dan and I separated. I crossed the road and headed into the jungle on the other side. I wanted to get down to the house where Capt. Nhu's staff was working, hoping to see him in person this morning.

Upon reaching the house, I crawled underneath the flooring and waited for the staff to arrive. Through the small splits in the wood flooring, I could see well enough to identify objects; and this would be the best way to look inside of the two locked rooms.

I didn't have to wait long — the door opened and in walked Capt. Ngo Dinh Nhu, with his staff following close behind. He was an averaged-sized Vietnamese man, with a heavy head of black hair. His North Vietnamese uniform had very little wrinkles in it, appearing to be recently pressed. His boots were in need of a shine. He quickly checked a stack of papers, then barked orders to a young officer, and everyone began to get busy.

The captain and the young lieutenant walked to one of the locked doors; and after the young officer unlocked the door, both men entered the room. A lamp was lighted and light quickly flooded the room. I moved slowly to where I could see up into the room.

It appeared this room was for their supply records; three old filing cabinets sat along one wall, with nothing much else in this back room. Shortly, they picked up the kerosene lamp and left. I only had to move a few feet to see them enter the other locked door. The room was flooded with light as a soldier held the lamp up high to show that a large map covered one wall. Fluorescent yellow highlighted the Ho Chi Minh Trail. Also in the room was a small desk and chair; a single cot was placed along a wall. This must be Capt. Nhu's office.

Soon, the young North Vietnamese officer left, leaving Capt. Nhu alone. Nhu began to study the map, then placed his finger at a location on the map and began to mumble something to himself. Soon, a knock came at the door. Nhu said something and a staff orderly brought in a pan, a pitcher of water, and a towel. Removing his shirt, Nhu began washing his face and neck after he was once again alone.

Capt. Nhu was in his late twenties, the son of a respected Hanoi businessman before the war. Before the French were defeated, his father operated a large successful shipping business for many years. Ngo Dinh Nhu helped his father for one year after graduating from Hanoi University. Then, he was summoned for military duty three years ago. The experience of working with his father gave him the knowledge of handling large shipments of various materials.

After joining the Army of North Vietnam, young Lieutenant Nhu worked hard to obtain the respect of his superiors as he moved up in rank. Now as a captain and a trusted officer, he ordered, shipped, and distributed war materials for the Viet Cong Army in South Vietnam. Nhu had been doing this job for the past 11 months.

Nhu knew that if shipments and distribution went well, the rank of major would be forthcoming within the next few years. His father was very proud of his accomplishments.

After he had finished washing his face and neck, Capt. Nhu put his shirt back on and called the orderly to bring him hot tea — *a taste he had acquired from the French*. While sipping his tea, he walked over to the large map and concentrated on a certain point on the map that indicated where troops were escorting a large shipment of weapons, ammunition, and field radios. The supplies in northern Laos — still three to four days away — moved slowly via oxen carts and trucks down the mountainous Ho Chi Minh Trail. Three days behind them was another convoy consisting of more weapons, ammunition, and medical supplies.

These two convoys would help provide the Viet Cong with enough weapons to overrun the South Vietnam Army very soon.

Hanoi always radioed him as each convoy left and headed down the Trail. Through experience, he had learned that it generally took 13 days for a convoy to reach him if there were oxen pulling carts or pack mules. A convoy of just trucks usually made the journey in six days.

Capt. Nhu had not yet decided what to do with the South Vietnamese female spy they had caught attempting to send radio messages five nights ago. He had instructed the officer of the security guards to question her personally. She had been spying on their shipments arriving from Hanoi and listening from the rear of the radio shack whenever a supply request went by radio to Hanoi.

She had worked as a cook at the camp for four months until they caught her in the radio hut providing information to her superiors in the south on convoy movements.

Maybe he should have had her executed right then; but for whatever reason, he was letting her live, for the present. If she would not supply the information Nhu wanted, he would throw her to his men as a war trophy, then have her shot when they tired of her.

I lay under the floor and watched every move Nhu and his staff made for nearly two hours, and then I eased out from under the building and moved back into the safety of the jungle. Shortly, I would try crossing the bridge during daylight by hanging onto and climbing across the maze of timbers on the underside of the bridge.

My next objective was the hut that held the woman prisoner, guarded by at least two soldiers. I stayed just inside the jungle as I approached the hut, silently creeping completely around the hut and again locating the two guards at about the same places they were the other night. Quietly, I then eased up to the side of the hut and peeped through a small opening. Inside, I saw the woman lying curled up on the floor. Taking a small pebble that I just picked up, I tossed it through a hole the size of a softball toward her curled-up form.

When the small pebble landed near her and rolled against her thigh, Lo Lei rolled over, looked at the little stone, and began trying to determine where it had come from — she looked toward the small opening, but saw nothing. She was afraid it might be the North Vietnamese officer or his guards. He was very forceful, always striking her in the face and yanking her hair. He enjoyed exposing her body for him to look at and touch.

Lo Lei became frighten, her flesh cringing at the thought of the officer. Then something very strange came through the small opening — a soft camouflage jungle hat with a U.S. Marine emblem on it. She picked it up quickly and studied it. One of Lo Lei's ankles, secured with wire and fastened high on the wall beyond her reach, allowed her movement about the room, but the stiff wire around her ankle prevented her from reaching either of the doors.

Lo Lei was able to get to the small opening, and heard the American say, "I'll help you tonight," in a rough Vietnamese language attempt.

Her heart leapt with joy — could he be interested in setting her free? The American then whispered, "Hat please!" She pushed the hat back through the hole. She had not spoken a word. She had only listened.

I had seen the woman's swollen foot, as well as her bulging face from the beatings she had received. I knew I must get her out of there tonight before they killed her.

I returned to the bridge by way of the jungle, crossed it again, and slipped back into the jungle quickly and quietly made my way back to the warehouse. There I remained hidden, lying in the edge of the jungle only 15 yards from the building for the remainder of the day, observing the activity of the guards and Nhu's staff.

From this vantage point, I had a view of the office, warehouse, and bridge. I could only see a little bit of the road below the bridge.

The guards had changed shifts at 1300 hours. At 1500 hours, Capt. Nhu left the office building and walked across the bridge down toward the barracks and radio hut. Nhu did not return. Again, the guards were relieved at 1900 hours. Nhu's staff turned out the kerosene lamps in the office and left for the day. The guards who were relieved walked back up the hill to their barracks.

I waited another 30 minutes and then slipped back to our campsite. I had hung around to see if Nhu would return, but he did not. Dan was already at camp. We ate, and Dan then placed our radio call to HQI. I had Dan inform HQI that tomorrow at 1500 hours, we would begin to execute our mission.

After Dan completed the radio call, I told him we would take the woman from the hut tonight at 2300 hours. Soon, I had briefed him on what had happened at the hut today. I explained the condition of the Vietnamese woman's foot and ankle. Dan said he would carry her if necessary. I told him he needed to make a pallet for her to sleep on once we got her safely back here tonight.

Dan then reported on the activity of the NV troops up at the guard barracks, the radio hut, and staff barracks. I shared the activity of the guards at the office and warehouse, Capt. Nhu's and his staff's activity, as well as the two guards' routine at the hut where the woman was held. We prepared ourselves for tonight's venture. I told Dan of my plan to rescue the woman, explaining how we would get her back to camp tonight safely.

At 2210 hours, we left our small camp and slowly moved down toward the hut where the woman was. Fifty minutes later, we were within 50 yards of the hut. There was no light showing; the hut was dark. This meant the officer wasn't around. We slowly crawled toward the two guards. One was near the front, the other at the back of the hut. Dan was to take out the guard at the front, and I would eliminate the guard at the back.

When we reached the hut, we both crawled underneath it and very slowly eased toward the guards. When I was within 10 yards of the sentry at the rear, I paused long enough to get my K-Bar in my hand. I moved slowly to avoid making any noise. The guard was looking around and scratching his crotch, completely unaware his life here on earth was about over. When I reached the end of the hut, I eased up off my stomach, getting to one knee near the steps. I was up on one knee when the guard turned and began moving toward me. I froze! He was now within five feet of the back doorsteps.

In the darkness of the night, he did not see me until it was too late. He did not have time to defend himself. I turned the knife sideways so it could easily penetrate between the man's ribs. I sunk the eight-inch K-Bar knife deep into his chest. He put his hand on the knife handle and looked into my black and green camouflaged face, his eyes wide with fear. His fingers let go of his weapon and my knife deeply embedded in his chest cavity. He tried to cry out, but no sound came from his lips; there was a small stream of blood running out of his mouth. I turned the blade toward his heart and begin a slashing motion, then pulled my knife free, wiped the blade on his shirt, and finally let his lifeless body sink to the ground.

After easing him to the ground, I waited until Dan disposed of his sentry and joined me. We then dragged both of the bodies off into the jungle a short way. I took an AK-47 and ammo from one guard for the woman.

We entered the hut through the rear door. There on the dark floor lay the woman. I motioned for her to be silent by putting my finger to my lips and tried to hold her still so Dan could gently removed the wire from her swollen ankle. Dan had brought his small pair of cable cutters to the hut just for this purpose.

Once free from the wire she tried to walk, and we could tell it would be better if Dan carried her. I motioned that Dan was going to carry her. I could see she did not want to be carried, so I instructed Dan to put her on his back. We had to leave now. The guards would be changing at 0100 hours.

One hour and 17 minutes later, we arrived back at camp. We attended to the woman's ankle by washing it, applying ointment, and then wrapping it tight in an ace bandage. She then washed her face, and we fed her.

She ate like an animal; she probably had not eaten much during the time the NVA had her imprisoned. I tried to ask what her name was in Vietnamese. She did not answer. Again, I tried. I knew my Vietnamese was not very good. This time she said, "Lo Lei Lauh," in English. Dan and I were shocked! We were not expecting her to speak English.

I asked, "How do you know the English language?"

"I graduated from the University of Ottawa in Canada, but when the war broke out between the North and South, I left Canada and came home to Saigon," Lo Lei answered. "Soon I joined the war effort as a spy for my South Vietnamese government. I was sending out information on the supply shipments so the Southern armies could intercept them after they entered South Vietnam territory. But, they captured me this time before I could give out very much information." Her capture five nights ago was at the radio shack, while she was trying to send a radio message when the radio operator left for the toilet.

"There is a large supply train coming down the Ho Chin Min Trail now. In another three days, the convoy will arrive here. The convoy is bringing many truck loads of ammunition and weapons," Lo Lei added.

"Would you like to help us destroy the convoy by helping us find them, or, would you like to go home now?" I asked.

"I want to help you, if you are really going after the supply train," she stated emphatically. "I could lead you to where the supply train might be located," she said.

"OK, let's do it," I said.

I knew her knowledge of the terrain, plus being able to speak our language, was a big factor in my decision to ask for her help. Lo Lei looked at our map and showed me where the supplies should be tomorrow night.

"It will take us about eight hours to reach them," she stated.

I figured we could get a few hours sleep and start out at 0500 hours in the morning.

"You two get some sleep; I'll wake you both at 0330 hours," I said.

At 0330 hours, everyone was awake; we ate, took a quick nature break, loaded up everything, and broke camp. We left nothing behind, not even any sign that we had been there. Using part of the bedding as a broom to sweep away any sign of intruders; all of our tracks quickly vanished.

The weather looked like it would turn nasty at any moment. A light rain began falling. There was lightning off to the West, moving toward us. We had walked about two miles when I thought it was now safe to use the PRC-77 radio, so I asked Dan to let HQI know where we were going and with whom.

We stopped just long enough for Dan to establish communications with HQI. We were lucky to be able to contact them with this weather front moving in on us. After providing them with the essential details, HQI thanked us for the information, and requested we contact them before making physical contact with the NVA supply train.

When we informed HQI about Lo Lei, we also asked that HQI contact her superiors and let them know that she was now with Dan and me and leading us towards the convoy.

Dan finished signing off just 20 minutes before the heavy rain began. It was a hard, cold rain that chilled you to the bone. The route Lo Lei selected was a direct route, avoiding villages and civilian population. Four hours later, I noticed a limp in Lo Lei's steps; so, we stopped for a breather and ate some lunch. Dan checked Lo Lei's ankle and re-bandaged it after applying more ointment. Eager to prove she could hold her own, she carried her weapon. She was ready to move out when we were.

The next time we stopped was three hours later, when Lo Lei said we were close to the trail. I asked her if she knew a place where we could get a good view of the trail. Half an hour later, she stopped and pointed below.

There, 200 meters below us was the famous Ho Chi Minh Trail.

From this advantage point, I also saw two large heavy wooden bridges the convoy would have to cross. There was no way around them in these mountains. The bridges were about 350 meters apart, and each spanned a very deep ravine — a perfect spot for explosives! Soon, the three of us were at the first bridge. Dan would rig each bridge with the C-4 and electrical detonators. I gave him my C-4 and detonator. This would be enough plastic explosives to blow the two bridges when the supplies and troops were on them.

While Dan was busy planting the explosives, Lo Lei and I scouted the area along the Trail for possible ambush points we could use. Three hundred meters beyond the second bridge, we located a smaller third bridge. It was about 90 feet long, spanning a very deep and narrow ravine. The road was slick and muddy and this meant the supply column would be moving fairly slow when approaching the first bridge.

We went back and found Dan just finishing up with the first bridge. He had tied the string of C-4 explosives to the timbers under the bridge and made sure the wiring going to the electrical detonator was secure and hidden. Dan had rolled enough wire out to reach 60 meters south of the bridge and there he hooked up the electrical detonator. Dan and I hid the wires so they were undetectable from the road. Dan now skinned the ends of the two wires so they would be ready for the detonator when we needed them.

The three of us worked to get the second bridge's explosives rigged in a like manner. Lo Lei and I installed two claymore mines and more C-4 explosives at all the bridges. I then informed Dan about the third bridge, and he and I headed south to wire it with explosives. Dan and I also installed three claymore mines, one just north of the third bridge, and two south of it. The rain suddenly stopped. Hopefully, this would be to our advantage.

Within three hours, we had completely rigged all three bridges with explosives, plus put claymore mines and C-4 between the first two bridges. We were now all heading back to the second bridge. I looked at my watch — 1540 hours.

Dan would blow the first bridge on my signal and if the fighting separated us, I would signal with a red flare. In case I could not signal, Dan had orders to blow the sucker when the last of the vehicles were three-fourths of the way across the first bridge. This would trap the entire column between the bridges with no way to retreat.

Lo Lei and I would be on opposite sides of the road taking out as many troops as possible with our rifles and the mines. She wanted to kill as many Cong as she could.

We would fight a retreating type fight until the three of us had all crossed the second bridge.

Dan would then blow the second bridge; we would again fight our way back to the third bridge, and then blow that bridge after we crossed it. I had selected a small gully 100 meters south of the third bridge for our designated meeting point.

We left the radio here between the second and third bridges until we returned for it. I asked Dan to make radio contact with HQI and send our last message before we confronted the column. Dan then began calling!

"'Delta-Two-Foxtrot' calling 'Hotel-Nine-Alpha'. Come in 'Hotel-Nine-Alpha', Come in! Come in!

No response.

"It's probably the rotten weather interfering and hampering our effort," Dan said, as he tried again. Still there was no response. Again, he tried!

"'Delta-Two-Foxtrot' calling 'Hotel-Nine-Alpha'. Over,..."

Then a familiar voice said, *"Delta-Two-Foxtrot', this is 'Hotel-Nine-Alpha'. Over,..."*

"'Hotel-Nine-Alpha', informing you that within the hour we should make contact with the supply column. Our time is now 1557 hours. Over,..."

"Roger, on your time and contact time. You must be at designated mail box tomorrow night at 2330 hours, for your return airmail. Over."

"'Hotel-Nine-Alpha', Roger on mailbox tomorrow at 2330 hours. Over and out!

Lo Lei had scouted the column and pinpointed its position. She reported there were 12 vehicles total — two cars and ten North Vietnamese army trucks, plus five large ox carts bringing up the rear that also carried supplies — that should be reaching the first bridge in about 20 minutes. Lo Lei said that most of the troops were in front or walking on both sides of the convoy. There were at least 100 troops guarding the column.

I passed this information on to Dan, as he and I had already decided the proper time to blow the first bridge. We had set out almost all of our explosives, but retained two C-4 bars each in our sacks, in case of extreme need during our run for the border. Dan hurried back to the detonator — located about 60 yards south of the first bridge — and waited in hiding.

Ten minutes later, the column scouts — a 12-man squad — approached the first bridge. They crossed the bridge, meandering 40 meters south of the bridge when the main column came into view. This group appeared more strung out than I had hoped it would be.

Here was where the rubber meets the road! Our hard work was going to pay dividends here in a remote mountainous region of Laos, or we would become meat for the buzzards to dine on.

Lo Lei was hidden behind rocks 100 meters south of the first bridge; she was to take out any troops she desired, after the fireworks began. I was on the opposite side of the road, 80 meters south of the bridge. I could see the supply column starting onto the bridge. I wanted to take out the last third of the column in the initial bridge explosion.

This would cut off any means of escape, eliminating any retreat back across the bridge. Also, any rear security would be left on the other side of a very deep ravine. The bridges length would only allow about six or seven vehicles on it at a time. So, as the last truck and the five ox carts got on the bridge, I signaled Dan to blow it.

In a split-second, the scene in front of our eyes changed dramatically. A large orange fire ball illuminated the darkening evening sky — pieces of timber and body parts of men and animals were engulfed within it and flying out in every direction.

Secondary explosions from the ammunitions created an even larger inferno. The vehicles and carts carrying the supplies blew apart, their cargo destroyed and scattered in the deep ravine. The bridge — completely wiped out. The remaining column could not retreat.

Shouts filled the air as officers and sergeants began giving orders. Troops began wildly firing their AK-47s, even though they could not see anyone. Lo Lei detonated a C-4 explosive as two trucks were trying to get past her position. One truck turned over, the explosion gutting the lead truck and sending flames skyward. Troops were screaming and trying to get away from the explosions. The second truck went around the overturned one and raced toward the second bridge.

As the second truck tried to get away from this chaos to get its cargo to safety, Lo Lei detonated another C-4 she had buried further down the road. The fast moving truck seemed to lift off the muddy ground as the explosion rocked its frame. It ended up on its side, burning. The driver began trying to crawl out, but Lo Lei was too fast for him. She cut his body almost in half with bullets. Within minutes, the ammo and weapons from both trucks went up in a huge explosion, which sent truck pieces flying everywhere.

I saw Dan was below me as he began to make his way back to the second bridge. His M-14 was spitting out rounds at troops as fast as he could possibly operate it. Firepower was the key element at this moment.

I fired the Weatherby .300 caliber magnum sniper rifle at officers and sergeants to systematically further reduce their morale.

I glanced toward where Lo Lei was fighting about six VC; that little woman was one terrific fighter. She was ruthless, a killing machine — yet, she had a mystic grace about herself that I greatly admired.

Two VC brought my attention back to the present; a hail of bullets from their AK-47s pelted the rocks close to me. I turned my attention back toward them and dropped the closest man with a well-placed head shot. Taking this opportunity to change positions, I jumped up and ran down the embankment, then quickly ducked behind a large boulder. Then I eased my head up just in time to see a VC coming down the embankment to flush me out from hiding. Again, I took a head shot and saw him fall; once again, I jumped up and ran zigzagging, back toward the second bridge. More troops from up on the road were now taking pot shots at me.

The convoy was still in disarray; they had not tried to move vehicles past the two lead trucks, which lay burning in the road. I caught up to Dan, and quickly asked, "Can you take out the rear truck in the convoy with your M-79 grenade launcher?"

"Suppose so," he replied. "Been hoping I'd get the chance to try it in the field."

Dan took out the little weapon that resembles a single barrel shotgun and breaks open the same way as a single barrel shotgun. The biggest noticeable difference is the size of the barrel, large enough for a full-grown squirrel to crawl into; and, the M-79's length is almost as long as a riot shotgun.

The shell it shoots looks like a giant oversized .45-caliber cartridge. When fired, it has a 'woomp' sound; but when the round hits a target, it blows everything to smithereens.

Dan's first round hit 20 meters beyond the truck. The second round was a lot closer, hitting just behind the truck. The driver put the truck in gear and raced toward the head of the column. The other trucks began moving toward the second bridge. Getting the convoy moving again might enable us to complete our mission of destroying the entire supply train. I wanted to blow the second bridge with convoy trucks on it.

With the convoy moving again, Dan and I headed toward the hidden detonators south of the second bridge. There were bullets getting real close, so we ducked down behind some large boulders.

As it was getting darker, I saw that I would need Dan's assistance in dispensing flares so I could identify my targets. I was now ready as Dan launched the first flare; I brought my eye to the 9X scope and viewed the roadside scene, trying to locate any officer. I found a young officer trying to get a burning truck pushed to the side of the roadway. I looked further back and found another officer sending his men down the embankment after us. In less than four seconds, I had located and selected him as my first target.

Since he was only 187 yards away, it would be a simple shot — I let the cross hair settle upon the side of his head, which exploded like a melon upon the bullet's impact. His lifeless body kicked, twisted, and fell backwards about five yards.

Quickly, I looked for an NCO, and located a couple of them nearby — this time a frontal headshot. The head just exploded as the 173-grain bullet tore his head almost from his shoulders. The body of the sergeant went backwards, ending up in a heap on the muddy ground. The sergeant's troops could see his near headless body lying just a few feet from them. These VC fighters knew this was the work of a sniper! Each time the sniper fired, one of them died. Their fear was apparent as some scrambled for cover!

I could get off one or two more shots before the flare faded, but I must hurry! I moved the scope back to where more troops were coming down an embankment. A sergeant was halfway down when I shot him through the chest. Picking a soldier next to him, I picked the same location — chest. Both bodies began rolling down the embankment.

Dan launched another flare, and I kept killing those coming down the embankment. At the realization that a sniper was picking them off, most that descended the embankment began to climb back up the side of the hill. They knew death was all about them, and they feared dying. Systematically removing the heads of officers and sergeants dramatically affected the soldiers' morale.

Another sergeant foolishly jumped into position to direct orders to the troops. He pointed down toward my position just as I fired. Again, his whole head exploded and his body flew backwards. His men began running away, trying to find any place safer than this spot. I shot two soldiers in the back as they tried to run.

They had witnessed three of their leaders getting their heads blown off by a sniper or snipers. These men began crawling under trucks or behind trucks, trying to escape the awful death that awaited them out in the open.

Another flare!

I searched for officers and sergeants. I located an officer standing on the running board of a truck, giving orders to its driver. My scope stopped in the middle of his back, and I squeezed the trigger. The officer clutched at the truck door, then began sliding down into the muddy roadway beneath the truck. There would be a large hole in his chest where the bullet exited.

Locating another sergeant who was commanding troops to follow him down the embankment, I stopped the scope on his chest and squeezed off a round. The man lunged backwards, and then his lifeless body slid sideways down the embankment. More of the convoy guards began running around on the road looking for a safe place to hide.

Again, we jumped up and ran toward the second bridge detonator. This time Dan and I made it. We both ducked behind large rocks again as a VC flare illuminated our area, and a hail of bullets rained down around us. It appeared we could detonate before the trucks were on the second bridge, as they were having difficulty getting past some of the wreckage on the slippery road. I wanted to locate Lo Lei's position. I heard more automatic rifle fire and knew she was about 60 yards south of Dan and me.

* * * * * * *

Lo Lei had already crossed the second bridge and gone back on the opposite side of the road, killing any Viet Cong soldiers that gave her the opportunity. She must hate them with a burning passion.

Four Viet Cong fighters were trying to flush out Lo Lei. They were taking turns moving toward her. She waited patiently until the four were just 20 yards from her — as they ran together toward her position, she detonated a claymore mine when they were within a few yards of it. The four seemed cut in half by the 1,000 buckshots packed inside the claymore anti-personnel mine.

When Lo Lei saw that no one else was shooting at her now, she zigzagged through the rocks toward the second bridge. She was less than 100 meters from the bridge when she felt a bullet slam into her left leg. The force of the bullet knocked her down, and she lost her AK as she fell onto the rocky ground.

Lo Lei knew she had to get to the rifle to have any chance of surviving. The VC would be coming after her now that they knew she was injured.

Lo Lei saw the AK-47 resting five meters from where she had fallen. Her leg felt like it was on fire as she began to crawl toward the rifle — but she couldn't stop until she reached the rifle. Within a minute, she was clutching the rifle again. As she quickly checked to make sure the clip had bullets, she heard voices coming from close behind her.

She was lying on her side with the barrel pointed toward the sound of the voices. She waited until the two Viet Cong stepped from behind the large boulder into the open. They saw her just 15 meters away as she opened fire on them. The bullets from her AK tore huge holes in their bodies. These two were careless, just as she was when she was shot in the leg. Lo Lei ripped off a strip of her pants leg and tied it as a tourniquet around her leg to slow down the bleeding.

Staggering to her feet, she walked and stumbled south toward the second bridge. She could hear single shots being fired, saw the night flares, and knew the Marines were still north of her. They would help her when she crossed the bridge — but first, she must get there alive. She knew she had to keep an eye out for the VC as she retreated, because there were no more claymores until she reached the bridge where the firing device and mines were already set.

Darkness gave her the cover she needed as she painfully made her way to the bridge.

Upon reaching the bridge and finding no soldiers nearby, she crossed the bridge and hid in the place where the Marine Sergeant had shown her earlier. She had heard the soldiers yelling and screaming on the road — they were afraid of the sniper. They had said that *when the sniper fired his rifle, one of them died — he did not miss!* Some soldiers were so afraid they refused orders to move from under the trucks.

Lo Lei looked at her left leg — about five inches above her knee was a nasty looking hole, but luckily, the bullet had gone all the way through. She tightened the strip of cloth she had earlier tied around her leg. This would restrict the blood flow to her foot, but she would not lose so much blood.

As Lo Lei looked out from her hiding place at the small bridge, her thoughts were on her late husband, Maj. Nan Cha Lauh. They had both attended the same college in Canada as exchange students. They fell in love and married while in Ottawa. She had lost their only child, a boy, at birth. That was in their third year at college. Ten months after the two of them graduated, the war in Vietnam began. The North Communists were fighting against their beloved South.

Both she and Nan Cha left Canada, as they wanted to return to Saigon to help their country fight the communist who were using Viet

Cong fighters from both the north and south to help wage war on Saigon and the South.

Nan Cha, assigned the rank of Captain, upon entering the Army was trained as a spy to gather information, which could be beneficial to the South's cause. A year later, the Viet Cong killed Nan Cha in a raid. Lo Lei felt she now must fight for both herself and her dead husband.

She hated both the North Vietnamese Communist and the ruthless Viet Cong. Killing them was beyond duty — it was a pleasure she enjoyed.

* * * * * * *

Every time Dan launched a flare, I found at least three or four targets to take out.

Now, I was just shooting Viet Cong, because finding officers and sergeants was just a waste of flares. They were scared of the sniper, as he had shoved death in their face! He had already killed over half of the officers and many sergeants during this attack.

I had to stop shooting as the flare burned out. I lost track of the number of flares, and I was out of 173-grain sniper rounds. So, Dan and I moved south through the rocks and boulders along the ravine, trying to reach the smallest bridge.

Reaching the small bridge, we discovered Lo Lei was already there.

"I've been hit in the leg," Lo Lei said, as she grimaced in pain.

"Look after her wound, while I take a closer look at the convoy," I said to Dan.

"You be careful, Sarge," Dan replied.

I saw that most troops were under the trucks and the drivers had left their trucks sitting in the middle of the road. The wreckage from the three lead trucks had blocked the road and kept the other vehicles from getting by on the narrow mountainous muddy road. Here, trapped between the first and second bridges, retreat or advancement was impossible. Dan blowing the second bridge caused entrapment of the supply trucks along with troops guarding the supply convoy between the two deep ravines, with no way to deliver their supplies or escape.

What a target for our jets! Complete destruction of the remaining convoy was now possible.

If only HQI would buy it. It was the simple solution to a problem. This extra firepower would also be the distraction we needed to pay a visit to Maj. Nhu's depot and possibly eliminate it before the chopper pickup tomorrow night.

We had salvaged all the unused C-4 plastic explosives and claymore mines for later use before blowing the second bridge. Our new count was now six C-4 explosives and only one claymore anti-personnel mine with electric detonator for later use.

Upon reaching our radio, Dan contacted HQI and read what I had written down.

"Hotel-Nine-Alpha', this is 'Delta-Two-Foxtrot'." After receiving an answer from Hotel-Nine-Alpha, Dan read our message: *"We have crippled the convoy, leaving it trapped between two blown bridges on the Ho Chi Minh Trail, 15 miles west of the South Vietnamese border in Laos."*

Dan then gave the coordinates of the convoy's location.

"Request air power to knock out the remaining convoy trapped on the mountain road, and we will pay a visit to one Capt. Nhu. Will wait for your reply to our urgent request. Over,..."

Dan sent the message; and within 10 minutes, we had the green light to pursue Capt. Nhu. But, HQI requested we stand by to act as ground spotters for the strike on the convoy.

Three Navy jets would take on the convoy shortly after daybreak. We could leave the area once our jets destroyed the convoy. The strike would be at 0620 hours, which gave us nine hours to get in some much needed sack time.

It had been a long time since we had eaten anything, so I suggested we get some food while we could. The three of us stuffed our stomachs, and then we took turns sleeping after moving further back from the bridges and road.

I roused both Dan and Lo Lei from their sleep at 0530 hours, giving us nearly one hour before the air strike on the convoy. We heard the sound of jet airplanes at 0620 hours and looked skyward to see three F-4 jets overhead. We watched as they banked and started their approach run on the convoy.

I told Dan and Lo Lei we should all seek cover, because the pilots could not know if we were friendly or foe. We all ducked behind some large boulders, and watched as the jets came in real low. The pilots must have had the convoy in their cross hairs, because the lead jet fired rockets at the convoy, then banked sharp right and climbed skyward.

The other two jets followed the lead jet in, also firing rockets. Explosions, fireballs, and black smoke filled the canyon once again. The jets came in again very low; the lead jet again fired rockets, but the other two fired their 20-mm cannons at the trucks and troops — more explosions filled the air.

After the third low-level run at the convoy, the jets climbed back into the sky and headed home. The attack had taken just four minutes. Observing the columns of black smoke lifting skyward, I knew the convoy was totally destroyed. Dan called HQI and gave them the report on the fate of the convoy.

Dan had also fashioned Lo Lei a crutch during the night. Now, the three of us began our journey to Capt. Nhu's camp. We still had a deadline of 2330 hours tonight to keep a date with the chopper for our air ticket home.

With Lo Lei's bad leg slowing us down, it took nine hours to reach Capt. Nuh's encampment. I had already decided to keep Lo Lei out of any firefight. I wanted her away from the action because of her injury. I could also use her AK. As we neared the encampment, I whispered my wishes to Dan. He just nodded and continued walking.

Dan and I crawled to where we could observe the four troop barracks at Nhu's camp. Time was now 1615 hours. As we peeked over the edge of the cliff, it appeared that everything was normal — guards not on watch were in either the barracks or playing a game of ball outside. A lone sentry in the guard tower watched the game.

When we returned to where Lo Lei was waiting, Dan walked behind her and knocked her out with a small chop to the base of her skull. He then picked her up and disappeared with her — 30 minutes later he returned. We went over our plan, detailing where and when we would be putting what type explosives, time of detonations, and where we would later meet, etc.

The encampment layout on this mountainside made our job more difficult. The camp had three main areas: (1) the four troop barracks, almost 100 meters above; (2) Capt. Nhu's office and warehouse; and then (3) 50 meters down the hill from the bridge was staff quarters with a kitchen and the radio shack. So, our blasts needed to be coordinated to be the most effective. I gave Dan three of my grenades, just in case he ran into trouble with the troops at the barracks.

He would destroy the four troop barracks, ammunitions shack, and guard tower. I would take out the storage warehouse, Nhu's office, and radio shack and radio tower. We had six half-pound blocks of C-4. Dan used three of the C-4 explosives and the lone claymore because he would be dealing with the most troops.

I slipped through the jungle and down to the radio shack, setting a single C-4 explosive to take out the radio shack and tower at 1705 hours. Then I headed up toward Capt. Nhu's office and quietly crawled under it and installed a little gift of C-4 and my last two grenades just for him. I placed these under the floor of the office area and tied everything to a floor beam.

Capt. Nhu's sleeping quarters were just a few yards away. If I got lucky, the blast would also get him. I set the timer to detonate at 1705 hours and 10 seconds. I eased out from under the office floor and made my way over to the warehouse. I had to destroy this warehouse with something besides explosives, because I was fresh out.

I would use fire — that usually always did a good job.

After slipping inside, I began gathering materials that would burn. I emptied a large wooden crate of clothes upon other boxes full of clothes stacked against a wall. I laid the empty wooden crate on top of the pile, took two .45 caliber pistol rounds, removed the lead bullets with my K-Bar, and empted the powder upon the pile. This would intensify the flame, giving it a good start.

I stepped back, surveyed the warehouse again, and was satisfied that all of it would go up in flames. I checked my watch. It was 1701 hours, four minutes before the first explosion at the radio shack — I had just a couple of minutes to start this fire and hide in the jungle. Capt. Nhu's office would explode in a fireball 30 seconds after the radio tower was demolished. Taking out my lighter, I ignited the pile of clothing; then, I moved rapidly to the back wall of the warehouse and eased myself outside. Quickly, I slipped into the jungle that was just 30 yards away.

Once in the jungle, I moved just far enough into the vegetation that I could still see around the warehouse and office; but if anyone was looking for me, they could not detect me. I looked for the three security guards and saw only one. He was 60 yards away and walking toward the warehouse. The other two guards must be on the other side of Nhu's office. I couldn't see them! As the guard approached the warehouse, he began shouting very loud — he must have seen the smoke, because he began trying to unlock the large padlock on the front doors with his keys. I glanced at my watch — still one minute till the first explosion!

The other two guards and Capt. Nhu came running up as the first guard finally managed to open the doors to the warehouse. They all stood in the doorway briefly, looking at the fire. Capt. Nhu began shouting orders. They could not see me kneeling with the AK-47 pointed in their direction. I centered the front sight on the left half of Nhu's back, about seven inches below his shoulder blade. I dared not wait any longer — squeezing off two quick, accurate rounds, I saw his body fall in a heap on the ground. The guards turned and looked my way. They were raising their weapons to fire in my general direction, when suddenly. . .

A deafeningly loud explosion!

The roar indicated an almost simultaneous ignition as the radio shack was now out of operation and the ammunitions hut and contents were blown skyward. Within seconds, there was another very loud explosion; this time it was Capt. Nhu's office. The explosion was so close that the force of it picked up the three guards and threw them toward me. I jumped to my feet and ran as fast as I could toward where the three guards and Capt. Nhu lay sprawled on the ground.

All four men appeared to be dead. Nhu had blood all over his back and chest. I quickly grabbed one of the guards' AK-47s and took his bandolier of ammo. I quickly turned my attention back to completing this mission and getting back to base safely. Within seconds after Nhu's office blew up, I heard the explosions from up at the troop barracks and knew Dan was taking care of business. The flames were beginning to engulf the warehouse now. Soon it would only be a pile of ashes.

I raced toward the bridge, and as I passed the Nhu's burnt-out office, I glanced toward where the building once stood. It appeared all members of the office staff in the building at the time of the explosion were killed. Small arms fire reverberated from up Dan's way, and I knew Dan was mopping up at the troop barracks. Glancing back over my right shoulder, I saw the warehouse was now totally consumed by flames.

Running across the bridge and into the jungle on the opposite side of the road, I slowly made my way down to the single shack where I first saw Lo Lei. Our predetermined meeting place!

No one was there! So I eased back into the cover of the jungle, near the shack, and waited for Dan. I made sure the AK I had just picked up was in good operating order and was fully loaded. Twelve minutes later Dan appeared with Lo Lei slung over his large shoulders. Her hands were tied and she was gagged for her own safety.

We needed to put some distance between this place and ourselves fast. There had to be other Viet Cong in the area who would come to investigate the explosions.

"Can you jog with her on your shoulders for a little while?" I asked Dan. He assured me he could, if I carried the radio. I gave him her AK and we lit out as soon as I slung the radio upon my back.

Two hours later, I stopped and Dan eased Lo Lei off his shoulders and onto the ground. I could see she was awake and plenty mad. I explained that the gag and ropes would stay in place until she calmed down. In a few minutes, she had quit kicking and fighting the ropes that secured her. So I had Dan untie her and remove her gag, and then I explained why this action was necessary.

"You would have been an additional responsibility I didn't need during the fight, and I wanted to make sure we got you back alive," I told her.

She was soon over her anger, and the three of us headed for Vietnam as fast as she could go — for we had a date with a helicopter.

At 2012 hours, we stopped again for Dan to check Lo Lei's leg wound and bandage which he had put on earlier in the day. We quickly ate; and glancing at my watch, I saw we had been here for 15 minutes. It was time to get moving again.

"Let's move!" I commanded as I got to my feet and swung the AK-47 across my forearms. In another minute, everyone was ready. We had three hours and 18 minutes to get to the helicopter's LZ. The chopper would be there at 2330 hours.

I stayed on a seldom-used trail that Lo Lei showed us. This was the same trail she used coming here a few weeks ago. We had been moving along at a swift pace on this trail for nearly two and one half-hours when Dan said, "Looks like she could use a break, Sarge."

Then suddenly, we were taking automatic weapons fire! Whoever was shooting at us had a good spot because bullets were chewing up the vegetation and ground all around us.

We all hit the deck about the same time the first shots were fired. *'Who had escaped from Capt. Nhu's compound to ambush us?'* I was also trying to figure out if we had a way out of the ambush. How bad were we outnumbered?

Thoughts raced through my head as I tried to think how we could get away from this situation. We had a deadline to meet the chopper. We would not survive if we missed it.

Returning their assault, we fired at their muzzle flashes. It appeared they were doing the same thing when they returned fire on us.

"How many M-79 rounds do you have?" I asked Dan.

"Four!" he stated.

"Get their yardage and drop a few rounds on them," I ordered.

Dan pulled the M-79 grenade rifle from his back and inserted a shell. After adjusting the sight for a 60-yard shot, he was ready to fire on my command.

When they fired again, I yelled, "Now, Dan!"

In a split second, a bright flash and explosion brought forth the sounds of screams from our attackers' position. Dan had scored a direct hit among them. I instructed Dan to leave the radio so we could move faster. Dan ripped off the antenna and pried off the control knobs, but to be sure the VC didn't take it, Dan said he would pull the safety-pin from a grenade if I would lay the radio on it. I picked the radio up and gently eased the radio downward. Both of Dan's hands were on the grenade as I eased the big radio down onto his hands. Holding the grenade with his left hand, he positioned the radio exactly as he wanted it with his right hand, and then gently removed the safety pin.

The Viet Cong who picked this radio up would be blown to pieces along with anyone standing close by.

As we all got to our feet, I said, "Dan, you move out at a run, down the trail and then

Lo Lie and I'll bring up the rear ... Move!" We all ran!

We had spent almost 20 minutes in that firefight — 20 minutes we didn't have.

I knew the VC would be close on our heels like a pack of dogs. They wanted us too badly to let us get away. Our only chance — just maybe — was to throw caution to the wind and literally race them to the landing area. As Dan was picking his way down the trail in the dark, the VC was only about 75 yards behind us. Every once in a while, they would fire a burst at us, hoping we would return their fire, so they could spot us. But, as long as they didn't close the distance between us, I was not going to return their fire. Dan set the pace at a fast trot as he picked his way down the dark moonlit path.

Down in my gut, I knew we couldn't allow these VC to follow us all the way to the landing area. That would also put the chopper and its crew in danger. I knew that somewhere soon we would have to face them again. But if and when we did, I hoped it would be on my terms — not theirs.

My lungs began to burn with the pain of not getting enough air. My legs were also beginning to feel the toll of running. I quickened my pace, and in a few minutes, I caught up to Dan.

"How are you holding out," I asked.

"I'm OK, but Lo Lei isn't going to make it much further," Dan replied.

"How is your ammunition holding out?" I asked.

"I've got two full magazines — enough to last for another short firefight," he informed me.

"We'll stop shortly, when I spot the right place to fight," I said breathlessly.

"Let me know when to stop, Sarge," Dan replied.

Again, I dropped back to our rear, keeping an eye out for any place that would give us decent cover and the element of surprise.

Time was running out for us. According to my watch — 2250 hours — 40 minutes left! I knew we had to find a place to set our own ambush soon. I was constantly checking the VC behind us, as well as trying to locate an ambush point. How I wished for a few 'claymores' to slow these VC fighters down.

I was watching our back-trail so intensely that I didn't see Lo Lei and Dan had stopped, and I ran smack into them. They had stopped without me knowing it, and Dan reached out and caught me as I came by him.

Needless to say, that almost caused me to crap in my pants.

"Look here!" Dan exclaimed as he pointed to good-sized stream cutting across the trail just in front of us. It meant we would have to lie down in the water to use the cover of the two-foot high banks.

This was perfect, it would provide what we needed, both cover and surprise!

We waited as the VC troops approached. It took them just minutes to reach our position. The three of us fired on my command, and we took them down like a bolt out-of-the-blue.

Two of the lead VC died in our initial burst, and the others crawled off into the jungle. Again, we jumped to our feet and raced toward the landing. The VC stayed further back from us this time.

Dan located another ambush point a quarter-mile farther down the trail. A large fallen tree laying alongside the trail would provide protection as we waited for the Viet Cong to approach. Lying on our bellies behind the fallen tree, I again checked the time – 2312 hours – 18 minutes left before pickup. Soon, we saw them approaching in single file, as they quietly slipped through the jungle without a sound being made.

"Fire!" I screamed when they were almost on top of us.

Again, they had miscalculated and were totally surprised. The first three troops were wasted, but the rest dove for cover in the thick jungle and began to return our fire. Judging by the number of different muzzle flashes I counted, I surmised there must be six to eight VC still left.

Dan again dropped an M-79 round into their position. As the flash from the exploding M-79 round lit up the darkness, we jumped to our feet and again raced off toward the pickup point, still a few hundred yards away.

Upon reaching the designated pickup point, I instructed Lo Lie to watch our back trail while Dan and I scouted the surrounding area to insure no VC were lying in wait for the chopper or us. Ten minutes later, we both returned to where Lo Lie was guarding our back trail. The landing site appeared clear.

We waited only minutes before the big chopper came over the clearing. It was about 500 feet above the jungle floor when I popped a green flare and tossed it into the clearing; the big helicopter circled and landed. As the chopper was sitting down, the three of us ran out toward it with a sense of excitement racing through our weary bodies.

What a sense of relief, knowing we were finally going home. After liftoff, I looked over at Lo Lei; she was smiling, because one of the helicopter gunners had given her a piece of chocolate. I looked toward Dan who was just sitting there with his eyes closed — probably thinking about his Kathy. I removed the case from by back, containing the sniper rifle.

We had been airborne only a few minutes, when suddenly, there was a small explosion, and the helicopter pitched wildly to its side. The sudden change in direction almost threw the three of us out the open doors.

The pilot yelled, "We've been hit with ground fire." "Brace yourselves in case we have to make a rough landing."

He got on the radio, giving our position and screaming into the mike, "May Day—-MAY DAY!" I kept thinking, *he's got to be joking!* But the spinning chopper was evidence that he was serious.

The last thing the pilot yelled was "HANG ON TIGHT!"

We slammed into some large trees, and then everything went black for me.

When I regained consciousness, I tried to move, but my right leg felt like it was broken and my head was bleeding and hurt terribly — but, I was alive. I called out to Dan, but didn't get a response. I called for Lo Lei, and there was no answer. The pilot called out to me. He was hurt bad, but had also survived the crash. I looked up and I could see lots of stars in the night sky. This was when I realized that half of the helicopter was missing! Suddenly, I felt sick to my stomach and threw up.

The helicopter broke into two large pieces upon hitting the palm grove. I lay in the smaller section that had just the pilot and me. Both of us were thankful to be alive. He said he was busted up inside. I crawled to where I could see outside. What I saw put real fear in my heart. I began crying uncontrollably and threw up again.

The other section of the helicopter lay burning 30 yards away. The tail was angled up toward the sky and the entire section was engulfed in flames. I screamed Dan's name repeatedly, but did not get an answer. I smelled like vomit and my head was hurting, yet I knew I could not let myself pass out because the Viet Cong would soon be swarming all over us. Surveying our situation, I saw that both of the helicopter gunners were missing, and both machine guns had been ripped from their frames in the doorways.

My sniper rifle was missing! I had quickly taken it from my back and laid it down beside me when I first got into the chopper. But the AK and my .45 caliber pistol were OK. I surveyed the ammunition and found I had maybe enough left to last 20 minutes, if I used it sparingly. The pilot had an AR-15 and a .38 caliber pistol. There were two 20-round clips for the AR and a handful of .38 pistol cartridges. Maybe we could hold them off for a while.

Deep down I knew we would not be able to keep the Viet Cong off us very long with just these small weapons.

I crawled to the pilot, unstrapped him, and pulled him out of his seat. He screamed when I moved him. Somehow, I managed to pull him back to where I had laid the AK-47. Then I returned to retrieve his AR-15 and ammunition. The 38 caliber pistol was in a holster around his chest. For the first time I really looked at him — he was a young first lieutenant. He had hollered loudly when I pulled him from his seat; he had something busted up inside for sure. My right kneecap — cut open and broken — was the victim of the crash. I managed to tie my belt off above my knee and let it serve as a tourniquet.

I thought about praying again, but felt that God wouldn't listen, because I hadn't kept any of the promises I had made to Him in the last year. But, would God even hear me?

I had nothing to lose by trying, so I began to pray aloud.

"God please let Dan be O.K., and help the pilot and me get out of......"

Automatic rifle fire! Bullets were hitting all around us. I peeped outside, trying to locate the VC. I saw their muzzle flashes. They were shooting from a location about 50 yards away, staying behind some heavy vegetation.

I fired a short burst from the AK, just to let them know some of us were still alive and able to shoot back.

For the better part of an hour, this exchange went on — the VC shooting at us and me and the lieutenant returning a few shots to keep them at bay. Together, we only had enough ammo to fire a few more rounds. When our ammunition ran out, they would jump us. That would be the end!

Then there was this mighty roar, and we heard the sound of machine guns. The pilot smiled, and I looked toward the night sky and saw two helicopters over us. They had come to our rescue and arrived just in time. The VC just slipped back into the jungle.

Our people loaded the four bodies of our dead in one of the helicopters. Afterwards, the pilot and I were loaded onto the other chopper on stretchers. I thought again about the prayer I had been praying when the VC opened fire on us. *'Was I just lucky again? Or, did God really hear my prayer, and answer it?'*

Two days after arriving back at base, the hospital nurse informed me that I had a couple of visitors. Gunny and Capt. Swanson came by to ask a few questions about the mission. I did not feel up to talking just yet, and told them that. I was to report to Capt. Swanson after being released from the hospital in a couple more days.

I lay there in that bed with my right leg hoisted up by some pulleys, thinking about what went wrong with the mission and how I had lost my best friend in that terrible crash. I wanted to blame myself, not the Viet Cong.

One of my responsibilities was to get both of us safely back to base. I failed!

* * * * * * *

Four months later, I was preparing to leave Vietnam — it had taken my best friend. Dan died in the helicopter crash along with Lo Lei and both of the gunners. I lost a part of myself in that crash. Dan and I were much more than comrades in arms — we were real close buddies and a very good sniper team; each knew what the other was thinking in the field. He had saved my butt more than once — I owed him my life. The two of us had been through so much in the last five months. At first, I was always rescuing him; but then, in the last couple of months, Dan had returned the favor. I could not stay for another tour and train a new partner as HQI wanted.

Gunny tried telling me that things were going to heat up soon in Vietnam. He told me how Marines like Dan and I were needed here and promised I would get my choice of spotters, if I would stay and lead another sniper team.

For the first time in a year, I discovered that the thrill of an upcoming hunt was gone.

The only thing I felt was sadness, fear, and anger. I didn't want to train another Marine to be a killer, then standby and watch him die. I couldn't do it again. Nobody could ever replace Dan Gibson. He was the finest Marine I'd ever known. Our mission was a huge success according to headquarters. But not in my opinion!

I would never allow another Marine to get that close to me again. Dan's death had left such an empty hole in my stomach that there was no way I would stay for another tour in Nam, or in the Marine Corps.

I had killed too many to try to count, yet I received a sense of pleasure in knowing I had helped a government and its people from being overrun by Communist troops. I was also buying my country time to get our combat forces in Vietnam. But, I also knew that our troops would face a determined and skillful fighter in the Viet Cong and North Vietnamese forces. I was lucky to fight the VC on my terms, usually without him knowing I was present. This was the advantage of being part of a good sniper scout team known as *'Delta-Two-Foxtrot'*.

I knew that after I got back to stateside, one of the first things I wanted to do was visit Dan's family and Kathy. I wanted them to know what a wonderful son and Marine he was. I needed to spend a day or two with them and visit Dan's gravesite. Maybe when I could see his grave and talk with his family and Kathy, I could put this thing to rest.

Could I ever get rid of the emptiness and guilt that have consumed me since Dan's death? I still felt like I was somehow responsible for his death — it was my responsibility to get us back safely.

On this important part of our mission, I had failed miserably.

* * * * * * *

I boarded the large jet in April for the trip back to the States. After storing my carry-on bag overhead, I sat down again at a window seat; and, as the plane gained altitude, I looked out at the countryside, just as I had when I first arrived in Vietnam.

Only this time, **I did not see the beauty in the landscape.**

About the Author

He writes with such personal passion and emotion the reader becomes captured by the books powerful human interest and explosive heart stopping action. They will laugh, cry, and also feel the pain that was so real. His desire is to let the reader feel and see everything through the sensitive nerves and eyes of the sniper and through the eyes of a young boy that grew up without a father. He wants his readers to feel as though they are being drawn into the very pages of the novel where they become part of the drama and action, experiencing a journey like no other.

"United States Marine Corps from September 1, 1961 through December 20, 1965".

'Semper Fi'

LaVergne, TN USA
10 September 2010
196516LV00005B/1/P